# Sandigras Canyon

Other novels by Alfred Dennis

Chiricahua
Lone Eagle
Elkhorn Divide
Brant's Fort
Catamount
The Mustangers
Yuma
Rover
Yellowstone Brigade
Shawnee Trail
Fort Reno
Ride the Rough String

# Sandigras Canyon

*by*

*Alfred Dennis*

WCP

Walnut Creek Publishing
Tuskahoma, Oklahoma

Sandigras Canyon



This novel is a work of fiction. Names, characters, places, and incidents are either the product of the author's imagination or are used fictitiously. Any resemblance to actual events, locales, organizations, or persons, living or dead, is entirely coincidental and beyond the intent of either the author or the publisher.

ISBN: 978-1-942869-05-4
Second Edition Revised, Paperback
Published 2015 by Walnut Creek Publishing
10 9 8 7 6 5 4 3 2
1. Western  2. Action/Adventure  3. Western Romance

Books may be purchased in quantity and/or special sales by contacting the publisher;
Walnut Creek Publishing
PO Box 820
Talihina, OK 74571
www.wc-books.com

This novel is dedicated to Ron Kennedy
of El Reno, Oklahoma. My good friend,
Naval Aviator, and a great American.
USS Ranger-Vietnam 1962-1964

# Introduction

Fort Worth, Texas, the year 1874. The great gathering point of many Texas trail herds heading north, following the Chisholm or the Great Western trail. Most cattle herds are gathered and start further south, down around Austin and San Antonio. Further north, the great towns of Dallas and Fort Worth are surrounded by huge cattle ranches and thousands of longhorn cattle. Cattle drovers, farmers, gamblers, and storekeepers all depend on the cattle industry to make their living. These same men, tired from long hours of toil, frequent the many saloons and gambling halls of the cattle towns to relax and spend their money.

Tonight is no different. The White Elephant Saloon in downtown Fort Worth, known for its gambling tables, good whiskey, and wild cowboys is crowded as usual, but tonight it is uncommonly quiet. Every man present has their full attention riveted on the card table at the rear of the building. Not a sound is heard throughout the saloon, except for the few words spoken by the men sitting at the round poker table.

Five men sit around the table, two gamblers, a storekeeper, a rancher, and a tall man dressed in the typical clothes of a cowboy. Everyone at the table knows this man is no ordinary cowpuncher. The cold grey eyes, the low positioned gun at his side, and the quiet disposition of the man speaks volumes. Here sits a gunfighter, if they didn't miss their guess. Every man present has seen plenty of gun hawks in their day. They know this man, whoever he is, fits the bill. Here is a man to walk a wide berth around, probably a man for hire, a killer. It doesn't pay to get crossways with this man.

The older rancher in the game clutches his cards hard as he studies the pot, glancing around the table. Several thousand dollars lay piled on the felt table, along with the deed to a huge ranch in Arizona. The Overland Stage Company and the U S Mail just delivered the deed, to the far-off property today. A heavy manila envelope, laying atop the stack of money, contains the papers from his lawyer and the previous owners who live in the east.

Relatives of Sandy Burris, who inherited the huge Sandigras Ranch from their deceased uncle, decided to sell the ranch before losing it, because of past due taxes. These people aren't ranchers or cattlemen, nor have they ever taken an interest in the ranch or even set foot in Arizona. They practically abandoned the ranch, letting it fall into disarray. Rustlers stole it blind, running off the cattle. Other ranchers took advantage of the absentee owners, grazing their own cattle on the ample range and using the ranch buildings for their own hands. Finally, back taxes forced the sale of the ranch at auction. Jonas Webb, informed by his attorney of the upcoming sale, temporarily became the new owner, until he found himself in the White Elephant Saloon, sitting at a high stakes poker game. Webb just sold a large herd of longhorn cattle to a passing cattle buyer. He was having a quick drink at his favorite saloon before heading home when he was talked into sitting in on the game.

Jonas Webb looks at his cards one more time. "Well gunfighter, are you betting or not?"

The grey eyes study the deed, placing it back on the table. "I'm raising you, Mister Webb." Placing his cards face up on the table, the rancher smiles confidently, paling as he watches the man fan four treys and turn them over for all to see.

"Well, Mister Wes Tobin, you just won yourself an Arizona ranch."

"Thank you for the afternoon entertainment and this ranch." Tobin gathers several dollars in cash and the deed to the Sandigras Ranch.

Webb smiles. "Thank me son, when it's really won; when it's over."

Wes looks at the man curiously. What does he mean; when it is really over?

# CHAPTER 1

Only silence beckons from the dark doorway of the smoky White Elephant Saloon. Inside, the dimly lit room is deathly quiet, not a sound emits, except for the soft tinkling of glassware being cleaned and stacked along the bar. All eyes around the room are intently focusing on five men playing poker, watching the drama play out around the well-lit card table in the rear of the building. Two coal oil lamps, hanging suspended above the round table, cast their eerie light across the intense faces of the card players. Several men stand about the room, clutching beer mugs, whiskey glasses, or smoked down cigarette butts, tightly in their hands. The drinks and unfinished smokes are held, but they are all but forgotten. Bystanders, barflies, cowboys, and farmers, all watch intently as the cards are dealt slowly to the players. Word spreads through the town like wildfire as the game progresses throughout the afternoon, and into the early evening. The pots become larger and larger, as gold, silver, and paper money piles onto the table.

Curious town loafers, drunks, spectators, even business owners, men from all walks of life, have piled curiously into the already crowded saloon as word of the game passes around town, among the towns-people. Poker games or any game of chance, is common in any saloon in Fort Worth, rarely gaining the attention of anyone, except the players. Seldom did a game contain the amount of money that has been won and lost around this table throughout the afternoon. Most of the watching spectators to the game have never seen this much money in their lives. They are fascinated, nothing can pry them away from the game as they have to see the outcome.

Five men sit at the table, five men intently studying the card's laying before them. Some have their hats pulled down low, halfway concealing their faces. The others, let the heavy smoke of several cigars, hide their anxiety as the cards are dealt.

The game is five card stud; one card down and hidden, three so far have been turned up, with one to go. By the fine cut of their clothes, the diamond stickpins in their collars, and the gold rings, two of the men in the game are gamblers, along with a rancher, a storekeeper, and a tall man with cold, slate blue-grey eyes. A man, who by the looks of his clothes, could have been almost anything. Only the low-slung holster, with the forty-four army issue pistol protruding from it, gives him away.

Gunfighter; the other four men know at a glance, exactly what he is. The ever-watchful eyes, a man who by habit sits with his back to the wall, yes they know. He has the trademark of a bad man. Few men dare look directly into the cold eyes. No words emit from the man. He sits quietly playing his cards as the afternoon passes and the dark night falls. Not particularly a big man, still he's above average in height, straight through the shoulders and narrow at the hips. It's the grey eyes, framed by a square jaw and high cheekbones that make men take a closer look at him. The straight hard stare can look plumb through a man. He seems to have the ability to see inside, what they're thinking and feeling. The hard stare can temporarily paralyze a man, not so much from fear, but the intensity of the eyes as they appear to numb a person. Many, who witnessed the game, later describe the grey eyes as being ice like, cold and hard as iron.

The barmaids, working the White Elephant that night, described the stranger as not being dashing or overly handsome, but they said he has a rugged wildness and rough chiseled face that drew their attention. They all know this quiet stranger is a gunman. They aren't sure who he is, but they can feel the danger emitting from the man. It's a feeling that sends chills down their body, but excites them at the same time. They seem mesmerized, unable to remove their eyes from the tall man.

Not a player at the table knows how many times the cards were dealt out. No one cares. Only the money, falling onto the felt covering, holds their attention with fascination, drawing them tighter into its web. As the pots are raking in, by first one, then another, they just want the cards dealt in a hurry, anticipating their next draw, somehow feeling lady luck is riding with them tonight.

The night passes and the hour is getting very late. The poker game has almost finished, depending on the turn of the last card. This hand, and perhaps the entire game, is coming to a close. Adding the last of his money to the growing pile, one of the gamblers drop out, along with the storekeeper. The pot in the middle of the table is once again heaped high with silver, gold, and paper money. Several spectators to the game, try to count the money piled on the table, but finally give up.

The older rancher is betting heavily, trying his best to bluff the tall man and the other players out of the game early. He only succeeds in building the pot for one of them, but which one. Who will be the lucky one? As they say, who will be the last man standing?

The rancher, Jonas Webb, looks across the table smugly at the small pile of money before the tall man, piling several bills onto the table. "Five hundred."

"Too rich for me; I'm out." The second gambler pulls the smoking cigar from his mouth and turns his cards face down, tossing them into the pot. He then picks up what little money he had left before him. Tipping his hat to the players left in the game, he shakes his head sadly. "My congratulations to one of you gentlemen."

The grey eyes look over at the gambler and nods, studying the pot for several seconds, before looking into the weather-beaten face of the rancher. "Alright, I'll see your five hundred."

The first gambler to fold out of the game deals. Quickly, he checks the pot and deals out the fifth and final card, face down. The rancher quickly pulls the last card into his hand and fans them, as a slow grin of satisfaction spreads across his face. The tall man lets his last card lay where it fell for several seconds before picking it up slowly, deliberately, his cold eyes never leaving the rancher's laughing face.

"It's your bet, Mister Webb," the gambler dealing the cards looks over at the rancher, "at your convenience, sir."

"Five hundred." The rancher glances across the table, arrogantly tossing his money onto the growing pile. The smug look of a man, who knows he has won, crosses the older man's face.

The tall man slowly spreads the two cards in his dark tanned hand, studying them for a second. He looks over at the rancher and slowly drops his gaze at what is left of his money. "Lot of money, Mister Webb." The words come out slow, carrying a heavy Texas drawl. "Yes, sir, that's certainly a lot of money."

"We're playing for table stakes; you in or out?" The words come crisp and hard. The rancher can see there is hardly two hundred left in front of the other man. He is anxious, anticipating the outcome. He knows he has the pot won. Jonas Webb is a very rich and successful rancher, money means little to him, but as with most wealthy men, he has to win. He has to feel the power of his money over other inferior men.

"Table stakes, huh?"

"Yeah, table stakes and you look kinda short to me," the older man smiles jubilantly once more. "Kinda hard luck, ain't it?"

The grey eyes study the rancher and look down at what is left of the older man's money. "Don't reckon you'd take my voucher?"

"Not hardly; I don't know you stranger, sorry." The beefy hand of the rancher clasps his cards tightly.

"Figures." Nodding, the grey eyes turn to the man's face again. "Just so you know me the next time we meet, the name's Wes Tobin."

"Tobin?" A voice whispers hoarsely from the crowd. The room turns silent, quieter than a cemetery during a funeral, as all eyes turn on the man. "It's Wes Tobin, the El Paso gunman. I thought I recognized those eyes."

"He killed Tulane Bannock." A shorter man drops his forgotten burned-out cigarette. "I saw him gun a man down in the streets of Laredo, two years back."

"Yeah, and how many more?" Another man whispers.

"Wes Tobin; I should have remembered you. It's been a while." The smaller gambler, who is dealing, studies the dark tanned face across from him. "Yes sir, quite a while at that."

"Why should you remember me, mister?" Wes looks at the man curiously, not recognizing him. "I don't recall ever having business with you."

"No, we haven't, I'm still alive." The gambler smiles.

"So?" The voice turns suddenly cold. "Where do you remember me from?"

"I was in El Paso when you killed the Rachin brothers." The gambler nervously downs his drink in one gulp. "You've aged some, sir."

"Five years have a way of doing that to a man." Wes studies the man closely to see if he can discern any hostility in his actions.

The gambler nods, smiling nervously. "In your line of work, I imagine it would."

"This ain't a social club." The rancher studies the tall man impatiently. "You calling Mister Tobin, or folding?"

"Neither, Mister Webb." Wes looks once more at his cards, as the rancher starts to show his cards. "I'm raising." The smugness leaves the rancher's face as he watches the tall man remove a money belt from around his waist. Gold coins click with a thud as they're placed in neat stacks near the pot. Laying the half empty belt on the table, the tall man looks over at the rancher and nods. "A man needs to be careful what he wishes for Mister Webb."

Counting the pile of coins, the tall man stacked in the center of the table, the rancher pales slightly and looks at his own cards. "You're raising me a thousand?"

A gasp comes from the crowded room as the spectators come to grasp with the amount of money that has just been wagered. Expectant eyes turn on the rancher, waiting to see what his reaction will be. Most present know Jonas Webb. They know he is a wealthy rancher, but a thousand dollars, plus the money that is already laying on the table.

"I thought I would at that." The hard eyes look clear through the shocked face of the older man. "Like you asked me, sir, are you calling or folding?"

"I ain't got that kind of money on me here." Perspiration suddenly beads on the man's forehead, running down his cheeks. "Not near that much."

The tall man's grey eyes never waver from the rancher's eyes. "You remember table stakes, don't you, Mister Webb? Your own choice of words, I believe."

"I've got close to two thousand, maybe more in that pot, Tobin."

"I'd say that's a pretty good accounting of the money you've bet." The face becomes even harder as Wes looks over at the sweating rancher. "You've been trying to freeze me and these other men out since you sat in, now bet or toss in your cards."

The rancher studies the grey eyes for what seems like several minutes. "I'll have to send to my ranch for the money."

"Table stakes Mister Webb, and again like you asked me, are you betting or folding?"

The rancher looks across the table at the pile of money, then once more at his hold cards before looking down at the saddlebags laying beside him on the floor. Pulling the leather bags into his lap, he unbuckles the straps and takes out a manila envelope, roughly wrapped with a piece of leather thong. Studying the bundle for several seconds, he tosses it on the table. The packet makes a stir as it lands on top of the pile of money. "That, Mister Tobin is the deed to several thousand acres called the Sandigras Ranch or Sandigras Canyons in Arizona Territory." The rancher looks again at his cards, then over at the tall man. "I'll call, if you agree to the wager."

Reaching his long arm across the table, Wes pulls the packet to him and unties the leather cord. Opening the heavy envelope, Wes unfolds the deed and looks the paper over, reading it slowly, line by line. Pushing the legal papers across the table, to the storekeeper, he sits back in his chair. "Do these papers look intact to you, sir?"

"I don't lie Tobin, they're good." The rancher takes offense, his face turning red. "You may be Wes Tobin, the deadliest and most feared gun hand in Texas, but no man questions my honesty, not even you."

Tobin ignores the outburst from Webb and waits for an answer.

Handing back the papers, the store man nods. "I've never known Jonas Webb to welch on a bet, or cheat a man in any way. If he says they're good, Mister Tobin, I'd stake my life on it."

Wes smiles coldly and nods. "You just did Mister Store Man, you just did."

"They're good, Tobin." Webb repeats, glancing at his cards again.

"How much you reckon this, what did you call it, Sandigras Ranch? How much you figure it's worth, Mister Webb?" The grey eyes bore into the rancher.

"A whole lot more than your thousand Mister Tobin, a whole lot more." Webb studies the papers. "The cattle alone will probably bring well over a thousand."

"You must be pretty certain of your cards, Mister Webb."

"Is it a bet or not?" Webb is becoming frustrated. He knows he has wagered far too much against a piddling thousand dollars.

"What's on it now?"

"I just bought it, sight unseen, through my lawyer. Never laid eyes on the place, myself. All I know for sure, it's supposed to have a ranch house, outbuildings, deep well, and corrals. Any livestock presently on the property branded with the Circle S belongs to you, providing of course, you win this pot."

"How many acres in all?"

"You can read. It says every inch of land in the Sandigras Canyons." The rancher shrugs. "Figures to at least twenty thousand acres, give or take a few."

"You must be holding a mighty good hand, sir." Wes leans back comfortably, making the wooden slatted chair moan. "Yes, sir, it must be a ring-tailed twister to wager all this on a single hand."

"Well, speak up, man. Is it a bet?" The old rancher is beside himself, halfway cussing himself for making such a bet and getting himself in this fix. He knows he holds the winning hand, he can feel it, but he also knows the Sandigras is worth twenty times the amount the pot holds. He knows he is being foolish for making such a wager, but he has come too far. He is in too deep to just fold his cards. His pride and arrogance won't let him back out now.

Tobin studies the rancher's face for several seconds. "Alright Mister Webb, you can use the deed. It's a bet." The tall man looks around the table at the other players. "All of you men are witnesses. I'll expect every man at this table to endorse these papers, stating I won this ranch fair and square."

"We will, providing you win the hand, Mister Tobin." The store man smiles.

"You've yet to win." The rancher watches as the other men at the table nod, then studying his cards one final time, afraid he may have misread them. Laying the two cards slowly on the table, he spreads them out beside his other three for all to see. "A full house, kings over nines."

"Good hand, Mister Webb." Wes studies the cards, laying his own face up on the table. "Very good sir, but not good enough; four treys."

Slowly, a sickly smile crosses the rancher's face. Raising his whiskey glass to the tall man, he nods. "Congratulations Mister Tobin, you now own an Arizona Ranch."

"Thank you, Mister Webb." Wes raises his glass to the rancher. "It's been a real pleasure."

Webb looks across the table and smiles as he signs his signature to the deed, adding a few last words. "Providing you're man enough to keep it."

"Well, sir, I thank you, and I'll sure do my best, to hold it, that is." Wes rakes in the huge pot and starts stacking the money in neat piles. "May I buy you gentlemen a drink before I depart?"

"You can buy me one, Mister Tobin. You've temporarily cleaned me out." The dealer smiles as he adds his name to the deed, along with the others. Wes nods, and then starts refilling his money belt. "Drinks for everyone, on me barkeep."

Jonas Webb stands, raising his glass. "Here's to you, Mister Tobin. You've won yourself a real cattle ranch if I ain't mistaken."

"I hope so Mister Webb." Wes looks up as a tall, thin man enters the saloon. "You sir, are a gentleman and a gracious loser, it's been a pleasure to have played cards with you."

"You know what they say Mister Tobin?" Jonas Webb studies the thin man as he hands over the ranch deed to its new owner. "There's no fool like an old fool."

"What's he talking about Wes?" The tall man walks up to the table, watching as Wes reties the manila bundle.

"Let's ride Pole, I'll tell you later." Wes scoops up his winnings and the encased deed. "Where you been all day?"

"Business, old hoss, business," the tall lanky man grins.

"I'll bet, what was its name, rye or beer?" Wes asks, nodding at the rancher. "You ever need a place to hang your hat Mister Webb, come to Arizona."

The old rancher watches the two men exit the saloon and raises his glass to them, mumbling to himself. "If I don't quit gambling so wild, I just may need a place."

The store man hears the last words and laughs. "Not you Jonas; you may have lost tonight, but I've seen you win a lot more."

"True enough," the old rancher smiles, remembering past games. "I've won my fair share, haven't I?"

"Yes, sir, you have."

"I believe the Sandigras is a place I should have visited, at least once." Webb exhales. "Oh well, easy come, easy go as they say."

"Ain't this exactly the way you started many years ago?" The store man's eyes follow as Wes and the other man exit from the White Elephant. "We were pilgrims out here back then. I had just started in the store business and you were working as a cowhand when you won the Big W, in a game just like this one."

"Your memory is still good Silas, that's why I'm kinda glad to see that boy win his chance at the same life."

"Boy, what boy? That's Wes Tobin, a gunman and a killer."

Webb looks at the swinging doors and shakes his head. "You're wrong Silas, that's now Wes Tobin, rancher and cowman."

"You think he'll make it to Arizona and his new ranch Jonas?"

"He'll make it, I'll bet you." Webb laughs. "If I haven't misjudged that man, he's a winner."

"Well, maybe you're right, but I doubt if we'll ever know or hear about him or the Sandigras Ranch." The store man shrugs. "Ever."

"We'll hear, I'm betting on it." Webb smiles and raises his glass at the vacant doorway. "I've seldom misjudged a real man, and there old friend, just went one."

# CHAPTER 2

Atop the high Arizona Mesa, Wes sits his horse as he studies the sloping trail winding its way down into the valley, spreading out plainly below him. As far as the eye can see, swells of grass wave gently back and forth as the warm breeze blows softly across the beginning of the Sandigras Canyons.

He thinks back to Fort Worth and the poker game with Jonas Webb, and still can't believe his luck that night. These beautiful green valleys are actually his, plus everything laying within the confines of the canyons. Ranch buildings can be seen, off in the distance, nestled dead center in the middle of a wide canyon floor. Cattle, along with a few horses, dot the grassy landscape, all across the valley that runs up against the steep sandstone cliffs, a natural barrier to anything that cannot fly. Studying the canyon walls, Wes doubts a lizard can escape over the sandy barrier.

Smoke drifts skyward on the horizon from the chimney of a large ranch house in the distance, then disperses into the clear blue sky. A small creek can be seen, even from this height, meandering slowly through the center of the tree studded valley.

"Looks like somebody's home, Wes." Pole Nichols sits alongside Wes, his brown eyes fixed on the smoke, coming from the house in the lower valley. "Maybe they got us some supper on the stove."

"It appears that way alright; maybe they do." Wes gazes out, across the long narrow canyon, and back at the wagon that holds a man and a woman. "If y'all are ready, I reckon we'll just ride down and introduce ourselves."

"Looks like a good incline down that stretch." Pole looks down the long gravel and sand trail, leading to the canyon floor and shakes out his lariat. "We better tie onto the wagon, just in case that brake don't hold. We sure don't want Miss Ellen and Monte to run off on us."

Wes nods and dismounts, tying his own lariat around the back axle of the big wagon. "We best remember this climb if we ever want to head back up this way after supplies."

"Let's get to the bottom first, before we start remembering," Pole laughs. "See if we're still around."


A little over a month has passed since the poker game, back in the White Elephant Saloon, in Fort Worth. Wes Tobin, the new owner of the Sandigras Ranch, in far-off Arizona, finished his business and rode out of the cattle town with his good friend and sidekick, Pole Nichols. Three heavily laden pack mules follow quietly behind them. Three hundred miles further west, into the grasslands of Texas, they stopped at the dusty little town of Abilene. The last hundred miles, or so, amounted to nothing but sand, sand, and more sand. Wes can't figure how people or cattle could survive out here in this hot, dry land.

"You plumb sure Monte and his wife, are supposed to be around here somewhere?" Pole studies the windblown buildings lining the street. "It's been quite a spell since we've seen hide or hair of old Monte."

"Last I heard, he was riding for the Crown Ranch." Wes noses his dust covered horse up to a tie rail. "I 'spect someone around here will know them."

"The Crown Ranch, I've heard of the place." Pole studies the storefront. "Supposed to be a rough bunch of boys, riding for the Crown."

"That's the story I've heard."

"Another thing, correct me if I'm wrong, pardner," Pole smiles easily, pushing back his felt hat, "Last time we saw Cousin Monte, you and him weren't exactly on speaking terms."

Wes grins and rubs his tanned jaw thoughtfully. "That's true, but we're still blood cousins, despite our little differences."

"Well the cousins part is true enough. That's one way of putting it, I reckon. But, if I recollect correctly, last time y'all were together, you two went at it like two bulldogs fighting over a bone." Pole nods. "It took over two weeks to heal yourself up enough to walk straight up like a man."

"You're right again old pard, but we need him." Wes smiles slightly at the memory of that set-to. "Just remember, me and him are still blood kin, and blood's thicker than water."

"Maybe it is, then again, maybe it ain't, and I agree, we do need him in the worst way." Pole nods agreement. "That's the plain gospel truth, ain't neither one of us farmers."

"Ranchers," Wes corrects, the smiling scarecrow of a man.

Thin and willowy as a blade of grass, Pole's looks can be deceiving. Over the years, many found out just how tough the likable Pole Nichols can be if he were riled.

"Whatever, farmers or ranchers," Pole spits. "Me and you together, wouldn't make a pimple on a real cowboy's bottom."


The second store, they stop at, Wes hits pay dirt. He finds out his information was right. Monte Belton did indeed work for the vast Crown Ranch. The storekeeper, though tight lipped and slow with his words, finally divulges that Belton and his wife Ellen are working fifteen miles west of Abilene. At least they were, the last time he saw them when they came in for supplies, almost a month earlier. Pole smiles at the information. They will head west and that's the right direction.

As the storekeeper looks out through the dirty window and points them on the right road out of town, he warns them the Crown Ranch isn't hospitable to strangers. "Don't let that worry you none store keep, old Wes here ain't exactly what you'd call sociable either." Pole reaches for the makings. "No, sir, he ain't exactly the friendly type."

"Yeah, I know who he is." The man nods as he looks Wes up and down. "With his reputation, I thought he'd be bigger."

"He's big enough, mister. Too many men made the mistake of underestimating him over the years."

"Where exactly does the Crown Ranch boundary start?" Wes walks back over to where Pole and the store man stand, looking out over the street.

"Right at the edge of town, boys." The storekeeper nods. "It covers a whole lot of ground, has to."

"Why's that?" Wes is curious.

"You've seen the land Mister Tobin, takes a hundred acres out here to keep one cow in grass."

Wes nods. "Well, if that's Crown right there, we shouldn't get lost."

Outside Pole shakes his head and grins over at Wes. "You know Mister Tobin, you're becoming a well-known man in these parts."

Wes isn't impressed. He knows he's well known. He also knows the reputation he carries. "Maybe Arizona will turn out to be a healthier climate for both of us."

"Sure couldn't be any worse than Texas." Pole rolls a smoke. "You ever get the feeling we've worn out our welcome in these parts?"

"Yeah, I reckon we have at that."

Two streets further along, Pole points to a large sign, hanging over the board sidewalk. The Bulldog Saloon's beckoning sign and swinging doors swing silently in the light breeze, inviting a thirsty man inside to slack his thirst.

"One beer, then we're riding." Wes isn't a drinking man, but that doesn't matter much, Pole could drink enough for both of them.

"Now Wes, you know one little old beer don't even wet a man's whistle good." Pole protests innocently. "Shucks, two don't even tickle his insides real good."

"One." Wes holds up his finger, as they dismount and tie their horses. A scarecrow of a boy appears almost as if by magic, perching himself atop a tie rail as they turn from their horses. With his raven dark hair, Pole thinks the youngster reminds him of a crow sitting on a limb.

"For a nickel, mister. I'll watch your horses while you're having yourselves a drink."

Pole frowns slightly, glaring at the boy. "How do you know what we're fixing to do youngster?"

"I'd bet double or nothing on it." The lad is eyeing Pole up and down. "You look like a drinking man to me, mister."

"Why you little scamp." Pole steps toward the boy. "I ought to tan your backsides and teach you some manners toward your elders."

"I figure you could do that alright, you're bigger than me, but my pappy wouldn't like it much, no sir." The youngster grins up at the skinny man. "You sure ain't bigger than him."

Pole pushes back his hat and looks down at the boy. "Just who's your pappy? Is he the law hereabouts?"

"Nah, not the law, him." The small, slender finger points across the street at the blacksmith shop, where a giant of a man stands watching the proceedings. "He's my Pa. They call him Goliath around here, but his real name is Rufe."

"I can see why." Pole takes in the huge arms of the man. "He's a mighty big man."

"Yes, sir." The boy grins. "Last week, he got in a fight with a skinny feller just about your size. It was bad, real bad."

"He kill him?" Pole is curious. "What happened?"

"No, sir, but it took the whole town almost a week to untie the knots my Pa jerked in the skinny man's tail."

Glaring, Pole looks down at the laughing youngster. "A nickel's too much, you little whelp."

Wes raises his hand, putting a stop to the bickering before it turns into something worse. He sure didn't spot the youngster slip up on them as they dismounted. Must be getting old, he grumbles. "What you gonna do if horse thieves get away with our horses?"

"Well, sir, I reckon I'll have to give you back your nickel." The boy is young, but he has a serious look on his face. "I'm kinda small to be fighting horse thieves, you know."

A hard man by nature, Wes actually smiles. "I reckon, young man, we've got ourselves a bargain."

"What about his horses?" The lad motions at Pole. "You want them watched too?"

Wes looks over at Pole and laughs. "You mean one nickel ain't enough?"

"Shucks, no mister, that'd just be a penny a horse. A feller could starve to death at those rates." The youngster looks the horses over as they are tied up. "It's mighty hot and tiresome work watching this many horses, especially when their owners are getting themselves pickled."

Flipping a dime to the outstretched hand, Wes tousles the boy's hair and walks up the steps, into the saloon. Pole only scowls as he passes. "Dang little rustler, I only charged a penny when I was that age."

Passing inside the swinging doors, Wes grins again and shakes his head. "Times are changing, my friend."

"I'll say, maybe I should stay here and guard horses." Pole grumbles. "Seems like a profitable business."


The Bulldog Saloon sits in the middle of downtown Abilene, easily the largest building on the city square. Inside the floor is covered with sawdust and peanut hulls, plus gaming tables of every sort. Poker tables, roulette wheels, and dice tables crowd the ample floor. A huge mirror lines the east wall with bottles of whiskey standing along the back shelves. Unlike the White Elephant Saloon, back in Fort Worth, this drinking establishment is well lit and well stocked.

Pole looks up, swallowing hard, as his eyes focus on an almost nude picture of a woman hanging above the long mirror. Ordering two beers, Wes notices Pole's attention is glued on the naked painting, his mouth agape in total shock.

"Drink your beer Pole, before you choke on it." Wes shakes his head and pushes the cool beer in his friend's hand. The tall man only smiles and raises his beer mug toward the picture. "I ain't never seen nothing like that in all my born days."

"That be my wife, mister." The barkeep looks hard at Pole, as he finishes wiping a glass dry.

"She's your wife?" Pole stammers. "I sure don't mean any disrespect at all, but she sure is a sight to behold, looking down on us from up there."

"Yes, she sure was."

"Was? She dead or something?" Pole looks up at the picture again and over at the barman.

"Same as, ran off with a tinhorn gambler last summer. Ain't seen hide nor hair of her since."

Pole swallows hard. "That's a shame, mister. I bet you sure miss her."

"Nope, not a bit." The barkeep slams the glass down. "Got the picture, I have, it keeps me company, and it can't spend my money or sass back at me. No sir, I don't miss her one little bit."

"Uh huh," Pole figures that to be a lie.

"You fellers just ride in?"

Wes nods slowly, taking a sip of his beer. Pole takes one last fleeting look at the picture, turning his back in embarrassment as the barman walks away. He can't understand a man displaying a picture of his own wife that way. Still, he isn't about to say more, some men got downright cranky about their womenfolk. Still, he figures the picture probably brought in a lot of business.

Tossing a coin on the long bar, Wes and Pole finish off their drinks and head for the door. Pole can't resist one last lingering look at the beautiful woman. Catching the barkeep grinning at him and shaking his head, he knows he's been had. She wasn't the man's wife at all; he should have known. Pole drops his head and walks out to where the youngster sits watching the horses. Nodding at the boy, they mount up and turn the horses to the west.

Pole frowns when the boy holds up the dime and sticks out his tongue. "You know they hang rustlers, don't you?"

"I might get hung, but at least I didn't fall for the old wife trick." The youngster laughs and races over to his father's protection.

"Smart aleck." Pole shakes his head, knowing the kid must have been watching him more than he was watching the horses.


Three hours of steady riding, across flat, desolate land, brings them to a sign standing alongside the dusty road. Wes nods slowly as he reads it. The sign is rustic, made of old lumber, and nailed to an equally old oak fencepost. The meaning is clear enough, as it came straight to the point; Keep off Crown. Trespassers will be shot on sight, rustlers hung before sundown, and we ain't hiring. This means you! C. Stanton, owner.

"Friendly sounding bunch, ain't they?" Pole looks around the flatland at the vast mesquite thickets and open grasslands. "At least we found the place."

Kicking his bay gelding, Wes starts forward. "Let's go see just how friendly these folks are."

"If I get hung like the sign says, I'm gonna be mighty mad at you, Mister Tobin," Pole gripes. "I'm still thirsty. One beer doesn't even dampen a man's gizzard."

"Pole old friend, a gallon probably wouldn't reach your gizzard as long as your neck is."

The tall man feigns hurt feelings. "You shouldn't make fun of a man's looks. I can't help if I'm a handsome galoot."

Coming into sight of the ranch, they notice several riders closing in on their flanks and rear as they near the large buildings that speak of wealth and prosperity. None of the ranch hands come close, only shadowing the two riders as they follow the road into the ranch yard. Pulling their horses in at the tie rack, Wes and Pole sit easily, their hands in plain sight on their saddle horns, keeping them well clear of the low-slung guns hanging at their sides.

One of the riders, shadowing them as they approach the big house, dismounts and disappears quickly through the large doors. Briefly, he is out of sight, and a screen door opens as the rider reappears on the wide porch. Placing both hands, arrogantly on his thin hips, the man looks expectantly back toward the door.

Only seconds pass before a big man, dressed in a broadcloth coat and white shirt walks into view, making his presence known. There is no doubt, here is the he-dog of the Crown Ranch. Wes studies the man closely, looking around the yard where at least a dozen rough looking men are mounted or afoot, surround them. He and Pole have ridden and worked for many Texas ranches. Neither are cowboys. They were hired mostly for their guns. Over the years, he saw men like these before, all over the huge state. Ranch hands are all the same, cold and aloof, at least until they become acquainted with a new man. It only takes a nod from the owner of a spread and they would jump on a man like a pack of dogs. A rough life made them hard as nails. If the signal was given, they would tear a man apart if they didn't kill him outright.

"You men read the sign you passed back on the road, or can you read?" The tall rider, who hurried inside to tell of their presence steps menacingly to the edge of the porch.

Ignoring the rider, Wes looks directly into the eyes of the well-dressed man. "We read it. I come in looking for a friend."

"Who's your friend?" The big man walks to the handrail and leans on it curiously.

"Monte Belton."

"Monte Belton," the man repeats the name. "You got business with Monte?"

"You might say that, he's my cousin."

"That might just make you Wes Tobin, the El Paso gunfighter," Stanton smiles. "Yes, I've heard Monte speak of you many times. Y'all have a family resemblance, excepting he's a mite bigger than you are. That's how I'm guessing who you are. What you wanting with Monte?"

"Me, and my partner here, are heading for Arizona. We're looking to see if Monte might want to trail along with us."

The big rancher looks Pole over carefully, then turns his attention back on Wes. "They say Arizona has a healthy climate. Never been any further west than where we're standing myself."

"Is he here?"

"He's here, 'bout five miles due west of here is a line shack." Stanton points with his chin. "You'll find him there. The road leads right to the place."

"Good day then. Reckon we'll be riding on." Wes studies the man, "unless you have any objections to us crossing your range."

"No objections, providing you don't stop."

"We ain't lost anything in these parts, so I figure we'll keep traveling."

"You gonna send word back if he decides to go with you?"

"No, don't 'spect so, Mister Stanton." Wes looks across at the man. "We're not heading back this way; wouldn't want to wear out our welcome."

The tall rider, standing beside the owner glares down from the porch, irritated at being ignored. "I hear you're a real hard case Tobin."

Wes looks over at the rider. "Do tell?"

"You don't look like much from here."

Pole kicks his horse between Wes and the porch. "He'd have you for lunch, sonny."

"What about you skinny man?" The man touches the butt of his pistol. "You hungry?"

Looking over at the enraged puncher, Pole grins widely, flipped his smoke at the man's exposed boot. "Nah, I'm particular about what I eat."

"That'll be enough, Regan. Leave it be." Stanton stops the rider from leaving the porch.

"Yeah, that'll be enough, sonny." Pole laughs and follows Wes from the yard.

Glaring pure hatred, the rider watches the men ride away and looks over at Stanton. "Why'd you stop me boss? He needed a comeuppance."

The big man smiles as he watches the departing backs of the two men. "I figure that'd be Pole Nichols. He's killed at least five men in stand up shoot-outs. He rides with Tobin, and from what Monte told me, he's probably just as mean."

The rider pales slightly and stares after Pole. "Maybe you just done me a good turn, boss."

"Yes, sir, 'spect I did." The big rancher nods. "I figure I just saved your life. Now, get the boys back to work."

Pole looks back at the ranch as they clear the yard. "That's about the roughest looking bunch of cowboys I've ever seen."

"Let's ride."


Smoke drifts lazily from the rock chimney as Wes and Pole ride slowly up to the line shack and stop in the bare yard. Except for the well-manicured flowers peering from their dirt filled boxes, nothing grows near the house. Not a blade of grass, weed or bush of any kind, grows about the windswept ground. A lone horse stands hipshot in front of the building, his reins trailing the ground with his head hanging. The pony is tired, other than his ears pricking up and his head raising a mite, he barely takes interest in the two new horses riding in.

Hallooing the small line shack, Wes waits as the door squeaks open. The man in the doorway is dressed in the clothes of a wrangler, from his spurs and chaps, to the kerchief wrapped around his thick neck. Both the man and Wes are about the same age and height, the difference being Belton is slightly heavier and more muscular. The woman following him is small, slight of build, with yellow blond hair, and the biggest sparkling blue eyes. She is almost plain, except for the eyes and the smile, a smile of radiance, a smile of genuine honesty and softness.

Monte Belton stares disbelieving at the two dusty riders sitting before the small building. Raised on nearby farms, the two are cousins, their mothers being sisters. Growing up, they were close, the only difference being Wes was wild, always in trouble of some kind, whether it was fighting or causing mischief. While Monte was just the opposite, quieter, always trying to shirk trouble.

Almost like brothers, they were close, until Monte finally moved away to west Texas, trying to get away from Wes and his growing reputation with a gun. The last time they met, after the war ended in a brawl, leaving both of them beat up and bleeding. It had been a humdinger of a fight. Both men came away battered and bruised, and it was the last time they spoke, or even saw each other, until this day.

Monte headed west, into the prairie lands, looking for work, while Wes hired his gun out to the highest bidder. Pole Nichols was raised on another nearby farm and had, as long as he could remember, shadowed Wes, covering his back. He's known both cousins since childhood, but has always been closer to Wes. He and Monte fought many a time, as kids were prone to do, but never once did he and Wes have a disagreement. Pole has always been curious about the cause of the fight between the cousins, but Wes never mentioned it again.

"It's good to see you, cousin." Wes steps from his horse and sticks out his brown hand, tipping his hat to the woman, "and you, Miss Ellen."

Nodding, she takes his hand in her smaller one. Monte and Ellen were married almost two years before she ever met Wes. She heard all the tales of Wes, his fighting and shoot-outs, but other than the wild tales, she knows little of him except what Monte has told her.

"You two know Pole Nichols, I believe?" Wes turns to where Pole dismounted.

"You two still running together, I see." Monte shakes hands, ushering the two men inside. "You haven't changed much Pole, haven't put on any beef to that frame."

Pole grins and takes his hat off before entering the cabin. "Yes, sir Monte, I have to run with Wes. Nobody else will have anything to do with your cousin here and far as my skinny self, he don't feed me to well either."

"I believe that for a fact; ain't healthy." Monte nods seriously. "Just looking like him almost got me shot more than once, but he could feed you better."

Wes looks to where Ellen is removing tin cups from the wood shelves. His eyes wander the room, a typical cow operation, a small line shack with only the bare essentials, needed to stay the winter. Everything in it is small, from the bed to the table, to the small stove. Wes knows Monte has all he ever wanted from life, right here. He has Ellen.

Bringing his attention back to the conversation, Wes looks over as Monte speaks to him.

"What are you two doing this far west?" Monte strikes a sulphur to his smoke. "You boys roam a lot further south, and by the looks of them pack animals you're headed on a long trip."

"We normally do stay south of here, and yes, we are fixing to ride a ways." Wes answers both questions.

"Y'all get run out of the south country?"

"No, we just turned the horses loose and this is where they brung us." Pole grins broadly and looks about the room.

"We heard you took sides in the Murphy, Ford range war, in Parker County. We also heard about you killing Bass Rachin and his brother in San Antone."

Wes ignores the remark and comes straight to the point. "We come to get you Monte."

"Get me, for what?" The shoulders shrug. "I ain't wanted for nothing and I sure as shooting ain't no gun hand."

Ellen places coffee cups, in front of the men, and homemade apple-pie as Wes looks over at Monte.

"We need you, cousin. Me and old Pole here ain't much at ranching or farming for that matter."

"Ranching, farming?" Monte looks curiously across the table at Wes. "What the blue blazes are you talking about? Last I heard, you ain't got no ranch. Hiring out your gun sure can't earn you that kind of money?"

"He does now." Pole bites into his pie hungrily. "Man oh man, Miss Ellen you sure are some cook."

"Thank you, Pole." She smiles. "You eat all you want. Just don't you dare get a bellyache on me."

"Wes Tobin, the El Paso Gun slick, owns a ranch? Where?" Doubt shows in his eyes. "Is this some kind of joke. You're pulling my leg ain't you?"

"It ain't no joke, Monte." Wes looks out through the open door. "No more than trying to raise cattle in this forsaken country."

"We've got grass in places. It's just hard to see." Monte defends the ranch.

"No, sir." Pole chews happily. "It sure ain't no joke."

"So tell me, how many acres does this ranch of yours take in?" Monte is skeptical. He can't believe Wes Tobin actually has a ranch.

"Don't rightly know for sure." Wes sips on his coffee, ignoring the pie and Monte's remarks. "It's in Arizona Territory, somewhere around Tucson."

"Last I heard that's Apache country, good for only raising rattlesnakes, Gila monsters and chili peppers." Monte snorts.

"Don't rightly know about that either. Ain't never been in Arizona before." Wes shrugs. "If it is, they best be moving out, cause it's ours now, and Cousin Monte, I aim to claim it."

"You have a ranch?" Monte shakes his head in disbelief. "Shoot you wouldn't touch a plow handle when we were kids, unless your Pa beat you into it."

"This ain't farming or plowing." Pole grins.

Wes pulls out the manila envelope containing the deed and papers, laying it softly on the table. "A third of the layout is yours cousin, that is, if you throw in with us and help me and Pole run the spread."

Monte hesitates, studying the bundle for several seconds where it lay, then picks it up. Unrolling the document, he lets his eyes take in the map and deed, looking over at Wes, then back down at the papers. "By the looks of this map and the description on the deed, there's got to be several thousand acres in these canyons."

"You know, that's exactly what the man said." Pole mumbles after swallowing another piece of pie. "Just after he lost the place to Wes."

Monte looks over to where Pole sits looking hungrily at the pie that remains uneaten. "Where'd you get it or how?"

"Don't fret yourself. It's all legal. When we get to Tucson, we'll register the ranch three ways." Wes lights a match to his smoke. "Providing you and Ellen want in."

"And if I don't?"

Wes shakes his head standing up to leave. "Me and Pole, are heading for Arizona cousin. Whether you and Miss Ellen come or not, is strictly up to you."

"Sit down Wes and have your pie." Monte studies the map for several minutes while Wes and Pole watch curiously. Measuring the small lines with the spread of his fingers, he notes each landmark, clicking them off mentally. Glancing over at Ellen then back at the map, he finally lays the papers down and looks at Wes. "Me and Ellen have a good set-up here, cousin. We eat steady and the pay ain't bad. I'd hate to lose it on a gamble."

"It may be a gamble Monte, everything in life is. I'm betting this one pays off for us, and I very much want you two in on this. We need you; both of you." Wes looks around the room. "And I think you need us."

Absently, Monte sips on his coffee, looks over at Ellen and back down at the deed in his huge hands. "Alright Wes, you have your shortcomings, but lying never was one of them; count us in."

Pole yips in delight and Wes smiles as they all shake hands and slap each other on the back before turning their attention on the apple-pie. Ellen frowns at Pole as he bites into his third big piece.

"It's settled then. We'll head for Arizona tomorrow." Wes removes his hat and smiles over at Ellen.

"You remember?"

"Yes ma'am, I do." Wes nods. "No hats at your table."

"Thank you, Mister Tobin." Ellen smiles. "You are a gentleman, and you Pole Nichols, are gonna have a stomachache tomorrow."

"What a way to go." Pole chews contented. "I'll die a happy man."

"I'll have to notify Mister Stanton and the Crown."

"I did the notifying." Wes lights a smoke. "Come morning, we'll ride."

"Our wagon's out behind the barn cousin. We'll just have to round up my horses." Monte looks over at Ellen and smiles. "Maybe we have a home, Misses Belton."

"I hope so Monte." The voice is barely a whisper. "I hope so."

# CHAPTER 3

The land in southern Arizona, for the most part, is dry and arid. As Wes follows the heavy wagon down the steep grade of rough gravel, trying to keep the wagon from running into the straining team, he notices the land slowly begins to change. Grass, belly deep on a horse, grows in abundance along the small creek that he spotted from high on the canyon wall. Unlike the higher elevations, out on the desert floor there is plenty of grass and water for their livestock.

Pole unties his rope from the wagon and coils it up on his saddle. Pushing back his hat, he looks back up the trail. "Whooee that's high up. Kinda throws a man's senses."

"What do you mean?" Wes looks over at Pole. "You sick or something?"

"Nah, ain't nothing like that." Pole looks across the flat canyon floor. "I could have sworn those buildings and corrals were a lot closer from up there. Kinda makes a man dizzy is all."

"You're probably right. I figure the ranch is about five miles, straight ahead." Wes looks off across the valley. "It does look further from down here."

"That far?" Pole shakes his head sadly. "It's been a long time since breakfast. I'm pert near starved."

"We'll eat tonight in our own house." Wes smiles over at the thin man. The word "house" sounds mighty inviting to him. It's been almost nine years since he and Pole left home to fight in the War Between the

States. Since then, they sold their guns over and over to the highest bidder. He wasn't proud of some of the things he had to do, but he wasn't ashamed either. He killed, but as far as he knew, he broke no laws nor was he wanted by any.

"You get scared coming down that trail, Miss Ellen?" Pole grins at the little woman.

Laughing, she shakes her blond curls. "Of course not Mister Nichols, you and Wes were holding those ropes tight, weren't you?"

"Yes, ma'am, I was trying my best but don't know about Wes though."

Two miles into the valley, Wes pulls his horse in, stopping midstream of the slow running creek, letting the cool water lap about the gelding's legs. The small river is a beautiful setting, with green grass covering almost to the water, and round smooth rocks lining the river-banks as far as the eye can see. Cottonwoods, elm, and other trees grow alongside the riverbank. The stream is crystal clear and he can see several fish swimming in the water, just above the small pebbles covering the bottom. The horses paw and nuzzle the water, wetting their muzzles. Satisfied, they drink greedily from the cool stream.

"This stream must be spring fed from somewhere higher." Wes looks toward the far mountains. "We'll track it to its source when we have time."

"I'll betcha a beer, it'll come up out of the ground."

"Man, I could make me a good meal of them things." Pole's mouth waters, just thinking about fish sizzling in a frying pan. "They'd sure go good with a cool beer, right about now."

"You that hungry?" Wes looks back over his shoulder as Monte drives the horses and wagon into the creek.

"Told you already; I'm dang near starved to death." Pole pulls at his worn belt. "Done pulled up two belt holes since you drug me out here."

"It was for your own good. You were getting soft." Wes grins. "Too much easy living."

"Easy living? Shoot, I ain't slept in a real bed over ten times since the war." Pole pouts. "I smell like wood smoke, and if I get any thinner, you'll be able to see right through me."

"Well, get yourself ready, we'll fix that tonight." Wes kicks his gelding and leaves the water. "I'll bet Ellen will cook us up a meal, if we ask her real nice."

Kicking his own gelding into deeper water, Pole leans from the saddle, scooping up a handful of water. "Dang, the place probably doesn't even have a bed."

Wes is surprised as they near the ranch house. The buildings are actually made of plank siding, not the mud adobe he was expecting. Long porches, furnished with chairs, run down each side of the house. The chimneys, protruding from each end of the building, have smoke billowing from both of them. Turning in his saddle, to survey the rest of the ranch, he finds the barn and two smaller outbuildings, are of the same planking. Someone has gone to great expense to haul that much sawed lumber down the rough trail they just traversed.

The last town they passed through was Tucson, where they visited the Federal Land Agent and recorded the deed legally, in their three names. Tucson is the county seat, located almost fifteen miles back to the west. Whoever brought in the lumber was out considerable time and hard work, to construct these buildings. Wes doesn't remember seeing a sawmill in the sleepy little town. They rode in at early dawn, only staying long enough to record the deed, feed the horses, and eat breakfast at a small cantina, before pushing on. It's possible he could have overlooked a sawmill. They only passed through the main thoroughfare of the town. It doesn't matter, the house and barns are here, and they are theirs.

Several head of fat cattle, grazing peacefully on the lush grass, raise their heads curiously as the riders and wagon pass by. Wes notices a large S branded on the hip of most of the cattle. He also notices the few saddle horses, standing in the corral as they pull into the yard, carry a different mark, the Running H Brand. Whoever the horses belong to, are inside the house, and they are squatting on the place.

Dismounting, Wes surveys the other buildings carefully for any sign of life before hollering a long hello at the ranch house. Motioning for Monte to hold the wagon where it is, Wes steps closer to the building and waits as the door of the ranch house opens slowly. Five men and a woman walk out onto the porch and stare down curiously at the new arrivals. The men are all dressed like cowboys, except for one. The woman is the type found in every saloon between Tucson and Fort Worth.

A slender, middle-aged man steps in front of the others as they leave the porch and descend the steps into the sandy yard. Wes takes in the two tied guns, plus the menacing look and stance. Over the past ten years, he faced many such men as this one. He doesn't know the man personally, but he knows exactly what he is. A gunman, the way his guns hang on the slender hips, the swagger in the man's walk, and the cold half-open eyes, there is no mistake.

Wes knows regular cowhands never carry two guns. They only get in the way. Most cowboys couldn't hit the broadside of a barn with one pistol, no use in carrying two. No, this man is no ordinary cowpuncher, he's trouble. Probably a troubleshooter for someone, a man to do the rough fighting, if the need arises.

Pole steps down from his horse and drops the reins, waiting slightly behind, to the left of Wes. Monte pulls the wagon to a stop several feet behind them, out of danger, making sure Ellen is out of the line of fire.

"Watch him Wes, he's a Texas Sidewinder if I ever seen one." Pole whispers as he closely studies the rest of the men. "I've got the rest of these tomcats covered."

"Can I help you, pilgrims?" The slender man asks arrogantly, taking several steps forward of the others. "You folks seem lost."

"How's that?" Wes asks. "Cause you're sure a long way from the road to town." The man steps sideways, two paces, so he can see the wagon clearly. "I've never seen any of you people before."

Wes studies the group for several seconds, before bringing his full gaze to bear on the speaker. "No, we're not lost, mister. Yes, you can help me by vacating these premises pronto."

"Vacate the premises, you mean this ranch?" The man looks behind him at the others, then snickers. "Now, why would we want to do that stranger?"

Wes pulls the deed from his pocket and tosses it at the man's feet. "If this is the Sandigras Ranch and I believe it is, we own it lock, stock, and barrel. It's all deeded and recorded legal like, in Tucson. You people, whoever you are, have been trespassing. Now, haul your freight out of here, like I said, pronto."

"Just like that?" The man sneers. "You ride in here, out of the clear blue, order us off the place, then claim you own the Sandigras."

"I own it, there's the proof. I ain't repeating myself twice, mister." Wes makes a show of pulling the thong from his pistol. "Read that deed if you want, then ride out, now!"

"You push hard, mister." The man looks over at Pole then at the wagon, ignoring the packet. "You don't give a man much room."

"You and your men are moving out and we're moving in. You've squatted here long enough." Wes watches the man's eyes. "You and these people are trespassing, that's over. Now, light a shuck out of here."

"I don't think Mister Halleck would like us just turning tail, leaving his cattle and property, on your say so."

"Only brands I saw riding in are the Sandigras S. You climb aboard your horses and hightail it." Wes stares hard into the gunman's eyes. "I'm evicting you my friend, and your friends are going with you, one way or the other."

"I told you, mister, we can't do that." The man turns slightly. "Mister Halleck wouldn't like it. There's several head of his Running H stock down in these canyons."

"That so?" Wes nods. "You go back and tell this Mister Halleck that I'm taking possession of every head of Running H stock I find on Sandigras Range. Tell him they'll be back, due payment for all the grass he's used over the last few years."

"You talk mighty tough stranger." The man shakes his head. "You're awfully sure of yourself."

"Try me, or ride out."

No warning comes, not even a flicker of the eyes. The slender man's hand moves without warning. He's quicker than a striking rattler when he reaches for his gun. Two shots explode, sending echoes up and down the valley, as complete silence follows. Wes watches the slender man slump slowly to the ground, a surprised expression on his face. Turning his attention to the other men, who stand staring down at their leader, he notices the look of disbelief and shock on their faces. "You men have the same chance, one minute to catch your horses and vacate, or make your play." Wes holsters his pistol and looks calmly across at the men. "Make up your minds, boys. Frankly, I don't care which way you jump."

"We're riding, mister. We ain't no match for the likes of you and him." One of the riders nods at Pole, who has drawn his pistol and has it pointing at their stomachs. "We're cowmen, not hired killers."

"He had his chance to ride out in one piece, same as y'all do right now." Wes' voice is cold as ice. "You be sure to tell Halleck that he drew first."

"What about our possibles?"

"Take only your horses and the woman; now get!"

Turning, all the men start for the corral, except one older, bowlegged rider.

"You're a hard man, friend. Mister Halleck ain't gonna take kindly to you gunning down Les, or keeping his cattle."

"Like I said old-timer." Wes looks down at the dead man. "He had a choice. He took his chances and made his own luck. You take him back to Mister Halleck and give him a message."

"What's the message?"

"The Sandigras has new owners now, with a legal deed. You tell him to keep off Sandigras Range, and that my friend, includes this whole valley."

"Who are you, mister?"

"Wes Tobin."

"Yeah, we've heard tell of you even out here, from Texas ain't you?" The man starts to turn. "Hired gun-hand and killer, well I reckon you are that, since you just put out the lights of Lester Bodine there, something very few men would be able to do."

"I am Tobin. Don't forget my warning." Wes watches the man hobble away. "Everything in these canyons belongs to the Sandigras; everything down to the scorpions."

Stopping, the old man walks back to where Wes waits. Looking over at the wagon, he stares hard at Ellen and nods, turning his attention back to Wes. "This warning's from me, Mister Tobin. These canyons are a natural holding pen for cattle. That's not why Mister Halleck keeps so many riders here. The cattle take pretty good care of themselves."

"What are you getting at old-timer?"

"Apaches, they think this is their land, and I reckon by their law it is. If and when they see that yeller haired woman with only three men to protect her, they'll swarm this place like bees to honey."

"That's our worry, old-timer."

The rider nods slowly. "Yes, it is a worry I sure wouldn't want to be saddled with. If I were you, I'd hire me some riders, pronto."

"You want a job?"

"Not on your life, Mister Tobin." The old rider grins. "I've ridden for the Running H far too long, most of my life."

"What's your name, old-timer?" Wes likes the old cowhand's spunk.

"Bacon Hollister."

"You ever want a job, come on back Mister Hollister."

"You think you'll be here that long?"

"You can bank on it."

"I'll keep it in mind."


Pole is smiling from ear to ear. He has thoroughly explored the ranch house, corrals, bunkhouse, barns, and he is content. Ellen has outdone herself fixing dinner and the bunkhouse is full of real beds and warm blankets. The ranch is far better than he expected. The barn is huge and tight with several box stalls. The bunkhouse will sleep several riders and the ranch house itself is well built, strong and tight for the heavy winters that are sure to come. Here in southern Arizona, a man never knows what kind of weather to expect. It's only smart to prepare for the worst.

Whoever built the place planned well and built it solid. The corrals are high with heavy timbers, to hold the wild range cattle and equally wild horses. Pole smiles over at Wes. Mister Webb didn't know what he gambled away for a mere thousand dollars. The buildings alone are worth more than a thousand dollars, not to mention the land, or the cattle and horses roaming the canyons.

Monte sits on the front porch after supper, his feet propped up on a rail studying the red stain where the dead man bled out. "You ain't changed any cousin."

Wes shrugs. "He took his chances. He pulled on me first."

"You wanted him to." Monte looks to where Ellen walked out on the porch. "You prodded him. I couldn't see your eyes, but I could hear plain enough. You wanted to kill that man."

"I gave him a choice. He didn't make the right one." Wes shrugs. "Out here, we're on our own cousin; strength rules. Now, they know what they're up against."

Pole flips his smoke away. "He was a hired gun hand Monte, doing his bosses' bidding."

"Weren't talking to you, Pole." Monte glares over at the thin man. "I was talking to Wes."

"That's a fact, but I'm talking to you." Pole looks hard at the man. "I'm an equal partner here. I'll have my say, if and when I want."

Monte raises to his feet, frowning. "Both of you are the same. You think a gun solves everything."

"It's for certain a gun solved this little problem, once and for all." Pole looks Monte straight in the eyes, unflinching. "We won't be bothered by that gentleman again, I'm betting."

"Stop it, now." Ellen speaks from the doorway, before tempers flare more. "What's done is done. Now we've got a beautiful home here, for the first time in our lives, and we're going to get along and build a life here."

"Sounds like good advice to me." Pole turns toward the bunkhouse. "Thank you for the fine supper, Miss Ellen. I'm headed for bed."

"You know Wes, this Rowland Halleck, whoever he is, will ride against you before he just gives the Sandigras over." Monte watches as Pole walks away.

"You mean us, cousin."

Monte nods. "Us then, but he'll come."

"Maybe, but we've got clear title to everything in these canyons, filed and safely locked up in Tucson." Wes pulls on his cigarette. "All legal and above board, if he comes and we have to fight, at least the law will be on our side."

"What law? Way out here, we're on our own, more than likely." Monte growls, "we'll be doing our own fighting."

"You can pull out cousin."

"No, reckon I'll stick." Monte looks over at the door. "Like Ellen said, we've got ourselves a beautiful home here, at least for now. I reckon it's worth fighting for."

Wes agrees as he looks around the ranch yard. "It's all of that for sure, but will you fight to keep it?"

"If they ride against this ranch, you know I'll stand with you." Monte flips his finished smoke out into the yard. "I can't believe you didn't know that."

"I knew it all along Monte, just wanted to hear you say it, is all."

Monte turns towards the kitchen. "Well, you heard it. I'll side you, cousin. You know I will, but I don't have to like it."

"I aim to keep the Sandigras." Wes flips his finished smoke onto the ground. "No matter what, I aim to keep every inch of these canyons."

"No matter how many will have to die?"

Wes' jaw tightens at the question. "No matter. It's worth fighting for, and like I said, it's their choice, they don't have to ride against the Sandigras."

Monte nods slowly and looks down at his cousin. "I didn't think it possible, but I believe you have become even harder than the man I remember."

"Monte," Wes leans back and looks up at the big man.

"Yeah."

"If I were you, I wouldn't sell Pole short on fighting ability. I wouldn't prod him into using his gun."

"If he's survived riding with you all these years, I ain't about to." Monte watches as Pole disappears through the bunkhouse door. "No, sir, I know he's a tough one. I sure ain't no gun hand, as you are well aware of."

"Just so you know." Wes rolls another cigarette.

"Whose side would you take, cousin?"

Wes exhales and nods slowly. "Don't make me choose. You're my blood, but that man's been like a brother to me, backing me when most would have run. Two different times, he took lead for me and saved my life. No Monte, don't ever make me choose."

"I won't." Monte smiles. "I know how close you and Pole are."

"Goodnight, cousin."

Monte stops in the doorway and turns. "Tell me, are you planning on keeping any Running H stock on our graze?"

"You can count on it." Wes looks off across the dark canyons. "Monte, until this trouble is over, I plan on riding roughshod over anyone who rides against us."

"Is that the only way?"

"It's the only thing these people understand."

Wes and Pole ride out at dawn, scouting the valley, canyons, and trails that intertwine all along the roughs leading over the rim, onto the desert floor. The main valley floor itself, Wes estimates to be at least eight to ten miles long, with several smaller canyons branching away from it. All along the valley floor, numerous trails and washes lead up and out of the valley. The two riders don't have the time to scout out every trail on the first scouting trip, but they do follow the main road that leads away from the Sandigras Ranch. Fresh horse tracks are plain all along the trail the Halleck riders and woman used to leave the valley, making a beeline for the Rocking H Ranch and their boss.

Several miles further south and west, they work their way along a well-used trail, up and out of the canyons. Topping out, onto a large mesa, after a heavy pull on the horses, they can see the faraway silhouette of buildings off to the west. Pulling up in a stand of scrub brush, they sit and watch as three riders push a small bunch of cattle toward the ranch.

"I'm betting that's Mister Halleck's Running H place." Pole squints into the sun. "That is, if I were a betting man."

"You're probably right. It looks like a big layout from here." Wes nods. "We followed the tracks straight here from the Sandigras."

"We gonna ride in and take a look see?"

Wes turns his horse. "Not today, no sense asking for trouble. We'll just let Mister Halleck come to us, I reckon."

"Then what are we fixing to do?" Pole pulls on his smoke, tossing the leavings onto the ground.

"I'm gonna take that old man's advice and ride into Tucson and hire us some hands if I can." Wes looks off to the northwest. "You get back to the ranch and help Monte keep a lid on things. I'll be back just as quick as I can."

"How far a ride do you think Tucson is coming from this end of the canyons?"

Wes looks around and shakes his head. "I don't have any idea. It's far enough, I reckon."

"Okay pard, but you steer clear of the Running H and Mister

Halleck's men." Pole stops his horse. "You sure you don't want me to ride in with you?"

"I'm just hiring men, not shooting them." Wes smiles, "I'll be back by sundown tomorrow, with any luck."

"You watch yourself. Remember, this is Apache country too." Pole looks down the trail they came up. "You know a wagon could come up that trail quite easy, not to mention a herd of our prime cattle."

"I've been thinking the same thing." Wes nods. "We need to do something about it."

"Fences?" Pole looks across the flat dry land. "I ain't seen a fence since we left Texas."

"Draw Monte a picture of what you've seen when you get in." Wes turns his horse.

"Just remember, you ain't got me to protect your backside this time," Pole laughs, spurring his horse for the ranch.

"I'll remember, and Pole," Wes watches as the smiling face turns back. "I'll have a few beers for you, if you're still thirsty that is?"

The swear words coming from the thin man are indiscernible, as Pole disappears back down the cut that serves as a trail, leading down to the canyon floor. Wes grins, then kicks his gelding into a short ground eating lope, toward the northwest and Tucson.

# CHAPTER 4

Late afternoon finds Wes sitting his horse and studying the broad, dusty street in Tucson, Arizona, before riding into the town. They stopped here once, before on their way west, to record their deed and grab a quick bite to eat. Coming in from the other side of town, from the east, he is unfamiliar with the town called Tucson. How many times before has he seen the same kind of town, the same people, with the same trouble waiting?

Somewhere in the cluster of dusty wood and adobe brick buildings, he knows another fast gun waits, wanting to make a name for himself. There always is. A reputation made with the cost of blood, which Wes knows could easily be his own, if he isn't on his guard.

Nudging his gelding forward, he lets the horse walk slowly down the wide street. His feet make a clopping sound as they meet the sand and hard ground of the much-used thoroughfare. Reading the names over the stores, as he passes by, Wes notices several storekeepers and town loafers watching him as he rides past.

The dust lies heavy over the board sidewalks and drifts hotly on the air. Reining the gelding in, Wes dismounts in front of the first saloon he comes to. By the signs over the buildings, this isn't the only saloon on main street, nor is it the biggest, but it is the first, and he has to start somewhere. It has been a long tiring ride across the dry land and his throat is parched. He needs one of Pole's cool beers.

The breed of men he needs, hangs out in the local saloons, looking for female companionship and whiskey. Cowboys lead a hard, lonely life. Their wants and needs are always the same. Coming into town on their day off, they want to drink and blow off a little steam, spending their hard-earned wages. Normally they would depart for their home ranch with empty pockets, a hangover, and enough whiskey in them to last until next payday. Wes is no cowboy, but he understands their thinking. He doesn't hold them at fault for their fondness for a good time. He knows the hard living, free spirited men he wants, and he sure won't find them in a local church.

Dusting himself with his Stetson, Wes pushes the swinging doors open and steps slowly to the side, letting his eyes adjust to the gloom before approaching the long bar.

It always amazes him that most saloons he visits are dim and gloomy, but there is probably a good reason. He figures, some men frequenting the saloons don't want their faces to show plainly in a well-lit establishment. At least it's cool inside the room, a break from the heat and dust out in the street.

Ordering a beer, he puts the damp liquid to his lips and swallows thirstily, all the while studying the room slowly. Several cowboys play cards at a table, while others sit talking and drinking. Some have their feet propped up on the tables, their spurs digging gouges into the already scarred, hardwood furniture. No one looks his way or pays him any attention.

Studying each man carefully, Wes looks over the men, to see if any look like a gun hand. Over the years, he gained a sixth sense. He knows a gunman almost as soon as he lays his eyes on him. The way a man wears his gun belt, the squint of his eyes, or the proud cockiness in the man's demeanor. None of these men fit the description; none of them makes their way with a gun. All seem like honest, working cowhands, men he could use.

Finding an empty table, Wes unties the tie down thong on his holster, pulls up a chair and sits down. Placing his half-empty beer mug on the table before him, he surveys the room again. The sweat-stained felt hats and dark, sun-dried faces around the room identify most of these men as cowmen. Friendly jibes and the normal talk around a poker table, echo across the quiet room.

An older man, with a growth of beard, watches him closely from across the room, averting his eyes when Wes turns to him. Nodding to the rider, Wes watches as the rider nods back. The man is alert as he watches his surroundings, and Wes likes that. Motioning to the bartender, Wes waits patiently until the bald-headed waiter walks over.

"Bring me another beer, and set that gentleman up with whatever he's drinking. Ask him if I could have a word with him." Wes motions toward the lone cowboy.

"Much obliged." Watching as the barkeep approaches the man, he waits as the rider studies him momentarily, then he rises and approaches his table. He wears a sweat-stained felt hat, adorned with a rattlesnake hatband. His thin bowlegs encased in worn chaps, a leather vest trimmed with Mexican pesos, and a leather wristband, accompany the rider. The big Mexican rolled spurs, beat out a jingle against the floor as the man approaches the table.

"Thank you for the drink, mister." The voice is gruff, but friendly. "Harry said you wanted a word with me. What can I do for you?"

"You got me figured?" Wes smiles.

"I know who you are, if that's what you're asking?" The bowlegged rider nods. "Just ain't figured out what you want with me."

"And who am I?"

"You're Wes Tobin. Word around is you killed Les Bodine, Mister Halleck's second fastest gun, yesterday." The man's friendly blue eyes look out from under a shock of grayish brown hair and graying week-old stubble of beard. The man has a likable, friendly way about him. "Word is you beat him cold."

"Whoever put out that word is wrong. It was mighty close. He was fast, real fast." Wes takes a swallow of beer. "Tell whoever is doing all the talking, Mister Bodine made a choice, the wrong one."

"Well. Mister Tobin, Halleck has another gun working for him. The older man takes a sip of beer. "You ever heard of Waco Grange?"

"I've heard of him." Wes looks over at the man. "Comes from down in west Texas, the Pecos River country, I believe."

"He's the one, and he's meaner than a rattlesnake with a toothache."

"I didn't catch your name."

"Jenks Lohan." The man nods, but doesn't offer his hand. "I ain't no gun hand. Last time I shot at a rattler, I missed him so bad, the poor thing almost laughed himself to death."

"What line of work you in, Mister Lohan?" Wes already knows the answer. If he didn't miss his guess, before him stands a real live Texas cowpuncher.

"Cattle; all I've ever known is punching cows." Jenks laughs. "Rode before I walked."

"You ride for an outfit now?"

"Nope, I just pushed a herd to Colorado Territory. Some of the boys stayed up there. Me and three riders just got back."

"Why didn't you stay with the others?"

Jenks grins, his lined, weather-beaten face, almost cracking like an old newspaper. "Too cold, that's why. Shucks every morning we'd have to build a fire under our horses to unfreeze the poor critters."

"The women up there don't keep you warm?"

"Women cost money," Jenks smiles, "something I try to hold onto if I can."

Wes smiles easily and pushes an empty chair out with his foot. As Lohan sits down, Wes knows here in front of him is a bona fide Texas brush popper. Most Texans, he knows, could take the truth and stretch it six ways from Sunday. It just comes natural to them, same as bragging. If a Texan isn't blowing or shooting you a yarn about something, they're passed out drunk. Nevertheless, they are cowboys, the best, and most are loyal to the brand they ride for.

Ordering the old cowman another drink, Wes studies the rider closely. "You want a job with my outfit?"

"What outfit is that Mister Tobin?"

"The Sandigras Ranch, east of here."

"Canyon country, I've heard of the Sandigras."

"You interested?"

"Cattle or guns?"

"Cattle mostly, if we have Apache trouble I'd expect you to pitch in and lend a hand."

"How much you paying?"

"Twenty a month and found."

"Thirty." Jenks shakes his head. "Twenty don't stretch far."

"Are you worth thirty, Mister Lohan?" Wes studies the man.

"Every dime of it." The older man smiles. "Plus some when the going gets rough, and on the Sandigras, it's gonna get plenty rough."

Wes looks closely again at the man, nodding his head. "Alright, it's a deal, thirty a month."

"And found."

"You're the new Segundo of the Sandigras Ranch. We'll need two or three more good men."

"I ain't never been a foreman before Mister Tobin, wouldn't know the first thing about bossing men."

"If you're worth thirty a month, you better learn." Wes smiles, "and call me Wes, you can call my partners mister, if you're a mind to."

"How many partners do you have?"

"Two." Wes strikes a match to his smoke. "Why is the Sandigras in for trouble Mister Lohan?"

"Well, sir, besides the Apache, you'll have the Running H and Mister Waco Grange to contend with?"

"They're my problem."

"Plus the Flannery Clan," Jenks laughs lightly, "almost forgot them."

"Another ranch, with toughs huh?"

The puncher seems amused. "Well, sir, the Flannerys have their moments, but I believe you'll find that out yourself."

"Why's that?" Wes groans. All he needs is one more bunch of riders to fight with. "You got personal feelings toward them?"

"Nope, but I'd rather you find out about them boys yourself." Jenks shrugs. "Wouldn't want word getting out, I was talking about them."

"The Flannery's must be a rough bunch?"

"They're tough enough."

Wes nods. "Alright then, that's what I'll do."

Jenks finishes off his beer and sticks out his hand, across the table. "Good, then you've got yourself a deal. How many riders you want?"

"You ever ride for the Running H?"

"Nope." Jenks shakes his head. "Like my old pappy always told me, some things a man just don't do if he has any pride in himself."

"Three or four should be enough. I want to get back to the ranch quick as we can." Wes shakes hands and stands up. "I'll pick up some supplies and meet you over at the general store in an hour. If you can, round up some men by then?"

"I'll be there."

"We'll ride out tonight. I want to get back to the ranch sometime tomorrow."

"You got trouble back there?"

Wes shakes his head. "Not that I know of, but there's only two men and a woman at the ranch."

"I'll go round up the boys."

Sitting beside three tote sacks of supplies, on the store's porch, Wes does a double take, swearing under his breath. Coming down the street, toward the store, rides Jenks Lohan and two others. Slung across the saddle of a lead horse and tied on trusses, like a Sunday turkey, is a third man, seems more dead than alive.

"We're here boss." Jenks reins in and looks down where Wes sits. Flipping away a half-smoked cigarette, Wes steps down on the dirt street and looks the men over.

"What's the matter with him, drunk?"

"A little maybe, but mostly he didn't want to come along." Jenks smiles. "Took some convincing, but he finally agreed." The other two riders are not in much better shape, but at least they are sitting astride their horses, not lying across them. Not straight mind you, but at least they are aboard. The two looking at him are middle-aged men, younger than Jenks, but not by much. The one across the saddle is just a lad, by the looks of him. They are definitely a sad looking bunch of men.

"What's he gonna do when he wakes up?" Wes is already doubting his recruits.

"His name is Charlie Mack. He's probably gonna think he's dead, and wish he were."

"I take it he didn't want to hire on with the Sandigras."

Jenks wraps his skinny leg around his saddle horn and draws in on what remains of his stub of a smoke. "Didn't say that, Wes. No, sir, I didn't say that at all. I said he didn't want to come along."

"Tell me Jenks, what's the difference?"

"Well, sir, he didn't want to leave Joyce Ann back there." Jenks pokes his finger over at another saloon where a crying woman is watching from the porch. "He's kinda sweet on her and she is on him, at least she was until his money ran out."

"I see."

Jenks leans over from his saddle, looking Wes straight in the eye. "Am I your segundo, or ain't I?"

"You are; we made a deal, I reckon." Wes is doubtful about the whole deal. "Yes, you're my foreman."

"Then he's going." Jenks unwraps his leg and smiles. "He'll be fine come morning; might even be able to sit straight on his horse."

Wes doubts his decision, but he wants to get back to the ranch as quick as possible. By now, Halleck has been told there are only three men on the place and if he finds out one is in Tucson, he might ride against the Sandigras. The words of Jonas Webb keep coming into his thoughts. "If you're man enough to hold it." He remembers the words of the old rancher vividly, he sure doesn't want to lose the ranch as Webb predicted. Wes has no way of knowing how many Running H riders recognized him in the saloon, while he talked to Jenks, and there is still the Apache the old rider warned him about.

Pointing at the other two men, he is about to have them dismount and load the supplies, but changes his mind. They are having their own problems just staying atop their horses.

"This is Harley Raper and Nathaniel Newhouse. Most folks call him Nate." Jenks introduces the new men. "I already told you who the youngster is."

Leaving Tucson, Wes turns a critical eye on the supplies and his new hired hands. He makes a side bet with himself, which will stay on the horses longer, the men or the sacks. A tall man with a shiny badge, penetrating hard eyes, and a low-slung pistol, watches them ride out of Tucson. Wes notices the man shake his head, wondering if the Marshall is making the same bet himself.

They are a sorry looking bunch as they head east, toward the Sandigras. Jenks swears under oath, with a straight face, that when the boys sober up, if they don't up and die, they will all be top hands. He even adds the young feller, lying across the horse's back, is a top bronc rider. He swears the cowboy can ride a greased bolt of lightning, or a greased pig, whichever Wes catches first. Wes has to smile, more Texas tall tales.

Ten miles out of Tucson, Wes strikes a sulphur on his pistol grip, studying the surrounding terrain in the moonlight as he lights a cigarette. One thing is certain, the shape this bunch is in, he sure doesn't want to run into any of the Running H Crew or Apaches. However, it's dead certain, for a fact, when or if they do sober up, they have to get better as they sure couldn't get any worse.

Seeing the ranch house and the inviting smoke of the chimney, Wes breathes a deep sigh of relief. It's been a long night's ride, but his new hands have sobered up considerably at the first cold stream they crossed as Jenks dumped them all unceremoniously into it. With the cold night air creeping in on their wet clothes, all three men came alive and started looking for their coats. The boy seems even younger looking, sitting astride his horse, a lot younger than Wes figured. He couldn't be a day over eighteen.

Wes looks closely at each man and wonders what Monte is gonna think when he sees them. He knows Pole will not say a word, as he has been in the same condition, maybe worse, several times in the past. One thing is a guaranteed fact; any man who likes to drink is bound to wind up the same way eventually.

Entering the yard, the men line up in front of the porch, almost as if they were ready for inspection. All eyes linger momentarily on Ellen, then glance over at Monte and Pole. Wes stares at Pole almost daring him to mention the sorry looking state of the hung over men. Ellen wrings her hands as they are introduced, smiling awkwardly.

"Breakfast is almost ready. When you men get washed up, we'll eat."

Monte only grunts as he pulls Wes off to the side, out of earshot of the men. Knowing Wes is fixing to catch it, Pole grins and motions for the four riders to follow him toward the corrals and bunkhouse. The two cousins stand off to the side, watching the new hands and Pole until they disappear inside the barn.

"Have you gone and lost any sense you ever had?" Monte shakes his head as he fumes and fusses. "For cripes sake, Wes."

"They'll be fine after we get some grub into them."

"Really?"

"Really, they just got back from pushing cattle a thousand miles north."

"Where north?"

"Somewhere in Colorado, I reckon."

"That ain't no thousand miles."

"Whatever Monte, I hired 'em. They're my responsibility." Wes shakes his head, too tired to argue.

"You're right there, cousin." Monte turns toward the house disgusted. "They are your responsibility, 'cause they sure as shooting ain't mine."

"I've got me a suspicion Cousin Monte, you're gonna eat them words in a few days." Wes slaps the big man on the back.

"I doubt that very much."

Wes sits his dun gelding and smiles as he watches Jenks and another cowboy, named Harley Raper, head and heel a thousand pound steer, stretching him out between them as smooth as silk. Two weeks have passed since he brought the four men on the payroll and they have done the work of ten since then. For days, the men worked steadily from daylight to dark with only Sundays off. Ellen insists they keep the Sabbath. There would be no work done on the Sandigras, not on the Lord's day.

The tally score shows three hundred head have been branded and separated. Most are mother cows and calves, but many, like this old mossy horned steer, were missed by previous roundups and are as wild as a church house rat. Mud fat, in their prime, now rounded up and branded, they are ready for market. Prime beef that will bring hard cash money back east.

Monte is uncommitted, but Wes knows he has accepted the men as he pitched in and went to work with them. Even as kids, Monte would never admit to being wrong, nor would he apologize. Wes remembers his and Monte's Pa saying, apologizing was a waste of time. They figured if a man said it to begin with, he meant it down deep, there was no use apologizing, no sir, no use at all.

Pole worked, repairing gates and fences, needed to hold the wild cattle and keep them from beating a hasty retreat to parts unknown. The tall man wouldn't make a pimple on a real cowboy's backside anyway and with a rope, he is useless.

Monte makes a rough count, figuring at least two hundred head of the cattle in the holding pastures are ready to head for market. There's no need to hold them any longer. They are in their prime, mostly seven or eight year olds, they would gain no more weight. Now they're just eating up good grass.

Not a word was heard out of Halleck or his Running H outfit, but Wes knows they have been watching the Sandigras, studying every move they make. With Monte's urging, Wes relents and pushes all the Running H cattle they found, up and out of the canyons, back onto Running H graze. On several occasions, he found horse tracks and burned cigarette stubs on one of the high mesa's that runs the length of the ranch. Indians don't ride shod horses, and they sure don't smoke Bull Durham American cigarettes. No, it was the Running H boys nosing around. They probably reported the return of the cattle to Halleck.

Wes is like Pole, he's no cowboy, but he has sharp eyes and can read sign like an Indian, so he set himself to riding the Sandigras Range, watching and waiting, on guard for trouble. Another two weeks and they will have enough stock to drive to market, but where? Wes figures to ride into Tucson and try to find a buyer from the markets up north. At least he could find out where the other outfits were sending their cattle.

A warm breeze blows down the valley, making the tall grass wave back and forth out on the flats as it whispers gently across the canyon. Wes and Monte sit propped up against the barn door. Supper is done and the other hands ride off to Tucson. Cash money from their first month's labors is burning a hole in their pockets. Charlie Mack is just aching to see Joyce Ann and soon he will part company with his hard-earned money.

Pole rides with them, under the pretense of bringing back Miss Ellen some laying hens she had asked for, from one of the town's women. For a solid month, she has fussed about not having eggs to cook with until Monte finally sent two of the hands into town to get chickens.

Well, things didn't work out too well on the chicken buying trip. It seems the two riders, Nate Newhouse and Harley Raper, got themselves roaring drunk. They were three days sobering up and returning to the ranch. The worst is, they completely forgot about bringing Miss Ellen's chickens back to the ranch on their return trip. Looking like two young kids, with their hands caught in the cookie jar, they stand meekly beside their horses, expecting the worst as Monte gives them a tongue-lashing. Only Ellen, coming to their rescue and ushering them to the dinner table for a hearty meal, stops the tirade of words Monte is dishing out, or maybe the firing they were fixing to get.

Looking up at their savior, as plates are placed before them, the men blush, and apologize for their errant ways, promising they will never get drunk again. From where Wes stands beside the door, he grins, knowing the men will forget their pledge as soon as a whiskey bottle hits the bar in front of them. The chickens are temporarily forgotten.

They are good cowmen, none are any better. They like their whiskey, women, and cards, but all three could quickly separate them from their hard-earned wages. Even after the headaches and the money evaporating like smoke in the wind, the men soon forget and eagerly await their next payday and future trip into town.

Monte frowns as he watches the men gallop away. The lure of a good time is stronger than their fear of Apaches or losing their money, something he just cannot understand. Payday and Saturday night is their time to howl, and the men are ready and able to hold up to their part. Nothing gets their blood up and running like a good barroom brawl or a pretty woman.

Jenks strolls from the bunkhouse and pulls himself up a corral post to lean back against as he watches the riders head out in a cloud of dust, yelling their lungs out. Their leggy horses stretch out in a full run, their necks stretching to the fullest, almost as if they are hurrying to get to town themselves.

He grins and nods knowingly. "Those boys are gonna raise the roof in Tucson tonight."

"Probably the last we'll see of that bunch." Monte glares after the riders. "Just as well."

"You'd probably like that, wouldn't you, Mister Belton?"

"I would, if we didn't need to get our cattle to market." Monte looks over at the old puncher. "A man either rides for the brand or doesn't."

"Well, they ride for the Sandigras, but I do believe this is their night off."

"Let it go." Wes looks out across the valley. "They'll be back."

"You're right Boss, they'll be back." Jenks strikes a sulphur on the corral. "If I were you Mister Belton, I'd lighten up a little on them when they get back."

"You ain't me, Jenks."

"No, sir, that's a bona fide fact, I ain't." Jenks looks hard at Monte. "I'm the ramrod of this hacienda, and I'm telling you, they're good loyal hands, none better."

Monte dusts the sand from his pants and strolls off toward the ranch house without a backward glance.

Jenks watches him go and shakes his head. "He's a hard man to get to know."

Wes watches his cousin disappear inside the house. "He's a good man to have on your side in a fight."

"Well, if he doesn't back off, sooner or later we may have to find out how good."

"Don't sell him short, my friend." Wes warns. "He's rougher than a corncob that hasn't been shelled."

"Don't matter, he just can't talk down to grown men like they're kids." Jenks frowns. "It'll strike a nerve one day."

Nodding, Wes changes the subject. "Jenks, you know the Running H. What do you think? Will they attack us here?"

"I think Halleck will have to make a move against the Sandigras soon." Jenks exhales deeply. "Sad, but a fact, he's gotta show the country who's running this range, plus he needs your grass."

"You mean he's overgrazed his own range?"

"That he has. He runs more cattle than he can possibly find grass for."

"So he just takes over range that isn't his?"

"This range here in the canyons and more, all around Tucson." Jenks strikes another sulphur. "That's why he can't let you run him out of the Sandigras or others will try the same."

"Sounds like he's a greedy man."

"Halleck has always saved this valley for his winter pasture." Jenks draws on his cigarette and nods. "I heard in town, he's supposed to have a big herd of hot cattle coming up from old Mexico."

"Hot cattle?"

"Stolen, or cattle bought from rustlers down along the border."

"Did he ever own this valley?"

"No, but he might as well have, he kinda squatted on it for years, until you ventilated his hired gun. Since old Sandy Burris passed, maybe ten years back, his heirs always lived somewhere back east." Jenks smiles. "That's who the Sandigras was named after. He started the ranch, but whoever inherited it never took much interest in the place."

Wes rubs his chin thoughtfully. "I wonder how Webb got his hands on the deed to the Sandigras?"

"There was rumor of an article written in an eastern paper about foreclosing on the ranch." Jenks shrugs. "Maybe that's what happened, something about back taxes."

"Maybe that's how Webb found out about the Sandigras and bought it." Wes nods absently. "Wonder why Halleck didn't bother to bid on the ranch?"

"Couldn't say, never heard." Jenks shakes his head. "Don't forget about the Flannerys."

"Yeah, you mentioned them once before." Wes watches as Monte closes the door slowly. "Who are the Flannerys?"

"They have a ranch in the deep canyons, south of here." Jenks nods off toward the flats. "Even the Apache don't enter their range."

"Bad folks huh?"

"That's describing old Boston Flannery mildly, to say the least." Jenks laughs. "He's the he-bear up there. He's got himself four sons that are as bad as he is, maybe worse. Not counting all the cousins, plus that red haired girl of his."

"Sounds like an army."

"Might as well be; with that girl, two armies." Jenks shakes his head.

"What about her?"

"Name's Sarah Ann, rides and shoots like a man, and has a temper to match."

Wes grins. "She sounds half wild."

"That she is, wild as any of her brothers, but she's a looker for sure." Jenks laughs. "Got more curves than a rattlesnake."

"You say the Apache don't bother them any?"

"They may butcher a cow or steal a horse now and again, but they don't bother the Flannery Ranch at all." Jenks flips his smoke. "Tried once, a long time ago, didn't work out so well."

"What happened?"

Jenks shakes his head. "Old Boston Flannery, that's what. That old heathen mounted up his kinfolks and chased the Apache all the way into Mexico, destroying every Rancheria he passed on the way."

"He sounds like a rough one."

"Like you told me about Monte, don't sell him short."

"We've got two hundred fat steers ready to sell." Wes changes the subject.

"Where would you go with them?"

"East would be a guaranteed sale, but north to the gold fields in Colorado will bring you double, maybe even triple the money."

"You sure Jenks, about the market up north?"

"I told you, we made the trip already, yep it's there alright." Jenks nods in affirmation. "Them miners work hard, they need beef, and there's only one direction to them, that's due north across the mountains."

"How long a drive?"

"Well, with good weather, and not walking the weight off the cattle, maybe five, six weeks."

"How many punchers you gonna need?"

"It'll take a few days to settle the herd and get them trail savvy, so they won't stampede at every spook they see." Jenks nods slowly as he remembers. "Then we can probably get along with five or so, then I'll send the rest of the men back here."

"You won't push 'em hard."

"About two miles an hour, I figure."

"That seems slow."

"We won't take a chuck wagon, just tote the supplies on packhorses and travel light." Jenks figures on his fingers. "I figure, if we can start soon, we'll have an easy time driving through the mountains."

Wes looks along the canyon walls and nods. "You'll have to handle the drive. I need to stay here to handle the ranch."

"Or wait till spring and take them east." Jenks shrugs.

"I've got some cattle coming in from the east in the spring. I want these steers and bulls off this range before they can mix with the new ones."

"What about the cows we left in the canyons?"

"I aim to cross these longhorn cows on the new Hereford Bulls I'm bringing in and upgrade our beef herds."

Jenks scratches his whiskers. "Herefords, what kinda critter is that?"

"They're red and white cattle, with three times the beef on them than a longhorn, and a whole lot easier to handle."

"You don't say?" Jenks scratches his head. "Can one of them bulls kill a grizzly bear, or survive a cold winter?"

"Can a Longhorn?"

Jenks nods. "I saw an old Longhorn bull after he gutted a big bear. Man, they tore up half of Arizona, but the bull won. He was mighty tore up, but he survived to fight another day."

"That's something I would like to have seen."

"Well, me and old Harley didn't see the fight, we got there after it was over, but that's what happened alright."

Wes looks over at his foreman. "Old man, are you up to heading a drive north?"

"Who you calling old, you young scamp?" Looking up at the sky, Jenks nods. "I reckon I am, but the weather could turn bad any day now."

"Then we'll start getting things ready tomorrow." Wes looks over at the house. "Tell me Jenks, about the Apaches, I've heard about them back in Texas. Just what are we up against?"

Jenks shakes his head, rolling another smoke. "Wish I had me a bottle of rye."

"You thirsty?"

"No, sir, but just the thought of them red boogers gives me the shakes."

"They that bad?"

"They are. One could be sitting right out there behind a bush, or buried in the sand, and you'd never know it, until they put a knife in your liver."

"That sneaky are they?"

"Don't underestimate them, they're fighters." Jenks draws in deeply. "Not only are they sneaky, they're the meanest and cruelest tribe I've ever heard off, worse than the Comanche back in Texas, far worse."

"You ever fight them?"

"If you want to call it fighting, it's more like chasing a wisp of smoke through the mountains." Jenks shakes his head. "Only time you see them is when they want you to."

"Army?"

"Uh huh." The finished smoke goes flying. "Mostly the army is useless, unless it comes to burying folks."

"I wanna meet with them."

"Meet with who?"

"The Apache."

"You what?" Jenks stammers, not believing what he just heard. "You lost your senses, or what?"

"They're just men, ain't they?"

"No, sir boss, they ain't." Jenks removes his dusty hat and runs his hand through his thinning hair. "Not by a long shot they ain't."

"Jenks, we've got Halleck, the Flannerys, and Apache to contend with."

"Don't forget Waco Grange." Jenks adds.

"We've got to trail cattle north." Wes looks over toward the house. "We have a woman to protect. We just don't have the men to cover all that territory."

"You aiming on making a deal with the Apache, ain't you?"

"It's a thought," Wes nods, "if we could make some kind of treaty with their chiefs."

"Yeah, a thought that's liable to get you dead." The older man frowns. "They're a treacherous bunch boss, you just can't trust them."

"Jenks you got any ideas on how to talk with the Apache without losing our hair?"

"Reckon you could ride over to the fort. There's always a few tame Apache hanging around, mooching drinks." Jenks shrugs. "You might hire one of them to contact the wild ones and set up a meeting."

"Who's the main leader out here?"

"If you mean chief, take your pick. Cochise, Mangas Colorados, Victorio, Nana, there's plenty to go around."

"Well, we need some kind of truce." Wes looks over at the older man. "We can't work this place and be fighting with everyone."

"Suttero's people are the nearest to the Sandigras."

"He the chief?"

"He is, and probably the cruelest of all the Apache leaders." Jenks looks over at Wes. "I sure wouldn't want to put much trust in him though."

"Sounds like a bad one."

"He's the youngest of the chiefs, and he hates whites with a passion."

"He's the one I want to talk with."

"You're crazy boss," Jenks protests. "He'll have your eyeballs frying over an ant bed."

"Can you arrange it?"

"I know we don't have the men that Halleck or Flannery has." Jenks lights another smoke. "I'm telling you hoss, making a truce with the Apache ain't the way."

"Getting the Apache to leave us alone, would be a start, even if we have to bribe them." Wes looks off across the valley.

"Are you saying they just can't be trusted?"

"If an Apache gives you his word, you can believe him, I reckon."

"If they don't?"

Jenks shrugs his shoulders. "I know a half breed kid at the fort who runs with the wild ones. He may be of some help."

"You think so?"

"I helped him out once, found him with a broken leg and fixed him up. Injuns don't forget a favor."

"Good." Wes pulls out the makings. "When the boys get back from town, you ride over to the fort and see what you can arrange. Meanwhile, I'll get the horses shod and the supplies you'll need, ready for the drive."

"Well, have everything ready when I get back, it's getting late in the season to be pushing cattle north." Jenks stands up. "We've got to move."

"I'll have everything ready."

"And boss."

"Yes, Mister Lohan." Wes grins at the man.

"If you find yourself minus your hair, and strung over a hot fire, don't blame old Jenks."

Wes watches Jenks walk away toward the bunkhouse as he builds himself a smoke. Drawing in on the cigarette, he nods solemnly. Yes, he had won them a ranch, but the pot also contains a whole pile of trouble to go with it. He is beginning to understand what the rancher Webb meant when he questioned whether Wes could hold onto the Sandigras. He wonders, how Webb knew of the trouble he would face, here in Arizona. Shrugging, he flips the butt and smiles, shucks, there's nothing new about trouble. He inherited some kind of trouble, one way or another, from the day he was born.

# CHAPTER 5

The cattle are mud fat, trail branded, and just waiting to be lined out before heading north to Colorado. Most are steers and bulls with a few older cows far past their calving days. Longhorn cows are the best mother cows of any breed, capable of having healthy calves into their early twenties, which most of these are.

Jenks has been gone three days. Wes figures to start him on the drive with the cattle as soon as he returns from Fort Bowie. Two hundred head of mostly prime beef graze the lush canyon, cash money on the hoof. It's late summer, soon the snow will start to fall in the North Country, and there is little time to lose. The herd must be through the deep passes before the bad weather comes closing in on them for winter.

"You reckon Jenks will be back today?" Pole sits looking out across the valley with one long leg wrapping around his saddle horn.

"Maybe, hard to say for sure." Wes dismounts and pulls at his cinch. "I sure hope so, fall's coming soon. We need to get the cattle on the trail."

"You sending me with 'em?"

"No, I need your gun here on the ranch." Wes scans the valley. "There's trouble coming Pole, I can smell it."

The lanky man pulls a tobacco pouch from his shirt pocket and studies the grazing steers. "Those hides are gonna bring a lot of money up north, you trust them boys to come back with it?"

"I trust them." Wes reaches for the sack of tobacco. "They've never given me reason not to."

"Shucks hoss, we don't even know them fellers." Pole grins. "They could sell the cattle and keep riding."

"They could do that alright." Wes nods in agreement. "I know the type, working cowhands, they're honest men to a fault. I'm betting they'll be back."

"We'll see I reckon." Pole exhales.

Wes knows his partner. Something else is nagging at him. "Speak up Pole, what is it?"

"You know, Monte is overdue getting back with our new hands, providing he could hire some."

Wes looks off toward the old wagon road, leading to Tucson, hoping to see his cousin riding in. "I know."

"You figure, he had trouble?"

"Doubt it, Monte's the peaceable kind." Wes watches as two old bulls push into each other. "He insisted on going and hiring his own men. He'll be okay."

"Well, something's holding him." Pole unlimbers his long leg. "One thing for certain, it don't take this long to ride to town and he ain't a drinking man."

"Like you said, he may have had trouble finding hands in Tucson." Wes shrugs. "Maybe he had to go on to Bisbee to find men."

"Unless he ran into Apaches."

"If he ain't back by morning, we'll ride out and look for him." Wes worries. "He'll be back."


The ranch buildings come into sight with the setting sun. Sundown also brings on the coolness of the night as soon as it's warming rays go down in the west. Wes and Pole unsaddle, wash up, and enter the warm, pleasant kitchen. Hot biscuits, meat frying, and boiling coffee always give off the best aroma to a hungry and saddle weary man.

Ellen looks at each face expectantly, but doesn't speak as she sets food before them. The other Sandigras hands, Harley Raper, Nate Newhouse, and the youngster, Charlie Mack, don't look up, just continue to shovel food into their faces. Wes tried to convince Monte to take a hand with him to town, but Monte insisted he wanted Ellen protected.

"He'll be in tonight, Miss Ellen, don't you fret none." Pole read her thoughts.

Wes glares at Pole for making the remark, a remark he knows might not come true. "You boys got the horses ready to push north at sunup?"

"We're ready, Wes." Harley, the oldest of the trio, nods. "Reckon we ain't waiting for Jenks?"

"Nope, can't waste another day. I want the herd to pull out at daylight. He'll catch up." Wes thirstily empties a cold glass of fresh milk. "Man, that's tasty; better than beer. That old Jersey cow was worth every dime I gave for her."

Pole looks up from his plate at the remark. "Speak for yourself, Wes Tobin. For me, ain't nothing better than a cool beer, and you gave the liveryman way too much for that bag of bones."

"A skinny cow gives more milk than a fat one," Ellen laughs. "I can't say I ever recall seeing a round, fat Jersey."

"Beer's fine, but not at the supper table." Charlie speaks up, ducking his head as Pole glares over at him.

"What would a young pup like you, know about beer, Charlie Mack?"

"Well, Mister Pole Nichols, I just might know more than you think I do."

"Humbug!" Pole resumes eating. "Milk better than beer, ridiculous."

"Yes, sir, come morning, we'll be ready." Harley interrupts the argument. "Winter's just around the corner, we need to get moving."

"Pole will trail with you until Jenks gets back." Wes pulls out a chair. "I'll have Jenks catch you on the trail."

"Yes, sir." Charlie grins over at Pole. "That's good news, maybe he'll bring some beer."

"Youngster, one more word out of you tonight, and I'm fixing to drown you."

"In beer, I hope." Charlie deadpans, making everyone at the table, even Pole, break out in laughter.

"We're gonna be short of drovers."

Wes nods. "We'll make do."

"I'll lead the packhorses until Monte gets back with more men." Ellen speaks up from where she is sitting near the stove.

"Oh no you won't."

"You can't stay here and guard me Wes Tobin, and get the herd heading north at the same time." Ellen stands up. "I'll be going, and that's final."

Wes nods slowly and smiles. He knows, until the herd settles on the trail a few days, he needs every man and woman he has in the saddle to help push them. "Okay, Miss Ellen, and thank you."

The rattling supper dishes become deathly quiet as the sound of several horses break the stillness outside with the noise of their arrival in the ranch yard. Ellen is the first out the door, throwing herself into Monte's arms as he dismounts.

"Thank the Lord." She almost faints as he holds her up. "I'd almost given up on you."

Six mounted riders sit watching the proceedings as Monte ushers her back inside the kitchen. "Take care of these men for me, Pole."

Pole looks the recruits over slowly, then nods. "You fellers light down and put up your horses, wash, then come in for supper. Charlie boy, show 'em where to pen their broncs and where they can clean up."

"Yes, sir."

Pole looks over where Wes is standing and shakes his head. "At least, they're sober. They even sit upright on their horses."

Only a cold stare comes from Wes at the friendly reminder of the condition his hired hands arrived at the ranch several weeks back. He returns to his seat in the kitchen. Wes studies each face as the men eat hungrily at the supper before them. Not one to make a hasty judgment, he waits until the men finish eating, before saying anything. "Why don't you men tell us your names and where you hail from?"

Every new man at the table turns his attention to where Wes sits drinking his coffee. "Don't reckon we caught your name, mister." One of the new men answers.

Wes looks across at the older man and over to where Monte sits watching. "Introduce your new hands Monte, then tell them who we are."

Monte nods and turns to where the men sit. "This is Wes Tobin, men. He's the owner of the Sandigras and your new boss.

"We understood you to be the owner, Mister Belton?"

"This is Sam Wade." Monte nods at the speaker, ignoring the

question. "The other five gents are Luke, Cole, Lonnie, Tad, and Jacob. They'll tell you their last names if they decide to."

Each man nods as Monte introduces them. With the four Wes hired, plus Pole and Monte, the Sandigras crew now counts thirteen. Halleck and Flannery both have more men, but at least there is enough hands now to get the ranch work done, plus put up some resistance, if it's needed.

Dawn is still an hour away as the horses are hazed into the corral and saddled. Jenks rode in, sometime during the night, unsaddled, and rolled up on his saddle near the corral, falling quickly into an exhausted sleep. Wes discovers him as he makes his morning inspection of the corrals, just as the rest of the hands are sitting down to breakfast. Toeing Jenks awake, he hands him a lit smoke and waits for the man to get his eyes open.

"Thank you kindly, Wes." Jenks sits up and stretches before taking the smoking cigarette. "Reckon I was a mite tuckered out."

"Sorry I had to wake you, but breakfast is on the table and we're burning daylight."

"I'm fine, I can always sleep, but I sure can't get Miss Ellen's good cooking anytime of the day." Jenks rises and leans against the corral fence. "I must have been awfully tired to sleep this late."

"Yeah, it must be five o'clock already." Wes laughs.

Looking over, Wes can tell the old puncher is giving the newcomers at the table a good look over, as he sits down to breakfast. He isn't happy with Monte's selection of riders.

After breakfast, Jenks calls off the names of the riders he wants to accompany him on the drive north. He assigns only one of the new men to go on the trail drive. "I'll take Harley, Charlie, Nate, and the new guy Jacob with me." Jenks repeats, for all to hear, as he pulls his cinch tight on a fresh mount.

"That's only five men."

"Wade and a couple of the others can help us push 'em for a couple days." Jenks checks his saddlebags. "After that we should get along just fine."

Monte stands off to the side, listening. "You don't like my pick of men, Jenks?"

"No, Mister Belton, I sure don't. Like I said, I'll use the men I do know on this drive and that new kid, Jacob."

Monte stiffens and steps closer to where Jenks is tying on his war bags and blanket roll. "What's wrong with them or is it just me, you don't like?"

The old puncher turns to face the bigger man. Wes notices Jenks slips his pistol loose as he turns. "Mister Belton." The voice becomes hard as nails. "You got several pounds and a few years on me. If you want a fight so bad, you better strap on a pistol."

Wes has seen the look many times. Jenks turns stone-cold as he prepares to draw on Monte. Stepping between the two men, he holds up his hands. "Let it go Jenks, ride out."

"Yes, sir." Jenks uncoils, his facial muscles relax and the tenseness goes out of his shoulders. "We'll be back soon as we can."

"Good luck," Wes says, as Jenks turns to his horse, then fixes his attention to where Monte leads his horse toward the house. Monte is a hard man to know. Wes knows he is a good man, but the other men don't know. His cousin sure isn't about to explain himself or try to make friends with any of them.

"Good luck to you, while I'm gone, Wes." Jenks steps easily into the saddle and looks down. "Remember what I told you, if Martine can arrange a meeting with any of the Apache, he will come here."

"Can I trust him?"

Jenks grins. "Well, it's a mite late to worry about that boss. I figure you can trust him, at least more than some of your new men."

"You know something about them I don't?"

Jenks straightens himself in the saddle. "Most of them have ridden for Halleck at one time or another."

"Jacob or Sam Wade?"

"No, I can't say they have, not that I know, but the others have for a fact. I can't figure out why the dark skinned gent, called Wilson, is here at all."

"You know him personally?"

"I do, he rode for the Halleck brand the last five years and far as I know he wasn't fired. He sure didn't quit top wages to ride for less here on the Sandigras."

Wes looks over to where the rider Wilson is cinching up his horse. "I see what you mean."

"He's a top hand for sure, but don't trust him for a minute." Jenks reins his horse toward the canyon. "He can use that gun he packs, he's killed more than one man. Adiós amigo."

"Adiós." Wes watches as the five riders, along with Sam Wade, Lonnie Bud, and Jim Cole, disappear into the gloom. "See you when you get back."

Jenks' arm waves as the rest of the riders on the ranch, including Monte, start toward the canyon where the steers and old cows have been assembled. It will take every available man to push the cattle over the cliffs to get them heading north. Wes turns to where Pole waits, beside the barn.

"I take it Jenks don't approve of our new hands." The tall man hands Wes the reins to a raw-boned sorrel gelding.

"He don't for a fact, but they're Monte's pick, so we'll just kinda watch them."

"Kinda watch them?" Pole grins. "Uh huh."

"We have some ground to cover before sundown. Let's get to it."

Three days later, the hands sent to help push the cattle away from their home range and trail break them, return to the Sandigras. Reporting all is well, the small herd is traveling steadily on the trail heading north to the Colorado gold mines, the riders sit down to a late breakfast.

Monte motions for Wes to come outside to the corrals. "Cousin, our passes out of these canyons are too vulnerable."

"What are you aiming to do?" Wes lights up a smoke. "I plan to fence every pass leading out of the canyons." Monte looks off, across the valley. "That's what I aim to do."

"That'll take some doing."

"It's got to be done, or we won't be able to raise any beef." Monte waves his big hand toward the far canyons. "There's just too many passes leading out of these valleys."

"A good cow rustler has wire cutters and they'll use 'em." Wes blows smoke.

"True enough," Monte smiles, "and I'll hang every man I find on our range with wire cutters."

"Oh, and you called me cold hearted."

"I'm learning cousin. Take a wagon into Tucson and get me the wire, will you?"


Wes and Pole ride alongside the wagon as Sam Wade drives it slowly down the main street of Tucson, pulling to a stop in front of the large general store. Tying the horses off, the three men brush at their dusty clothes before entering the busy mercantile. Looking slowly around the store, Wes waits until the owner finishes with some town women and hands the man his list of supplies.

"I've got most of the supplies you want, but you've got an awful lot of that newfangled wire on your list, Mister Tobin."

"Yes, sir, it is a lot," Wes acknowledges. "That's what the man wants."

"You must be aiming on fencing half of Arizona," the storeman jokes.

"Well, what I've got is on the rear dock. Have your man bring the wagon around back."

"You may not become too popular, stringing this new wire, Wes." Wade looks over to where the wagon sits. "I'll drive the wagon around and load the stuff."

Pole grins from the sidewalk. "Shucks Sam, don't let that worry you none, he's never been known to win a popularity contest."

"Yeah, well this might be different." The man isn't joking. "Barbed wire is like poison around here, could get a man killed, or a whole lot of men killed."

The rolls of wire stack neatly in the heavy work wagon, followed by sacks of flour, sugar, and other supplies from Ellen's list. The storeman grins broadly, watching the last of the wire load then retreats inside.

The rolls of wire were a bad investment for him, taking up his floor space in the back for several months. He's glad to be rid of it and the trouble it brought. The man who originally ordered it was convinced, after a good beating by Halleck's men, to forget about picking it up.

"Let's go have a bite to eat and maybe a drink before heading out." Wes looks over at the two men as the wagon is loaded. "What do you say?"

"Sounds good to me." Wade climbs onto the wagon seat.

"I'll drink to that." Pole quickly swings into his saddle. "After all that work, I need me a beer."

"You'll drink to anything." Wes shakes his head.

"Most anything, Mister Tobin, most anything."

"The Grubstake Saloon has the best food." Wade picks up the lines and clucks to the team, "and cold beer."

"My kinda place exactly." Pole laughs and kicks his horse into a trot. "I'll thank you not to say a single word about only one beer, Mister Tobin."

"It's your money."

"It surely is, but you're buying." Pole laughs. "I'm working today, remember?"

"Why would I do that?" Wes shakes his head. "You're working for wages, not beer."

"Why, it's pay for my bodyguard services, which I do believe you'll be needing as soon as folks see this wagon loaded with wire." Pole laughs again, "and that comes extra."

Ordering steak and potatoes, Wes leans back and looks over at Wade then around the crowded room. "I take it you don't like wire, Mister Wade?"

"I don't like it at all." The man picks up his beer. "I've seen what it can do to critters caught up in it, even men."

"Maybe you best draw your wages then, cause old Monte is fixing to wire off the canyons." Wes looks over at the puncher. "Nobody will be affected except the Sandigras. It'll keep our stock from wandering away, by accident or any other ways."

Wade looks over the rim of his glass. "If you want me to quit Mister Tobin, say so, if not, I reckon I'll stick."

"No hard feelings Mister Wade, just giving you a choice is all."

"I'll stick." Wade sips on his beer. "This show might be interesting to watch, and you can just call me Sam."

The steak and potatoes are barely finished when the doors of the saloon bang open and several riders pour into the room. Wes watches Wade's eyes narrow as he recognizes the riders.

"Careful here boss, they're Halleck men." Wade whispers quietly. "That's Waco Grange leading them."

"Whose wagon is out front with the wire?" The man wears a tied-down pistol, low on his right, and a reverse draw pistol high on his left. The hard-set jaw, along with the deep frown, says all that needs saying. Waco Grange is on the prod, ready to make a fight of it.

Wes looks calmly from under his hat at the gunfighter, casually taking another drink of beer. "Who wants to know?"

The sharp cold eyes settle on the table, taking in its three occupants. "Waco Grange, I ride for the Running H."

"You mean you kill for the Running H don't you, Mister Grange?" Wes has his right hand hidden from sight, which Grange doesn't overlook. "That's my wire, what about it?"

Grange starts forward, only to be stopped by a gruff voice from the doorway. "Hold up there, Waco."

The man is big, bigger than Monte. His shoulders are covered in solid muscle, bunching under the vest and shirt.

"I was just asking the man a question, Mister Halleck."

"Waco, you and the boys have a drink on me, while I talk to this gentleman, who I believe claims to be the owner of the Sandigras."

Wes lays down his fork and studies the big man. So this is the he-bull himself, Rowland Halleck, owner of the Running H. The man is big, but more than that, he is proud and arrogant. He notices the way Grange backed away, like a whipped dog when ordered. He figures, here is one dangerous man.

"Claim, Mister Halleck?" Wes stands up. "Your hired killer, Mister Bodine, used that same term, just before he expired. Seems he couldn't or wouldn't, read my recorded deed to the Sandigras."

"You planning on fencing off the canyons, Mister Tobin?" Halleck leans heavily against the bar, reminding Wes of a bear scratching itself on a tree.

"I didn't buy that wire to look at." Wes nods. "I'm fencing every trail and gully leading out of the canyons."

The big man drops his eyes to the tied down pistol on Wes' side, then raises the flaps of his vest, showing his chest and hips. "I ain't an armed gun hand, if there's any fighting, it'll be with them." The ham like fists rise slowly, as the rancher smiles insolently.

"You seem to know me, Halleck." Wes glances at the long bar where the Running H riders stand silently, listening to every word. "So I won't bother to introduce myself."

"Why shouldn't I know you, Mister Tobin, you killed one of my men." The big man glares across at Wes. "You throw a wide loop."

Wes shrugs, stepping away from the table where he can watch the entire room. "Your man drew on me, didn't leave me much choice, and while we're on the subject, any loop I throw is at my own stock."

"I'm telling you, don't string that wire in the canyon." Halleck's fists clench. "You won't get a second warning."

"You told me, I hear real good." Wes smiles slightly. "Now Mister Halleck, I'm telling you, stay off Sandigras Range and keep your riders out of the canyons."

"Or what?"

"I'll kill every Running H man I find on my range causing trouble." Wes looks at the men standing beside the bar. "You people hear me good. From now on, the Sandigras is closed to all Running H riders."

Halleck studies the table where Pole and Sam Wade sit, wheeling about and exiting the saloon, motioning for his men to follow.

Wes smiles coldly, returning slowly to his seat.

"I'll be danged." Wade grins broadly and slaps his leg. "You bluffed him boss. You caused old rough-and-tumble Halleck to tuck tail and run."

Wes finishes his beer, then slowly stands up. "No, I didn't Sam, you don't bluff a man like Halleck. He just wasn't ready to make his play is all."

"Whichever it were, I ain't ever seen that man backwater from any man, never."

Pole finishes his beer, placing the empty mug softly on the table, nodding slowly at the empty plates scattered in front of them. "Let's head for home boys, while we can."

Wes grins. "You mean you don't want another beer?

"I suddenly lost my thirst, let's get."

Looking the street over good, before they step through the swinging doors, Pole and Wes mount their horses while Wade climbs onto the wagon. Halleck and the Running H riders are nowhere in sight. Wes can feel eyes on his back, as they ride slowly out of Tucson, but no Halleck riders show on the dusty street.

Wes rides the southern canyons while Monte puts the other hands to work stringing fence along the many small draws and trails exiting the Sandigras. Searching the far-flung skyline, Wes turns his bay gelding back toward the far-off ranch headquarters. Today, he is uneasy, jittery, and nervous. Only Pole remains at the house to watch over Miss Ellen and the ranch buildings.

Pole is a good man and Wes trusts him with his life. However, if they are attacked, would one lone gun hold off the raiding Apache? Jenks warned him several times before leaving, to be on guard and never let it down. The Apache Martine, the friendly half-breed from the fort, still hasn't put in an appearance at the ranch. For some reason Wes cannot throw his uneasiness.

Kicking the gelding into a hard lope toward the home ranch, Wes holds the gelding in a little, preserving the animal's strength for the long miles he has to cover. Two hours later, the blowing gelding slides to a halt in front of the ranch house as Wes steps lightly from the saddle.

Pole appears from the corner of the house and hurries toward Wes. "I thought the devil himself was after you the way that old pony was fanning the breeze."

"Is everything alright here?" Wes looks about the yard.

"Yep." Pole looks him over curiously. "What's got you spooked, hoss? You dang near ran that bronc to death."

"Don't know for sure, I had a bad feeling riding in tonight, a real bad feeling. It made the hair on the back of my neck stand up." Wes shrugs. "I can't explain it, just getting jumpy in my old age, I reckon."

Pole's eyes suddenly widen as he looks across the sweaty gelding, Wes is unsaddling. "Well, maybe that uneasy feeling of yours has just been answered."

Turning slowly, Wes focuses his eyes on several warriors, sitting their horses quietly across the yard. Six mounted Apache men watch the two whites from the trees lining the nearest corral. Naked, except for the breechcloths hanging from their waists to their knees. The dark-skinned warriors are all fierce looking young men. Some wear their hair flowing long and loose, down past their shoulders, others have theirs cropped short, just below their necks. No war paint shows on their dark faces, a fact that makes Wes breathe easier. The youngest looking of the warriors, rides slowly forward, stopping only feet from where Wes and Pole are standing beside the ranch house.

"I am the one called, Martine." The youngster stares down at Wes and Pole from his horse. "The white man, Jenks, come to fort, say you want me to ride here. Say you pay me to come to this place."

The face is young, but Wes senses the warrior is older and wiser than his appearance. Not as dark as most Apache, this one is half white and half Apache. According to most whites, a breed is the worst kind of Apache, mean as a full-blood and smarter. Many are mixed with Mexican blood which makes them even worse in the eyes of the Americans that populate Arizona. Not an ounce of fat shows on any of the young men. All are lean and smooth muscled with coal black eyes that seem to look into a man, almost as if they are reading your mind.

"Jenks said Martine is a friend of the whites." Wes walks nearer the warrior. "You are welcome here."

"I tell you this white man, no Apache is truly a friend of the whites, even a breed." The voice is soft, but the words are hard. "Your people have given the Apache no reason to like the white race."

"Perhaps we can become friends, Martine." Wes looks the young warrior straight in the eye. "As I said, you are welcome."

"And the others?" The youngster nods behind him. "Are they welcome?"

"If they come in peace, they are welcome here at the Sandigras." Wes looks over at the solemn warriors. "Come, sit with me. I will have food and drink prepared for my friends the Apache."

Ellen quickly heats leftovers from last night's supper. Pole tells her to stay in the house, out of sight, as he brings out the hot platters of food for the warriors to eat. Martine and the warriors bite hungrily into the beef, chicken, and potatoes, nodding with satisfaction.

"He is a good cook." The youngster nods at Pole, who retreats to the porch after bringing out the food. "Maybe he could teach the Apache to make food taste this good."

"Yes, he is." Wes laughs. "He might be willing to teach you."

"White man, is there to be trust between us?" The young warrior nods toward the house. "We know of the white woman with the yellow hair. We have seen her many times. She is the one who prepared this food."

Wes nods. "We are new here, Martine. We know little of your ways."

"Never lie to us, never. We can smell a lie on your tongue before you speak it." Martine looks over at Wes with a deadpan face, a face that is unreadable. "We may be stupid Apaches, but we can sense fear in a man's sweat."

"I did not lie. I just didn't bring the woman out here for you to see." Wes' face hardens. "Trust me Martine, no one here fears the Apache. We respect your people, but do not make the mistake of believing we fear them."

"Why did you bring me here?" Martine changes the conversation. "What do you wish from me?"

"I asked you here so I could talk with the chiefs." Wes motions to the other warriors who are still eating.

"These?" Martine snickers and speaks to the others in Apache, causing them to burst out laughing. "They are not chiefs. They are my friends from the fort."

"Your friends, they're not chiefs?"

"Do you think I would ride here alone?" Martine smiles and tries to joke. "This is dangerous country, white eyes ride this land." Irritated with his ignorance of the Apache, Wes ignores the sarcastic remark.

"I want to talk with the headmen of the Apache."

"Why?"

"I will pay you well if you bring them here to talk."

"Why?" The question comes again. "Why do you wish to meet with our chief?"

"I want peace with the Apache. I want to live in these canyons in peace." Wes tries to explain what he wants, careful to form his words. Jenks already warned him the Apache would consider any word of apology or hesitancy as a sign of weakness.

"You are afraid of the Apache. Maybe you have a weak heart." Martine snarls, thumping his chest with his closed fist. "Or maybe you have too many enemies among the whites here."

"I fear no man Martine, no people. I prefer peace with your people instead of war and fighting."

"The redheaded ones, the Flannerys are people to fear." The young Apache shrugs. "Are you, white man?"

Quicker than a blink, Wes lunges to his feet, firing the heavy pistol five times in an upright post in the corral.

The warriors look on in amazement, as five holes appear in the heavy wooden post, cutting it almost in half. Martine jumps backward from the porch, thinking at first, Wes is firing at him.

Reloading the weapon, Wes calmly places it back in his holster, ignoring the cocked rifles the warrior's point at him. "Like I said, I fear no man, but I would rather have peace than war with my neighbors, but I reckon that's up to you and your people."

Martine looks again at the bullet holes, nodding his head. "I have seen men like you who fight at the fort."

"Men like me?" Wes studies the face of the breed. "Bad men who kill for money." Martine tosses a piece of beef to one of the warriors. "Do you kill for money, white man?"

"I have, but now I have come here to raise cattle and maybe a family."

"I see death in your eyes. I smell death on you like the rabid dog. I think you like to kill, maybe."

"Apaches kill."

"We kill for our land, we fight Mexicans, Americans, but we do not kill our own people for money."

Wes changes the subject. "Will you bring the chiefs in for a talk?"

"Why should they come here?" Martine looks at the house. "This is a dangerous land for them."

"I will guarantee their safety on this land."

"From Flannery?" Martine points south. "The redheaded devils that live there, you cannot protect them from the evil one."

"I give you my word." Wes stares into the warrior's eyes. "I will protect the chiefs from anyone who causes trouble on this range."

"You would protect Apaches against other whites?"

"In these canyons, I protect everyone who comes in peace."

Martine shakes his head. "No, they will not come here. I will speak with them for you, but they will say where they will meet with you."

"Sounds like a good way to lose your hair." Pole speaks up. "Don't go to them, pard."

"It is the only way, if you want to speak with Chief Suttero." Martine looks over at the slender man and shrugs. "He will not come here."

"Set up a talk, we will come to wherever he chooses."

"This is good." Martine stands and wipes his hands. "You will bring gifts for the chiefs?"

"I will bring many gifts," Wes agrees. "What do they wish?"

"Guns, bullets, and maybe whiskey."

"You know I will not bring these things, but I will bring other gifts." Wes flattens his hands. "No guns, no whiskey."

"No whiskey?" Martine shrugs and looks at the house. "Your woman, the blond headed one, she watches from the house."

Wes stares at the youngster closely. "Ellen, come out here."

The kitchen door opens slowly as Ellen steps through it, standing straight and proud before them. The sun's rays make her yellow hair sparkle in its light. Martine looks Ellen up and down as she appears on the porch. Walking to where she stands, he touches her hair lightly. When she doesn't flinch or show fright, he smiles. Her big blue eyes stare unflinching across at him. "You are a lucky man Wes Tobin, she is very beautiful, and she is also a brave woman."

Wes nods. "Yes, I am a lucky man."

"An Apache warrior would give many horses to have a woman such as this one for his wickiup."

"Martine knows better than that. He has lived among the whites at the fort." Wes scolds the young Apache. "A white woman is not for the Apache."

The warrior smiles and moves toward his horse. Pulling a small gold cross and necklace from a leather pouch, he walks back to the porch and hands it to Ellen.

"You are kind señora, this is for the food." Ellen looks over at Wes, unsure whether to take the gold chain. Seeing him nod, she reaches out her hand.

"It is beautiful." She turns the cross in her hand. "Thank you."

"Yes, it is beautiful." Martine looks at the small hand holding the chain and cross. "It should be worn by one such as you."

# CHAPTER 6

Wes breathes a sigh of relief as he watches the warriors disappear. It is good they left before Monte and the men return from the canyon. Monte knew he was planning to meet with Martine, but he wouldn't expect to see so many Apache warriors in his front yard.

"You think it was a good idea, letting them see her?" Pole stands beside Wes. "It seemed risky to me."

"You heard Martine. They already knew she was here." Wes shrugs. "They've probably been watching the ranch for days. Sure wasn't any use to keep hiding her from them."

"Well, I doubt Monte will think it was a good idea." Pole grins. "Especially, if he saw that buck touching her hair."

"I'm trying to make peace with those people, Pole. Trust comes with it."

"Uh huh." Pole scratches a sulphur on his britches leg. "Boot hill is plumb full of folks who trusted their fellow man."

"They don't see blonde hair often, could be this was the first time." Wes shrugs. "It didn't hurt anything."

"Yeah, tell that crap to old Monte." Pole blows smoke into the air and laughs lightly. "While you're telling him about that buck running his fingers through Miss Ellen's hair, try to explain the little doodad he gave her."

"Some things are better off forgotten and not spoken of, Mister Nichols."

"Amen to that brother," Pole laughs as he walks away. "He ain't blind. He's bound to see that gold chain sooner or later."

"To refuse his gift, would have been an insult."

"You tell Monte that, then start ducking," Pole laughs. "Yes sir, this could get interesting."

The heavily loaded work wagon rolls slowly into the barnyard at sundown with Monte and his fence crew following it. Pole looks around to find Wes, then walks slowly out to the corrals.

"Where's Wes?" Monte pulls his saddle and wet blankets from the tired horse and looks around.

"He's here somewhere. At least he was a few minutes ago."

Monte just slung his saddle across a corral pole when Wes walks from the barn, stopping in front of the men. "You boys have a good day? No trouble, I hope."

"We finished fencing the passes, all except the west road to Tucson." Monte leans back against the top rail of the corral. "There was no trouble."

"Then I reckon Halleck or his men didn't show?"

"No, just us, the wire, and a few jackrabbits." Charlie Mack, one of the younger riders laughs.

The dinner bell sounds as Ellen summons the men for supper. Pole looks over at Wes and smiles as they head for the kitchen. "You best eat a good meal, old buddy."

"Why's that?"

"I figure when she tells Monte about that Indian touching her hair, you and him are gonna have another set-to like the last time." Pole watches Monte's broad back disappear through the door, then his arm wraps protectively around Ellen. "Can't say I would blame him much either."

Wes looks over at Pole and nods. "Thanks old buddy for worrying about my health."

"Think nothing of it, Mister Tobin."

There's little talk around the long table. The hands are busy eating, tired and famished from a hard day's work. A good supper, warm bed, and some sleep are foremost on their minds. Pole watches and waits, occasionally looking over at Ellen, and around the table. He knows

Monte's hair-trigger temper. It would only take her spilling the beans about the young Apache touching her hair and trouble will erupt sure as shooting. Monte smiles and looks over at the little blonde he loves so much as she takes her seat beside him. "Did you have a good day, Mrs. Belton?"

Pole swallows hard, his ears and eyes on point. He is shocked when she makes no mention of the Apache presence at the ranch, only that she had a good day. Wes only smiles as he begins to appreciate what a remarkable woman she is. Jealous and protective as Monte is of his wife, the wrong word, or any word about the Apache, could start a small war, right in the middle of the kitchen table.

Wes is surprised, the Apaches are never mentioned until Monte, Pole, and himself are all sitting on the back porch after supper.

"You trust the Apaches, cousin?" Monte listens skeptically as Wes tells about the visit from Martine and the others.

"I'll let you know after I meet with them again."

"Well, it's your hair I reckon." Monte shrugs. You take care of yourself. We can't afford to lose you."

"Thank you, Monte." Both Wes and Pole are shocked at the sentiment from the big man.

"Thank this warrior Martine for the beautiful necklace he presented my wife." Monte looks over into the blank faces before him. "It is beautiful and looks expensive."

"Ellen told you?" Pole stammers.

Monte nods. "When you get married Pole, if you ever do, you'll find there is no secrets between a man and his wife."

"She never mentioned anything about the Apache at the supper table." Pole shakes his head.

"She explained the whole thing to me in private, before my temper let me make a fool of myself and ruin everything we've got going here."

Pole and Wes look at each other amazed. Is this Monte Belton talking or an imposter? Never, in all the years growing up together, have they heard Monte make any excuses for his actions or temper.

"You ain't mad?" Pole asks.

"No, she made me realize they are just paying her a compliment on her cooking."

"Uh huh, I'm turning in." Pole takes one last look at Monte and walks away. "I ain't feeling well, don't think you are either."

Monte watches the tall man walk away, shaking his head. "You think the way he's acting I never apologized for my actions before."

"You haven't cousin, not once," Wes laughs.


Wes sits his gelding in a grove of tall cottonwood trees, studying the small trail leading off to the west. Somewhere over the high ridges, back in the deep gorges, he knows the Flannery Clan laid claim to the land and built their holdings. Before pulling out on the drive, Jenks drew him out a rough map of the area, warning him again of the bad tempered Flannerys.

As he enjoys a smoke, one lone rider suddenly appears, high on the ridge, a clear silhouette against the skyline. The early morning sun from the east makes the horse and rider easily visible from where Wes sits his gelding, hiding under a large cottonwood tree. The rider is looking down, studying the new fence blocking the only pass out of this end of the canyon. Monte and his crew finished stretching fence across this last pass only the day before. The wire shimmers brightly in the morning sun as it dances along the sharp barbs.

Wes watches and listens as the horse starts slowly down the narrow rocky trail that bottoms out onto the flats, almost at the fence. Small rocks and gravel cascade down the steep incline as the horse and rider reach the bottom.

Kicking his horse, Wes eases slowly forward, keeping the trees between him and the approaching horsemen, careful to remain hidden from the rider's view. He doesn't know what the man is up to since there is no reason for him to go further down the rough trail, unless he intends to cut the fence. The rider, whoever he is, can plainly see from the ridge above, there is no gate and the fence is solid.

Several minutes pass and Wes is still obscured by the line of trees. He is near the fence, near enough to stop the man if he has to. He can hear the horse moving toward the fence, bringing him closer, only yards from where he waits. Dismounting, he quickly ducks through the strands of wire and hides alongside the narrow trail.

Only the rider's lower body shows from where Wes waits, but he can plainly see wire cutters in the man's right hand. Lunging forward, Wes grabs the near leg and flips the rider, head first, off the side of the lunging horse. Slapping the horse forward, out of his way, Wes jerks the fallen rider to his feet, his balled fist ready to strike.

Shoulder length red hair falls out from under the felt hat as the rider fights and kicks like a wildcat. Wes is shocked, his hand grabs at the scratching and spitting girl as she tries kicking herself loose. Stepping quickly back, he releases the spitfire of a girl after making sure she isn't armed. The only weapon he sees is the rifle, which still hangs from her saddle horn.

"I'm sorry, ma'am." Wes steps back, away from the enraged woman. "I sure didn't know you were a girl."

The green eyes glance quickly over at the saddle, measuring her chances of reaching it. Quickly, scooping up a fist sized rock, she catches Wes dead in the stomach, then makes a lunge for the rifle. She's fast, only the sideways shying of the horse prevents her from getting her hands on the stock before Wes grabs her from behind.

As he wrestles her to the sandy ground, Wes knows now what it is like to fight a grizzly bear. She is strong for a girl, much stronger than he expected a mere female to be. Wes has never been indecisive when trouble confronts him, but this time he's at a loss at what to do. Not wanting to use his full strength against her, for fear of breaking something, he finds himself in a predicament. For once, he found something he can't shoot or punch. He is already bleeding from several scratches, not counting the blood seeping through his shirt from the sharp edge of the rock.

Flipping her to her back, Wes lands astride the lunging girl, grabbing for her hands. The green eyes spit fire as she takes a bite out of his wrist, and tries to kick him with her boots. Fingernails, teeth, knees, and elbows, as she throws everything she has at him.

"Lady, if you'll quit fighting me, I'll turn you lose and let you get up."

The girl doesn't answer, but she suddenly quits resisting and lies still. Wes remembers the last time he freed her hands. As she glares up at him, the eyes are still red, smoldering anger showing from her face.

"Alright, turn me loose whoever you are."

Wes relaxes his death grip on her wrists. "You gonna calm down and behave yourself, if I do?"

The red hair shakes as she nods. "I quit fighting didn't I, now turn me loose, I'll behave."

Before releasing her, Wes looks around on the ground for his pistol. He doesn't trust the girl one bit. If she gets her hands on his gun, he has no doubt, she wouldn't hesitate to use it. Standing up, he quickly backs off several feet and picks up the pistol as she stands slowly to her feet.

"Like I said, miss," Wes dusts off his hat, "if I knew you were a girl, I wouldn't have tossed you from your horse."

"Who are you, mister?"

"Wes Tobin, of the Sandigras."

"You are of the Sandigras." The redhead pushes back her long hair. "Now, mister, you're dead or will be soon."

"I hate to hear that I'm deceased, ma'am." Wes grins. "When do you foresee my demise?"

"As soon as my Pa hears that you and me have been rolling around on the ground like a couple of lovesick rabbits, you'll be deceased alright." The redhead glares at him. "I don't see anything funny about that."

Wes studies her face, and despite the anger showing, she is indeed a beautiful girl. Jenks was right, she is as rough as a man, maybe rougher, but she is definitely something to look at. The baggy overalls and oversized shirt, probably cast off from her menfolk, sure can't hide her well-rounded figure.

"What does that supposed to mean, ma'am?" Wes asks again, trying to get her to talk. "Is it a threat?"

"Like I said Mister Tobin, when my Pa and brothers find out about you and me here on the ground, you're a dead man for certain."

At the implication, Wes turns crimson red from embarrassment. "Now you know dang well I didn't know you were a girl, and besides, you were about to claw my eyes out."

"I wish I had."

Wes shakes his head, if her kinfolk are half as tough as she is; the Sandigras is in some serious trouble. "Couldn't we keep this between us?"

The green eyes glance at the fence. "You tear down that wire Mister Tobin, and maybe I will."

"Can't do that, ma'am."

"Would you stop calling me, ma'am. My name is Sarah Ann Flannery." Her chest heaves in and out, as she tries to catch her breath. "Most folks call me Rusty. You don't need that fence mister, we ain't cattle thieves."

"Well, Miss Sarah Ann Flannery." Wes grins at the girl. "I don't know that for a fact."

The girl advances a step, her anger welling up again. "Now you're making fun of my name and calling my family rustlers?"

"No, ma'am, I sure ain't doing neither." Wes holds up his hand and retreats. "I sure ain't tearing down that fence."

The girl watches as Wes jacks the shells from the rifle and replaces it on her saddle. Handing her the reins to the horse, he waits as she mounts. Pointing her finger at the scattered shells the redhead waits as he picks them up.

"You've got three days Mister Tobin, to get rid of that newfangled wire."

"Then what?"

She turns her gelding and twists in the saddle, looking back at him, her green eyes flashing. "I figure my Pa, brothers, and cousins will pay you a visit."

"I sure hope that don't happen, ma'am." Wes retreats toward the fence. "If they do, you best buy some shovels."

"Shovels?" The pretty face is curious. "What for, we ain't digging that dang thing up?"

"For burying folks ma'am, your Pa and brothers. Wes ducks back through the fence, the wire cutters clenched in his hand. "Good-day, Miss Flannery."

One final look, at the beet red face of the girl, causes Wes to grin broadly, as he walks to where his horse stands ground tied. Feeling the dry blood on his scratched up face, he unties his canteen and wets his handkerchief. He sure doesn't know about the rest of the family, but this Flannery is a scrapper.

Ellen looks across the dinner table at the long scratches, on the length of Wes' face. She also takes in the slow way he sat down in his chair.

"Did you get into some mesquite thorns, or did your horse buck you off?" Monte questions, he also notices the scratches.

Only a hard stare and frown come across the table as Wes picks at his supper. All the hands look him over, but none dare question what happened. Finishing supper, Wes motions for Pole and Monte to follow him outside.

Thanking Ellen for supper, as he passes around the table, he stops as she lays her hand on his arm. "You may fool them, but you sure aren't fooling me, Wes Tobin. Those scratches are a woman's fingernail tracks, or my name ain't Ellen Belton."

"Small bobcat, Miss Ellen," Wes grins. "Thanks for the fine supper, and especially helping with the Apache." Only an exasperated look comes from her as he laughs and walks through the door.

Rolling smokes, the three men find chairs at the end of the porch and light up. Pole is dying of curiosity himself, but he knows better than to ask. He knows Wes, when he's ready, he will explain the marks and the spot of blood on his shirt.

"Boys, we may be in for some trouble." Wes looks at his partners. "Real trouble."

"I knew it." Pole sits forward. "Tell us, what happened, and what kind of trouble are we in."

"I met up with the Flannerys today." Wes blows out smoke. "Near the last fence y'all built in the southernmost valley."

"How many?" Monte looks up sharply. "They didn't tear down my new fence?"

"Just one and believe me, she was plenty." Wes shakes his head. "No, she didn't tear it down."

"A woman did all that to your face?" Pole looks at the scratches. "Nah, you're just funning us."

"She did for a fact," Wes nods. "I've fought a lot of men, but never a woman like her."

Monte laughs. "You're telling us a woman whipped you, alone?"

"Well, I wouldn't say she whipped me cousin, but she sure put up a good tussle and fought me to a draw."

"Yeah, you look like she did," Monte nods. "A mere woman."

"A mere woman? No, sir, she was more like a tornado and cyclone all rolled in one." Wes shakes his head. "I'm telling you boys, she was a ring-tailed fireball, for a fact."

Pole shakes his head. He knows Wes is serious. "What trouble are you talking about Wes?"

"Jenks says the girl has four brothers, several cousins, and a Pa, that's kin to the devil himself." Wes rolls himself a smoke. "Who knows what else is back in those sand dunes."

"That's all or is there more good news?" Monte swears.

"She says if we don't tear down the fence, the whole bunch will ride on us here."

"Over one fence?" Pole shakes his head. "That much fuss over a piece of fence?"

Wes nods his head. "She says the Flannerys used that particular trail as a shortcut into Tucson for many years."

"Well, we sure ain't tearing all that wire and hard work down just on her say so." Monte flips his smoke and stands up. "Cousin, that is final."

"I didn't see any pass or trail they could use from that end of the canyon." Pole tries to remember a pass they might have missed.

Wes nods. "Then we better get ready, cause I don't believe that lady was bluffing."

Pole picks up his hat and looks up. "I took stock of what shells we got. I reckon we better ride into Tucson and stock up quick."

"He's right about that." Monte looks over as the ranch hands start a horseshoe game near the bunkhouse. "We're low."

"Me and Pole will ride in tomorrow." Wes stands up. "You stay close Monte, real close."

"We could put a gate in the fence and try to be neighborly." Pole draws in deeply on his smoke. "Don't 'spect that would do any harm."

Monte nods thoughtfully. "We may just do that if they give us time."


The horses kick spirals of dust up as the two men ride in a slow trot toward town. Wes studies the chaparral and small clumps of brush that dot the sandy landscape. It amazes him, as soon as they ride out of the Sandigras, the landscape changes to arid, dry desert, which they are now crossing over.

Both men are wary, two riders this far from their home range or a town are fair game to any band of Apaches that spot them. Neither light a smoke nor carry on a conversation, their eyes and ears stay completely tuned in to their surroundings.

Tucson town comes into sight about noon or a little after. Pole smiles, licks his lips, then kicks his horse into a little faster trot.

"We'll get the supplies first and then we'll have a drink." Wes can read his partner like a well-used trail. "Supplies first."

"Come on Wes, you can't be in that big a hurry to get back to the ranch?" Pole complains. "I ain't had me a drink in so long, my gizzard has shriveled up."

"I don't know the Flannerys, just what little Jenks told me about them, and now the girl's threats. Yeah, I'm in a hurry to get back."

"You're the boss."

"No Pole, I ain't your boss and you know it." Wes shakes his head. "I just want to get the ammunition back to the ranch."

"One drink and we'll head out." Pole shrugs. "Maybe two."

"Sounds good."

The chubby, storeman smiles, looking across the counter at Wes, as he places his order. First the wire and now the ammunition, the men from the Sandigras are spending a large amount of money in his store. Shrugging happily, he disappears into the storeroom and reappears with his arms loaded. When he finishes, well over a thousand rounds of rifle and pistol shells lay stacked on the counter. Across the room, Pole is sighting down the barrel of a newfangled Winchester, rubbing his hands over the finished stock and admiring the smooth action of the rifle.

"They don't shoot as many times as the Henry mister, but they're slick as pig fat to handle."

"Are they accurate?"

"Sighted in properly and with a good set of eyes looking down that barrel, they'll knock the eye out of a squirrel at a hundred yards. Sir, they don't make a gun more accurate."

"They jam or misfire?"

The man shakes his head. "Ain't had nary a complaint, no sir, you keep them clean and well oiled, they're like a well broke mule. These Winchesters will never give you trouble."

Pole hands the weapon over to Wes, who opens and closes the breech, then sights down the barrel. "They sure are dandies, Wes."

"There's open range behind the store, if you gents want to try one out." The chubby one points with his chin. "Shells are on me."

"How many of these rifles have you got in the store?"

"Seven left, altogether." The shopkeeper takes the gun from Wes. "They've been selling like hotcakes here 'bouts. Yes, sir, the boys sure like 'em."

"Halleck's men buy many?" Pole questions the man.

"They sure do. The Running H is one of my best customers. Those boys appreciate any kind of gun," the man adds. "That is when they save up the money to buy themselves one."

"Add them to the bill, along with a hundred rounds of ammunition for each rifle."

"Yes, sir." The man looks across at Wes. "You are paying cash?"

"Figure the bill, we're gonna have a drink, then we'll be back to settle with you, with cash."

"Yes, sir, Mister Tobin." The storeman smiles broadly. "Expecting Apache trouble out at your place are you?"

"Maybe, just figure my bill, we'll be back."

"They'll be ready and waiting." A wide grin spreads across the store owner's face as he watches the two men cross the street. "Yes sir, they'll be ready when you are."

The Oxbow Saloon boasts a wooden floor and a full mirror running the length of the oak bar. Chairs and tables set scattered around the room, among the gaming tables. Several gamblers sit playing cards, too engrossed in their game to look up at the newcomers that just pushed through the swinging doors.

"I hope the beer is cold like the sign says." Pole wipes his mouth expectantly, slapping the bar with his open hand. "Two beers, my good man."

Wes can only shake his head, as he has never seen anyone drink like Pole can, not even close. It never shows any effects on the man, no matter how much he tosses down. Hooking his heel on the rail, he turns his back on the bar and studies the men in the saloon. Most are common barflies, mingled with a few gamblers and cowboys, probably Halleck's riders. Wes takes a sip, as he turns back to the bar.

Pole polishes off his mug and then slaps the bar for another, when the bat wing doors squeak open. Five rough looking men, push through the doors and sidle up to the bar beside Pole.

"Beer, barkeep."

"Yes, sir, Mister Flannery." The barman's hand shakes as he places the beer before them. "Anything else, sir?"

Now, Wes knows what Jenks meant when he said these men were dangerous. Every one of them, stands over six feet and weighs well over two hundred. The matriarch of the bunch, Boston Flannery, is bigger than his boys.

Cutting his eyes at the men, Pole changes his mind about the beer. Instead, he nods at the swinging doors. "Let's get, while we still can."

"You satisfied your thirst already, with only one beer?" Wes grins slightly.

Pole looks sideways at the big men beside him. "Yes, sir, for once I sure have."

"All of a sudden isn't it?"

"Drinking too much can be dangerous to a man's health, sometimes."

"Well, sure sounds like good advice to me." Wes finishes his beer and follows Pole through the doors, taking a last glance at the broad backs of the big men. "Real, good advice."

Pole turns to take one last look, as he passes from the saloon, making sure Wes is behind him. With his eyes averted, he runs smack-dab into Sarah Ann Flannery, knocking several packages from her arms, dumping them onto the sidewalk.

"I'm terribly sorry, miss. I should have been looking," Pole apologizes, as he reaches clumsily for the bundles.

Not a word is spoken by the redhead as she stares unbelieving at Wes, who stands behind Pole. Wes looks back at the girl in shock, his mouth wide open in surprise.

"Well now, Mister Tobin, how convenient for you to be in town today."

Poles' hand stops in midair as he looks over at the shocked look on Wes' face. "This is her, this is Miss Flannery?"

Wes can't believe it, of all the people to bump into, especially with her menfolk within earshot, just inside the swinging doors, not twenty feet in distance.

"It's her alright."

The girl is about to say something, but as Pole stands and removes his hat, as if he is in a trance, she only stands there and looks up at him.

Wes looks at both of them as they eye each other. "Miss Flannery, I'd like you to meet my partner, Pole Nichols."

Looking at his extended hand, she nods and takes it in her own. "Can't say I care much for your friend here, Mister Pole Nichols, but sometimes you don't get to pick your own company, same with relatives, it just can't be helped."

"Yes, Miss Flannery, I know exactly what you mean." Pole still holds two of her packages in his hand. "May I help you with these?"

Wes can't believe it, not only did she not yell for her menfolk, there she is, walking down the sidewalk, smiling up at Pole like he is something special. Shaking his head, he looks back through the doors, where the Flannerys are still belly up to the bar. No one had seen or heard the ruckus so he figures now would be a good time to make a hasty retreat, across the street to the mercantile.

He never will understand women. One yell from her would have caused a killing right then and there, probably his as he was outnumbered and definitely outweighed.

Settling with the storeman, Wes ties the rifles onto their saddles, placing the cartridges in the saddlebags. Mounting his gelding, he leads the other horse to where Pole and Rusty Flannery stand talking, beside a flat wagon.

"Let's ride, hoss."

Pole makes a frown and tips his hat to the girl, smiling down at her. "Good-bye, Miss Rusty."

"Now, Pole now would be a good time to leave." Wes looks back at the saloon.

Wes can't believe his ears when she smiles sweetly and answers. "Good-bye, Pole Nichols." Then in the same breath, she looks up, where he sits his horse. "I ain't forgot about you either, Wes Tobin. Don't you think for one minute I have."

"Yes, ma'am."

"Don't call me, ma'am." She glares over at him. He watches in amazement as she changes again, smiling sweetly up at Pole. "We come to town every two weeks on Saturday."

"You know, come to think of it, I believe I have business in town the same day."

Pole stands switching awkwardly, from one foot to another, not knowing exactly what to say.

"Matter of fact, I know I do."

"Good." Rusty smiles broadly. Then, frowning over at Wes, she turns to the wagon. "As your friend here knows, I ride every day in the southern canyons."

"I ride there too," Pole smiles. "Every day."

Glancing up the street, she spies her father and brother's leaving the saloon. "You best be going. My Pa doesn't take kindly to strange men talking to me in the middle of the street."

"I'll hope to be seeing you, Rusty." Pole replaces his hat. "Soon."

"I'm hoping we meet again." She smiles innocently.

"What about me, ma'am, you hoping we meet again too?" Wes smiles.

"Don't press your luck, Mister Tobin."

"Yes, ma'am."

"I told you Wes Tobin, about calling me, ma'am." Her green eyes look to where Boston Flannery stands, watching them curiously. "You gonna tear down that fence?"

"That'll be up to my Cousin Monte."

"You remember what I said? That fence stays up and we'll probably meet again, real quick."

Wes looks over at the girl and smiles. "Is that a threat, Miss Flannery?"

Pole smiles shyly. "Don't pay any heed to him, Rusty. He's just rough around the edges."

"If y'all don't ride out quick, his edges are liable to get a lot rougher." She nods behind them where her menfolk are approaching.

Riding out of Tucson, Wes looks back at the Flannerys and over at Pole. "You two hit it off, right well."

"She's a nice girl." Pole speaks dreamily, looking back at the girl. "Real nice."

Wes can't believe it. He has heard folks talk about love at first sight, now he has seen it. He figures, one word from Pole, was all it would have taken, if he had popped the question to the girl. There would have been a wedding today, and maybe a killing.

Looking back, where the girl is still waving at Pole, like a lovesick calf looking for its mama, he sees the Flannery's watching them as they ride off. The bigger Flannery lifts her bodily into the wagon. Wasting no time, for the girl to change her mind and go to yelling, Wes kicks his horse into a lope. He distances himself from Tucson and the trouble that could have erupted with one word from her.

"I'm in love," Pole pronounces, turning in the saddle, straining to get one last glimpse of the redhead. "Smitten."

"With that spitfire?"

Pole frowns over at him. "She's a real lady underneath all that frowning and rough exterior."

"Yeah Pole, and I'm Robert E. Lee."

"Watch your mouth Wes Tobin, she's gonna be my wife." Pole nods seriously, his big Adam's apple bobbing up and down his throat like an apple in a water barrel. "I'm settling down as of right now. I'm through with hiring out my gun."

"What, have you lost your mind?" Wes looks bewildered. "I mean about the marrying, and all. We're both finished with hiring out our guns. We have the Sandigras now."

"No, I ain't lost my mind." Pole smiles broadly. "I've found the woman of my dreams. The woman that I want."

Wes shakes his head in amazement. "What do you think Miss Flannery would say about marrying up with you?"

"Don't know, I ain't popped the question to her yet."

"You ain't asked her. Tell me Pole, isn't it customary for the woman to know about such things."

"Don't fun with me, I'm serious." Pole nods his head. "I'm gonna marry Miss Sarah Ann Flannery."

"You can't be serious. You just met the girl today." Wes shakes his head. "Marrying is a big commitment. It's not like going to town on Saturday night."

"I'm telling you, I'm serious and I'm hoping she is too." Pole absently rolls himself a smoke. "She's beautiful."

"Yes, Pole, she is beautiful," Wes admits, "There is one other problem."

"What's that?"

"Her four brothers and one mean old Daddy, that's what." Wes looks behind him, expecting to see the Flannerys coming over the nearest hill in hot pursuit, with their guns blazing. "You're liable to be fighting with them tomorrow."

"I ain't fighting with her kinfolk, today or tomorrow." Pole shakes his head. "No, sir, I ain't."

"Great, you're gonna hang me out to dry, up against the whole clan?"

"I'll fight Apaches, the Running H, or rustlers, but I ain't fighting my intended's family." Pole shakes his head. "No, sir, I ain't."

"Pole, for crying out loud, she ain't your intended."

"Oh yes, she is." Pole nods. "Or, she soon will be."

Wes clenches his jaw tight and shuts up. There's no use arguing with a man with lovesickness. He's seen it before, but when a man is smitten, he is doomed. It's almost as bad as blind staggers in a horse. He'd seen that sickness once too, and like love, it's an incurable disease. Frustrated with the thought of marriage, Wes rolls a smoke and looks long and hard across the vast sandy land.

"I thought you didn't want to smoke." Pole notices the cigarette dangling from Wes' mouth. "Remember, there's Apache out here?"

"Don't see how it matters, you're already dead." Wes strikes a flame and lights up. "Or as good as, so I might as well join you."

"What you got against marriage anyway?"

"Nothing." Wes exhales. "No, sir, not one thing old buddy, as long as you're the one getting hog-tied and branded."

"It can't be all that bad."

Wes finally gives up and shrugs. "Good luck old friend, I hope you the best. With that gal, you're gonna need plenty of it."

"It can't be all that bad." Pole repeats, mumbling, as he rolls a smoke and clams up. "It can't be."


The Sandigras riders pass the Winchesters around the bunkhouse, each man admiring the rifles in turn. All the ranch hands fire five rounds out the back door to familiarize themselves with the weapon.

"Sweet, awfully sweet." The bandy-legged rider named Lonnie Bud passes the rifle back to Wes after firing it. Five well-placed shots make a small grouping on the target that Pole set up. "It's smoother than molasses over a hotcake."

"I wouldn't want to be the man that rides in here against these Winchesters." Another speaks up, sighting down the barrel. "Pure suicide is what it would be."

"Yeah," Pole looks over at Wes, thinking of the Flannerys and the girl.

"Well, let's hope no one does." Monte examines a rifle and nods his head. "I for one would sure like to live in peace."

Jenks has been gone almost three weeks with the cattle. So far, nothing was heard from him, which Wes knows is a good sign. Out here, no news is good news. With the fencing finished, Monte put all the hands to work with sickles and rakes, putting up what hay they can find for winter. The huge barn loft is packed with anything that resembles grass. When the cold winds of winter blow across the canyons, the horses and cattle will need all the roughage they can get.

Wes rides out every day but he's frustrated, as nothing has been heard from Martine. He hasn't returned as he promised. All across the Sandigras, everything is quiet, no Running H riders, no Apaches or cattle rustlers, nothing. Everything is peaceful, which Wes is glad of, but he is still worries, knowing it wouldn't last. Halleck isn't a man to give up so easily, no it was far too quiet, something is sure to happen.

Wes and Pole patrol the far-reaching canyons every day, splitting the timber and grasslands between them. Each man takes a section of the ranch and scouts the land, checking the fences for any damage. So far, they haven't been touched. With the rough terrain and smaller side canyons, it takes both men four days of hard riding, to cover the Sandigras range, from one end to the other. Normally they would meet at the bigger canyon in the late afternoon where the two creeks merge, riding back to headquarters together.

Wes rests against a cottonwood tree that stands along the bigger creek, studying the valley floor. He worries, as Pole is late returning to their meeting place. He knows the lanky man is never late for supper or a cold beer. Maybe the Flannery girl detained him. Looking down at the cigarette stubs littering the ground, he shakes his head. He has been wasting time, hoping Pole would ride up. Only two more hours are left in the day and soon the sun will start to set. Something must have happened.

Pulling his cinch tight, he turns his horse toward the west side of the canyons, as his eyes search the ground for any sign of another horse passing. A mile passes and then another, as he rides from one fenced in draw to another. Pole's horse left plenty of tracks on the ground and they're plain enough for a blind man to read. Pole rode through here sometime earlier in the day.

Monte has strung several strands of the new wire across each draw or trail that a cow or rider could use to get out of the canyon floor. The fences are necessary, as the Sandigras doesn't have the men to patrol every day, trying to keep the range cattle from wandering off the ranch. So far, all are intact and nothing seems amiss. Knowing he is wasting time as daylight is running out, Wes kicks the gelding into a lope, toward the south end. He heads for the same fence he ran afoul with Rusty Flannery, only three weeks earlier. This is the most southern trail leading out of the canyons, up to the crest of the mountains and onto the Flannery holdings.

Slowing his horse to a walk, Wes follows a small cow trail through the trees that leads to the fence. For years, until the fence was built, Jenks said this was the trail used by rustlers or honest cowmen to run their cattle into old Mexico miles to the south.

Sitting the gelding quietly, Wes stares at what was a fence. The posts were ripped from the ground and the wire was rolled into a useless tangle. Stepping down, he loosens the tie down from his pistol and approaches the fence cautiously. The passing signs of horses and cattle show along the narrow trail. Tracks of Sandigras cattle, being hazed and herded south over the rough trail, are plain to read.

Here in the shadows, close up against the canyon wall, it has become too dark to make out the tracks plainly. Cussing his stupidity, for waiting so long and letting dark close in, he leads the gelding slowly up the narrow rocky trail.

# CHAPTER 7

The trail leading out of the canyon floor, to the higher ridges is narrow, surrounded by steep banks and no trails branching out of it. In places, the tracks in the sandy soil are plain to read. Whoever is pushing the cattle is ahead of him, how far he doesn't know. The echoing sounds of his horse walking in the gorge are loud enough to be heard from afar. Wes has never been this deep into the upper southern canyons. He is now in unfamiliar territory. The trail could branch off or it could stay straight ahead, toward Mexico. As tall and steep as the canyon walls are, he just has to guess where the trail leads. He can't even see the stars plain enough to get his bearings. Pushing the gelding up the rough ground, Wes travels blind, with no idea where it will take him.

Wes feels his stomach grumble as breakfast was long gone and supper is no closer. Ellen fixed him some biscuits and side meat which he chewed on absent-mindedly. The sound of the tired gelding's shoes hitting on the rocky trail echoes up and down the steep canyon walls with every step. The trail climbs up and down, through canyons and timber, across small flats then over another hill. Wes rides blindly, following the dark trail, keeping close to the canyon walls.

The moon comes up full, casting its brilliance across the canyons, giving Wes some light to see by. Topping out of the gorge, a few hundred yards farther to the south, he reins the gelding in and studies the trail. For the first time it forks with one branch to the south, while the other starts down a grade to the west. Tracks of horses and cattle are dim, but they are there. They travel in both directions. He thought the ones he was following continue to the south fork, probably heading for the border, but even with the full moon, the tracks are almost impossible to make out.

Mulling over which direction to take, Wes finally slides from the tired horse, deciding to wait until morning to make his choice. With the sun, he could read the trail clearer. He doesn't know if Pole even came this way, but he knows his friend well enough to know if he found the wrecked fence, he would follow the rustlers responsible for tearing it up.

Leading the gelding slowly forward, looking for grass or water, Wes suddenly stops, as the trail turns sharply to the west. Ahead, he can barely make out dim lights of some kind. Far too many for a campfire, it must be the Flannery's Ranch buildings. He doesn't know the layout of the land or the ranches that sit back in the arid canyons, but from the way Jenks talked, the Flannerys own and laid claim to this entire country.

The far-off lights slowly become clearer in the early morning mist as he approaches closer. Stopping at a small water hole, Wes waters his tired gelding and decides to let the horse graze on the sparse grass and rest until full daylight breaks over the flats ahead. He must have dozed slightly as he awakes with the sun shining brightly down on his face. Lunging to his feet, as yelling from close by, brings him fully awake, he looks about to find the source of the noise. A young boy, out hunting, spotted the sleeping stranger and his horse, racing away toward the ranch, screaming his lungs out.

Mounting, Wes rides slowly toward the ranch buildings, his hand resting on his pommel, away from the pistol. He has been discovered so there is little use in trying to sneak in. Several men wait on the broad porch of the run down old house, while others watch his approach from the corrals. Wes knows at a glance, they are the Flannery clan. They are some of the same rough looking bunch he saw in Tucson. The family resemblance amazes him. They are all tall men with reddish complexions and sandy to red hair. He must have interrupted their breakfast as several hold coffee cups and biscuits in their hands.

The bigger man, the one the bartender called Mister Flannery, pushes to the front of the men and stares across the yard at him. No words are spoken for several minutes as the two men size each other up. Wes' eyes dart sideways as Rusty Flannery comes around the house, stopping dead in her tracks.

"Well now, Mister Tobin, are you lost or did you just come calling?" She laughs.

"No ma'am, but my friend Pole Nichols may be." Wes looks around the yard, counting at least twenty full-grown men watching him, not counting the women and kids.

Boston Flannery steps down from the porch and approaches Wes quietly for such a ponderous man. "Sarah Ann, do you know this man?"

"I met him and his friend in Tucson, last time we were there."

"Oh yes." The big man acts like he remembers. "You were awfully friendly with the other one."

She shrugs indifferently. "I don't hardly know either one of them, Pa."

"You don't huh?" He looks at the unhealed scratch marks on Wes' face and grins slightly. "Those marks on his face sure look like some of your branding. I've seen plenty of those same scratches on your brothers."

"He must have stuck his ugly face someplace where it shouldn't have been." Rusty glares across at Wes. "They sure ain't my doing Pa."

Wes looks over at the redhead. "I haven't met this lady, Mister Flannery, at least not formally."

Boston Flannery takes in the low-slung pistol and the cold eyes. "What do you want here, mister?"

Wes has never seen as big a man, not all in one spot anyway. Flannery has to weigh at least three hundred pounds, standing well over six feet. He carries extra weight around his middle for sure, but that doesn't diminish his stature in the least.

"Someone cut my fence and one of my hands has gone missing." Wes studies the big man. "I've come looking for the man."

"You think we are responsible?"

"I didn't say that." Wes stares into the blue eyes. "Exactly."

Flannery steps closer. "I don't know how you found your way here gunfighter, but suppose you turn around and ride out, now."

"Can't, I've got a good friend out here somewhere and I'm staying, at least until I find him."

"You could get buried right where you sit." Flannery looks down at

Wes then over at the girl. "The low canyons may be yours, but this side of the Sandigras is my range and we keep it private."

"I appreciate the fact it's Flannery property, and I respect a man's privacy." Wes looks across at Rusty then around at the other men. "I also realize I could get buried here, but when you dig the hole for me, make it big enough for two. When your boys open the ball, I'll try my best to see that you join me."

The big man stands motionless, studying the hard talking man before him. Suddenly, the wide mouth breaks into a wide grin and the matriarch of the Flannerys throws back his head, laughing deeply. "I admire a man with style and guts Mister Tobin, I surely do."

"You know me?"

"Who doesn't, any man that bucks up against Halleck and his Running H riders has to have talk going around about him."

"Have you seen my man?"

The big head shakes negatively. "No, but you rode past the trail that your friend probably took. The one leading due south to Mexico."

"I saw the trail, then I spotted your lights." Wes looks about him. "I don't know this land Mister Flannery. I figured I'd ride in and see if you folks knew anything."

"Ride to the south Mister Tobin, leave us be. We know nothing about your man or your cattle."

"I didn't mention the cattle."

"You didn't have to. Why else would someone cut your fence and why would your man go missing."

Turning his gelding, Wes nods. "Thank you, Mister Flannery."

Flannery holds up his hand. "Breakfast is on the stove, light and eat before you leave."

"I need to be riding."

Flannery motions at the house. "A few minutes either way won't matter much I don't reckon, and my missus is a real fine cook."

Nodding, Wes dismounts and follows the big man inside. His eyes widen as he stands in the kitchen. Never in his life has he ever seen such a huge table. Wes is curious, is everything on the place overgrown? The men return from the outside and retake their seats around the table, hungrily eating their breakfast. Feeling someone at his shoulder, Wes turns as Rusty places a plate of eggs and potatoes with fresh side meat before him.

Now, he knows why these people are so big. They had to be, eating the way they do. Not one of the men speak. Only the sound of hungry men and silver can be heard in the big dining room.

"You boys know who took this man's cattle?" Flannery looks around the table. "If you do, speak up."

"Halleck riders came up the pass and crossed the canyon early yesterday." A slender redheaded man speaks up.

"You see them, Rowdy?"

"I've seen 'em, Pa." The younger Flannery nods, then answers after he swallows. "Running H riders are pushing Sandigras cattle south with Waco Grange, leading them."

"Anything else?"

"There was a tall and skinny, ugly feller, sneaking along behind the cattle." The young redhead takes a swig of coffee. "He wasn't trying to catch up with the others. I figured he was hounding them for some reason."

"That be your man, Mister Tobin?"

Wes nods. "Sounds like Pole alright."

"Rusty." Flannery looks over at the girl. "Get your friend Mister Tobin a fresh horse, his looks played out."

"He ain't my friend Pa, but I'll get him a horse." She looks across at her brother and raises a skillet threateningly. "You call Mister Nichols ugly again Rowdy, and I'll brain you."

"Shucks sis, I thought you didn't know him?" The redhead laughs.

Blushing, she looks around the room at the upturned faces staring at her. "Well, it ain't polite to call folks ugly."

"You seem to be defending him."

"That's enough boy." Boston Flannery frowns at his oldest son, looking curiously at the girl.

"She's lying Pa, about knowing the skinny one and all."

"Rowdy, I said that is enough. Get outside and go to work."

Wes looks across at Boston Flannery, as he sits the fresh horse. "Thank you for your hospitality Mister Flannery, it won't be forgotten. I'll get the horse back to you."

"Good luck to you, Mister Tobin. When you return, we will have us another talk about the fence and my daughter."

"Yes, sir." Wes nods, blushing slightly before turning the horse. He likes the older Flannery, despite his hard ways and the many things that have been said about him. "I'll be seeing you soon."

Nodding over at Rusty and Mrs. Flannery, he tips his hat and kicks the fresh horse into a lope back to the south. Pole and the cattle are somewhere ahead on the trail leading into old Mexico. A dangerous and cruel country, he has to hurry if he is to be in time to help Pole and recover the cattle.

Rounding a bend, not far from the Flannery headquarters, Wes watches a rider walk his horse out from concealment behind some cedars blocking off the trail. The redheaded youngster, Boston Flannery called Rowdy, waits in the road, his rifle resting easily across his saddle.

Wes slows his horse to a walk as he approaches the rider then pulls the gelding in and waits for the young Flannery to speak. The calmness and uncaring attitude of the man before him infuriates the redhead.

"I'll let you ride out this time gun hand, but don't come back on Flannery range."

"And if I do come back?"

"It'll be your funeral." Rowdy Flannery swears, his green eyes spitting fire. "Here's a Flannery that ain't scared of your fast gun Tobin."

Wes nods, kicking his horse forward, pushing the young man's horse sideways out of his way. Stopping beside the rider, he looks across at the redhead.

"You're one of the Flannerys I seen back at the house. I think your Pa called you Rowdy."

"Yeah, I'm his oldest son."

"Well, Mister Flannery, I suggest you go to using that rifle instead of your big mouth."

"Next time gun-hand, next time." The rifle barrel points lazily toward Wes. "Heed my words, don't come back."

"You folks are kinda anti-social, ain't you?"

"We want to be left alone, alright. My Pa ain't no gun hand mister, but he'll surely fight you. I ain't about to let the likes of you kill him."

"I like your Pa boy, they'll be no trouble between us."

"Get off our range Tobin and don't come back."

Wes looks hard at the redhead. "I don't cotton much to being run off any place I want to be, mister."

"This rifle is running you right now."

"Flannery, I don't want to kill you, but if you don't turn that barrel away from me, I will."

"You that fast mister, with a rifle barrel looking dead at your stomach?"

"If you don't ride on," Wes' face hardens, "I reckon you're fixing to find out."

Uncertainty spreads across the young Flannery's face as he glares at Wes for several seconds. Cussing, he kicks his gelding hard and turns back down the trail.

Wes watches Rowdy out of sight and turns back on the trail and the cattle tracks leading south. Several miles, after climbing out of the broken canyons, the trail widens and joins what seems like a rutted wagon road, leading due south to old Mexico. Wes stops his gelding and studies where the trail he follows intersects with the larger road. It is well hidden. If a rider wasn't aware of the trail or wasn't watchful, he would ride right past the turn off that leads to the Flannery's. It seems, riders using the cutoff, purposely keep the trail well hidden at its junction, not cutting the brush or leaving tracks out of the canyons.

Studying the rutted road in both directions, he turns south. Whoever is pushing the cattle has ridden at least a mile into the rougher ground before turning the herd onto the smoother road. As the tracks materialize and bunch back together on the road, Wes pulls in his gelding and dismounts. Examining the tracks closely, he knows it's the herd from the Sandigras. One of the men pushing the cattle, rides a pigeon toed horse that leaves a clear track, making the small herd easy to identify.

Looking off to the northwest, Wes tries to figure just where the well-traveled road will lead. Unless he misses his guess, eventually it should make its way to Tucson. Now, he knows why the Flannerys wanted the pass left open. It has taken him a whole day of hard riding to reach where he is now. By crossing the Sandigras, a rider could save at least one day, maybe two.

It would be hard to push a large herd of cattle and practically impossible to get a wagon up or down the narrow draw. However, if a rustler or rancher wanted to just push a few head of rustled cattle south, like these men did, the small trail would do.

Boston Flannery has not only fed him and loaned him a horse, he had dealt fairly with him. When he returns, he will convince Monte to build a gate at the canyon mouth and let him and his family use the pass to go into town for supplies. With a little mutual help and persuasion, maybe the Flannerys would guard the draw from their side and become allies.

Wes notices the tracks of a lone horse, following the herd, keeping well off to the side of the road. He knows it's Pole, but with the drifting sand, the tracks quickly become hard to read clearly, he couldn't be sure. Kicking the gelding into a ground eating trot, he travels south.

The water hole is still muddy and stirred from the passing cattle, but it's wet. The gelding drinks deeply before Wes pulls him back, out onto dry ground. It is nearing dark. He has been traveling hard all day, trying to close the distance. The herd is still a few hours ahead, even at the slow pace they travel. Wes looks about at the sparse grass, then decides to let the hard ridden horse rest and graze before moving on, in the early morning. Staking the horse out on the best graze he can find, he kicks wood together for a fire.

Feeling his stomach grumble, Wes cusses his foolishness for starting the trail without provisions, but if he returned to the ranch for supplies and help, he would have lost another full day. Looking over at his saddle, he shakes his head. No blankets, no food, nothing. Well, maybe this will teach him a lesson about pride. He was too proud this morning to ask Boston Flannery to stake him to some grub and a blanket.

Rolling a smoke, he pokes at the fire and looks off, into the gloom. He knows come full dark, it's fixing to get cold. The fire will warm him on one side alright, but his other side will freeze. Well, he had his saddle blankets to roll into. They'll be a little damp on the bottom, but they will have to do. He sure couldn't eat them though, and again he thought of Mrs. Flannery's breakfast, which was a long time past.

A stick lands beside the small fire, causing Wes to whirl and draw his pistol. Rusty Flannery stands well back in the chaparral, staring smugly at him.

"Well, I see you found water by yourself, Mister Tobin." She leads her horse toward the stream. "That's something at least."

"What are you doing out here?" Wes is astounded as he looks at the girl then behind her, seeing if she is alone. "Where's your menfolk?"

"I've come after my man, same as you." She looks at the fire. "My Pa and brothers, ain't here."

"Your man?" Wes can't believe his ears. "You mean, Pole Nichols?"

"I sure ain't talking about you." Unsaddling the horse, she piles the saddle near his. "You bring any grub?"

"Nope."

"Blankets?"

"Nope."

Mumbling, she leads the horse to the watering hole. "You're something, Mister Tobin, really something."

"I was in a hurry." Wes stares at the redhead as she walks away. He can't help himself, she is a beauty. "Didn't have time to ride back to the ranch for supplies."

She hobbles the gelding and walks back to the fire. "I knew a man one time. He was always in a hurry out here."

"Yeah, what happened to him?" Wes piles more wood on the fire.

"Dang fool starved to death." She stares down at him. "You hungry?"

"Yeah, I'm hungry." Wes looks dubiously at the redhead. He hates being in her debt for anything, but he sure can't eat his pride and he's starving.

Wes watches as she brings out a frying pan and an old beat-up coffeepot. Rolling himself another smoke, he eases back against his saddle.

"You got another one of those things?" She nods at his cigarette.

"You smoke?"

"I sure ain't wanting to cook the dang thing."

Wes rolls another smoke and passes it over to her, watching amazed as she lights up with a burning ember from the fire. He has known a few women that smoked, but they were the type that kept behind closed doors during daytime hours. This girl is forward, bold is a better word. He doubted she got embarrassed about anything, but she is a lady, not a barroom woman.

"You reckon you could get yourself up and bring me those tins?" She stirs the skillet of beans. "If it ain't too much trouble."

Wes has to admit, she is a good cook, but then again, as hungry as he is, anything would taste good. Resting on their saddles as they eat, few words are spoken between them. Rusty Flannery rode here to find Pole. She hasn't forgotten or forgiven Wes for the incident back in the canyons.

Keeping their thoughts to themselves, they eat and watch as the sun, slowly fades away, off to the west. By the time they finish their meal, it is fully dark. The chill starts creeping in on the night.

"You wash." She points at the dirty dishes.

Wes picks up the plates and starts for the water hole. "Yes, boss."

"You're learning cowboy."

Piling more wood on the fire, Wes rolls them another cigarette as she spreads her blankets near the blaze. The glare of the fire brings the red in her hair out even more.

"Thankee kindly, Mister Tobin." She takes the smoke. "My brothers got me started on these things."

"It's a bad habit for a lady."

"Who said I'm a lady, Mister Tobin?"

"Why don't you call me Wes?"

"Call an older man by his first name, why that's disrespectful." She shakes her head. "That's downright sacrilege."

"Scratching my eyes out ain't disrespectful?"

"I was attacked, I was scared." She exhales. "I had to protect myself."

Wes draws in on his smoke and shakes his head. "Yeah, you acted scared alright. I was the one who was scared."

Looking over at him, she smiles and nods. "Okay, Wes it is."

"Just out of curiosity, does your Pa know where you are?"

"Nope."

"Now that's just great, I'm probably a dead man." Wes looks uneasily about him. "You get some sleep, I'll stand guard."

"For what?"

"Apaches." Wes looks across at her. "Or have you forgotten, we're a long way from nowhere, with a burning fire that can be seen for miles?"

"I ain't forgot," She laughs easily, her white teeth shining in the dark, "I don't think the two of us is gonna stand off an Apache raiding party alone. Do you?"

"Maybe not, but I sure ain't going to sleep and let them get my hair without a fight."

"Suit yourself, I'm going to sleep."

"You sure are sure of yourself." Wes shakes his head.

"They see this red hair and they'll skedaddle out of here, pronto."

"They that scared of your Pappy?"

"They are." There's no brag in her words, just fact. "They got themselves one dose of Boston Flannery and they don't want another."

Flipping the burned stub into the fire, Rusty rolls into her blankets. Only the green eyes peek out as she looks over to where he hugs the fire.

"Feels like it's gonna get cold tonight," she grins, "awfully cold."

"Keep digging Miss Flannery." Wes shakes his head.

"I was just passing the time."

"Well you've passed it, now it's time for little girls to go to sleep." Wes looks to where she lies watching him. "Thanks for the dinner."

"Is Pole married?"

"No, he ain't."

"Has he ever been married?"

"No, he hasn't."

"Good." She smiles and snuggles deeper into the blankets. "Sleep tight Mister Tobin, but don't you freeze on me now."

Wes looks over at her in disgust, pulling the damp saddle blankets tighter around him. They smelled of horse sweat and are covered with horsehair, but they're better than nothing. Shucks, after two days on the back of a sweating horse, he had to smell just like a horse himself.

The cold chill of the desert settles on the small camp. It amazes him how quickly the nights could turn cold out here on the desert floor. In Texas, the nights didn't seem near this cold. Slipping closer to the fire, he holds out his hands to the warmth.

"Cold ain't it?"

He looks to where the redhead has popped out from under the wool blankets. A mischievous grin spreads across her face, causing her ivory white teeth to sparkle again in the light of the fire.

"It is that."

"Come over here."

Wes swallows hard as she raises the blankets, inviting him to join her. "Now, I don't know about that."

"Come on over here, you'll freeze by morning, and I sure ain't got time to nurse you."

"Yes, ma'am, I mean Rusty."

Slipping his boots off and crawling under the blankets, Wes feels something hard pressing against his back. "What's that poking at me?"

"It's just my skinning knife, Mister Tobin." She pushes the knife tip a little harder. "So we understand each other."

"Well Rusty, I don't blame you." Wes grins and pulls the blanket around his head. "I do believe I understand your meaning quite well."

Breakfast consists of hot coffee and cold biscuits. Wes saddles the horses while Rusty washes up and breaks camp. Rubbing his cold hands together, he holds them out to the cheerful warm blaze. It's barely daylight as they down the coffee and take the trail south.

"You know, when your Pa finds out I let you follow me after these men, he's liable to skin me alive or worse."

"Well, Mister Tobin, don't tell him." She hunches down in her heavy coat against the cold of the morning. "Roll me a smoke, will you cowboy, and I'll never speak a word of it."

"You're too young to smoke." Wes blows onto his hands to warm them, pulling out the makings. "You always ride around out here alone?"

She studies the surrounding flats and nods her head. "It's beautiful, isn't it? And yes, I've always taken care of myself."

"I believe it."

"There's a small village just across the border." She takes the offered cigarette. "I figure that's where you'll find your cattle and maybe our friend."

"You've been there before?"

"No, I've never been that far south, but I've heard my brothers talk about a town called Corrales." Rusty draws on the smoke. "It's a holding place for hot cattle. There's supposed to be plenty of corrals and plenty of crooked ranchers to buy them."

"Convenient." Wes shifts in his saddle and looks over at her. "How far is the border and this town?"

"Eighty miles, give or take a few miles."

"Great." Wes turns in his saddle, studying his back trail, looking for the whole Flannery tribe to descend on them. "That's another two or three days."

"You don't like my company?"

"Partly, but it's your Pa and brothers, I'm worrying about right now."

"I figure they'll be along, sooner or later."

"That's just great."

The night's camp rests the horses and their riders. Wes kicks his gelding into a ground eating trot, carefully surveying the passing terrain. They are crossing some of the most desolate ground that borders old Mexico. Sand, cactus, and more sand, it is fit only for scorpions, rattlesnakes, Apaches, and Mexican Bandits. Dangerous and barren yes, but Rusty is right, it is indeed a beautiful and serene land.

Late in the afternoon, the horses suddenly prick their ears and pick up their pace. Seeing nothing suspicious in sight, Wes studies the trail ahead carefully, letting the horses set their own pace. Everything seems quiet, nary a bird or the wind as nothing makes a sound or stirs. Less than a mile passes before Wes discovers the shimmering of a small stream crossing their trail. The water is what catches the horse's attention. Thirsty from the dusty road, they hurry to the stream.

Dismounting beside the shallow trickle of water, they let the horses drink their fill. "We got company cowboy." Rusty reaches for her rifle.

"Don't touch it." Wes doesn't look up. He seems to be studying the water. "I see them."

"You do, well you're awful calm about it." She hardly speaks the words, when five Mexicans ride up, out of a small draw, halting their horses less than thirty feet away.

"They look like Mexican bandits." Wes cusses himself for riding up to the water so carelessly. The horses not only smelled the water, but they caught the scent of the other horses. "Bad hombres."

Rusty shifts slightly on her feet and smiles at the Mexicans. "Well cowboy, seems you're out in the cold again."

"When I start this dance, you duck for cover." Wes flips the tie down from his pistol hammer. "You hear me?"

The bigger Mexican raises his hand and smiles broadly. "It is a beautiful day, señor."

"It is that."

"And you Miss Rusty, what do you think?" The bandit looks at the girl. "Is it not a nice day?"

Rusty shakes her head and smiles over at Wes. "Si Ramone, it is a beautiful day."

"You know this Mexican?" Wes can't believe it, the little redhead is plumb full of surprises. He knows she just pretended to be scared.

"She better know me, señor. She is my Goddaughter." The Mexican laughs. "I gave her the first horse she rode."

"You could have told me." Wes looks over at the girl, exasperated. "I almost killed him."

"You didn't ask me." She shrugs. "Get behind cover was all I heard."

"Rusty." He glares over at her. "One of these days."

"Your Papa sent me word by Jose that you were missing." The big Mexican smiles widely, his teeth showing tobacco and coffee stains. "What do you do way out here with this one?"

"Where is Papa?"

"He rides for Tucson, he thinks maybe you went there to get married." The Mexican grins. "You are in much trouble, señor. The Flannerys are very upset that you have stolen one of their women."

"I didn't steal her," Wes swears. "If you're her Godfather, you know how hardheaded she is."

"Si, my friend, I know this but Señor Flannery doesn't, and she is his only daughter."

"You go back and tell him, I tried to send her home." Wes shakes his head and frowns. "Take her with you."

The big sombrero waves in the fading light as the Mexican shakes his head. "Not me señor, I like my head right where it is."

Wes sits beside the water and watches as the Mexicans dismount and kneel down for a drink. There is no doubt they are bandits. The Mexican holsters, the wide sombreros, the fancy vests, they are banditos alright. Normal Mexicans don't ride well-bred horses or carry bandoleros of bullets strapped around their chests. Most Mexicans are farmers and peons. Not this band, they are friendly enough, but given a reason or excuse, they would cut your throat without hesitating.

Few words are spoken as the men smoke and drink coffee beside the small stream of water. Rusty passes among the Mexicans, pouring coffee and laughing at their jokes. Sitting down next to Wes, she looks across at Ramone.

"Mister Tobin has had some cattle stolen, and one of his men is out here somewhere." She questions the man, her eyes studying his face. "Have you seen anything of them?"

The Mexican pokes the fire and looks over at her. "Si, the cattle are ahead. They will reach Corrales in maybe two days." He shrugs and nods at Wes. "The gringo who follows them, I think he waits for this one to come."

"How many men ride with the cattle?" Wes asks.

"Five bad men, señor. I think you should find your friend quick and go back to your home." Ramone watches as the other Mexicans nod their agreement. "I think you should forget the cattle and leave this place, muy pronto."

"Those men rustled my cattle and cut my fences." Wes shakes his head. "I aim to get them back."

Ramone shrugs. "They have only taken forty, maybe a few more. They are not worth losing your life over, señor."

"They're my cattle." Wes straightens and looks at the Mexicans. "One or a hundred, no one is rustling the Sandigras and riding away with them scot-free."

"The hombre who leads these men has killed many, señor."

"Who is he?"

"He is called Waco Grange, he rides for Señor Halleck."

"Halleck," Wes spits out the word. "You're saying the Running H is behind this cattle stealing?"

"Si señor, the Running H," Ramone nods at Rusty, "and this one, she should not be here."

Wes smiles. "Ramone, you know she does what she wants to."

"Si, I know this," Ramone smiles, "but she is the pride of her father and brothers, if she was to get hurt, señor."

"Maybe you should escort her back to her father." Wes grins. "Make her go home."

Ramone looks to where Rusty sits down. "No, señor. I do not think this is a good idea."

"You two talk like I'm not sitting here." Rusty stands up. "I'm going after Pole and that's final."

"Pole?" Ramone questions. "Who is this Pole?"

"My future husband."

Ramone laughs and looks over at her, saying something to the others in Spanish. "The one who follows the cattle is your husband?"

"He will be." Rusty raises her finger. "Ramone, don't you dare say one thing against him, not one thing."

Several of the other Mexicans snicker as she stomps away. Ramone looks across at Wes and grins. "Señor, por favor, I am sorry to laugh, but your friend, he is muy feo, so ugly."

"Well, he's skinny for sure."

"Skinny." Ramone laughs. "I've seen more meat on a buzzard."

"You better not let her hear you talking about her intended." Wes looks to where Rusty is unsaddling her horse. "Might not be healthy."

"She is something, high strung like a blooded horse, beautiful like a desert flower." Ramone looks over at the girl and smiles. "But, the temper, your friend may have much trouble with this one."

"Tell me Ramone, how did you become her Godfather?" Wes is curious.

"You mean me being Mexican and a bandit?"

"I reckon." Wes nods. "It is a curiosity to me."

Ramone takes a mouthful of the strong coffee, Rusty prepared the men. "The Apache attacked a wagon headed for Tucson to visit the doctor. They killed almost all the men in their first charge. My men and I were close by. Much noise comes to our ears, guns fired, and screams coming from the wagon. We come up behind the Apache and charge, killing several before they see us. The rest run away. When we got to the wagon, a woman, big with child, was in the back in much pain. She was having a baby."

"Rusty?"

"Si, the little one." Ramone nods. "I helped her into the world, then escorted them on into Tucson and the doctor."

"Old Boston Flannery was mighty grateful."

"Si señor, I became her Godfather, and a good friend of Señor Flannery."

"I imagine."

"He thinks very much of this girl. I think maybe you are a dead man, señor." Ramone shrugs. "Either the gringo Grange will kill you or Señor Flannery."

"Could be. How big is the town of Corrales?"

"It is a small place. Many gringos come to this place with stolen cattle."

Ramone's timing was right. At noon, two days later, the small town of Corrales lay in view ahead. Nothing stirs on the dirty streets as they ride near. It seems asleep, almost deserted in the early afternoon hours. Populated mostly by Mexicans, with only a few white travelers passing through, the town is blanketed in dust and heat.

The corrals they passed, on the outskirts of the small town, show the only sign of life. Several head of thirsty longhorn cattle bawl and stand about the lots. Saddle horses, their backs covered in heel flies are penned separately alongside the cattle.

Wes studies the horses closely then the buildings and corrals. None of their riders are in sight. Something is strange here. The horses in the corrals don't carry the Running H brand. Wes' attention is pulled away from the corrals, back to the festive music coming from the only cantina along the small street that traverses the town. Whoever rode these horses are inside and having a good time.

"Well, there's the cattle, but I don't see Pole anywhere." Wes looks at the cattle as they pass. The big S brand shows plainly on their hips, despite the dust that covers them. Ramone studies the noisy cantina ahead in the square. "You and the señorita wait here. Me and my compadres will ride into town and find your friend."

Wes nods. "While you're looking, find Waco Grange for me."

"You sure this is what you want me to do, señor?" Ramone looks toward the cantina. "I told you, this one you want is a very dangerous man."

"I'm sure. Tell him to come out into the street, with or without his men."

Ramone grins sadly. "Por favor señor, we ride here with you, but we are not gunfighters, we are banditos."

Wes flips a burned-out stub onto the sandy ground. "I don't want your help my friend. This is my business and mine alone."

The Mexican shrugs. "So be it, señor, it is your life also."

"Yes, it is."

Wes and Rusty follow the Mexicans into Corrales, but lag far behind, giving Ramone time to find Grange and deliver the message. Handing the girl a cigarette, he strikes a match. "You should wait here Rusty."

"I should, but I ain't letting you ride in there alone." She takes the smoke and thanks him.

"Pole will be in town somewhere, if they haven't killed him already."

Her face hardens. "If they have, I'll kill all of them myself."

Wes smiles over at her. He knows she means what she said. "I'm curious girl, you've only known him a short while."

"What made me take to him so quickly?" She smiles. "Is that what you're wondering, Mister Tobin?"

"Exactly." Wes nods. "Pole is my friend, but he's not exactly a ladies man, if you know what I mean?"

"Maybe not to you Wes Tobin, but to me, he's like a knight in shining armor of old, my mother use to tell me about."

"Really?" Wes has heard it all now, Pole Nichols a knight in shining armor.

She smiles dreamily. "He's a gentleman. Oh, I know he's killed, but the way he looks at me. No man has ever treated me, or talked to me with the respect and kindness he showed."

"I'll be danged Rusty, you truly do love the tall galoot."

The green eyes flash. "Yes, I do. I know it was real sudden, but that's the way we Flannerys do things, real sudden."

Wes smiles. "It was that, little lady, and I'm happy for both of you."

"Pole says you don't think much of getting hitched."

"No, ma'am can't say I do."

"Will we find him alive?"

"If I know Pole, he'll be alive and kicking when we see him," Wes laughs, "and probably holding a mug of beer."

# CHAPTER 8

The horses walk slowly along the streets of Corrales, their hooves kicking up dust devils with every stride. Not a soul moves along the street, not even the skinny town dogs that normally roam through the village. Wes studies the deserted streets, letting his eyes search out every doorway and alley.

"It's siesta time, Mister Tobin." Rusty, sensing his curiosity speaks up. "Everything in town is asleep."

"Everything?"

"Yep." Rusty pushes back a lock of red hair. "People down here are laid back. They take life pretty easy."

"You mean they're lazy?"

"Not exactly, it's just their way of life." She smiles, "It's a good way for them."

Pulling their horses to a halt at the edge of the town square, Wes studies the cantina and its dark doorway. "I'm riding on in; you wait here."

"Not likely." She kicks her horse. "I told you, I'm finding Pole."

The street is wider than most towns north of the border. It's also much dirtier, with litter along the storefronts. Wes dismounts and ties his gelding to a hitch rack in front of what looks like a mercantile store. Across the street, the music from the cantina still sounds loud through the doorway.

Wes is expecting Waco Grange and his men to come charging through the doorway at any minute and is shocked when Ramone, with Pole following, emerges from the bar. Rusty races across the street, flinging herself into the tall man's arms. Embarrassed and red faced at first, Pole finally breaks into a wide grin, pulling her to him.

"I didn't expect to see you down here, Miss Rusty."

Smiling, she cranes her neck backward and looks up at him. "When Wes told me you followed the cattle down here, I had to come."

"I'm glad."

"Okay, okay, let's break up this reunion." Wes stands watching the two smiling faces. "Where's Waco Grange and his men?"

"They sold our cattle early this morning." Pole looks over at Wes, then the Mexicans. "They lit out soon as the deal was finished, headed back across the border I reckon."

"Those are our cows over in them corrals." Wes looks back toward the cattle. "I don't care who bought them."

"Yep, I reckon they are, they're carrying the big S brand," Pole nods. "The new owners are in the cantina eating. They might dispute your claim a bit."

"They know they're stolen cattle."

"They know; seems they've been buying hot cattle from Grange for quite some time."

"You mean Halleck don't you? Waco Grange is just a hired flunky."

"Ok." Pole corrects himself. "They've been buying from Halleck."

"Sandigras cattle?"

"Mostly," Pole nods, "they didn't know who I was way off down here, so I hung around the cantina and picked up the local gossip."

"You just happened to have a few beers while you were waiting." Wes grins."

A few," Pole admits. "I was beginning to think I was gonna have to take them by myself."

"Didn't figure I was coming, huh?"

"Oh, I knew you'd come sooner or later, I just didn't know which." Pole looks down at the girl. "I wasn't about to let them take our cattle."

"It's good to see you, pard."

Wes unties his horse and leads him back toward the corral. Leaning over the top rail, he cusses, the cattle are drawn. They were pushed hard with little water or graze, but at least he has them back. Worn out as they are, pushing them back to their home range should be no problem. All they need is a good long drink of water and they'll be ready to travel.

"You want a job helping us herd these cows back to the Sandigras?" Wes looks over at Ramone.

Several cowboys emerge from the cantina as the Mexican is about to answer. "Si, señor, but first we will see what happens. Maybe you take these cattle, maybe you don't."

Wes looks across the street to where Ramone is staring. Four rough looking men, spread out in a long line across the street, walk slowly toward the corrals. Waving Ramone and his men back, out of the line of fire, Wes and Pole wait calmly as the oncoming men approach. Pole glances sideways to where Rusty still stands beside him.

"Get out of the way, gal."

"I'm staying, Pole."

"No you ain't, missy. You'll just get one of us killed, maybe both."

Reluctantly, she moves back to the stable door where Ramone and his men have retreated. The four cowboys walk to within thirty yards of the corrals and stop, silently staring at the two waiting men.

"You boys got something on your mind?" A heavyset man stands slightly in front of the others. "You sure seem interested in those cattle. We've been watching you for some time from over at the cantina."

"Yes, sir, you might say we're interested. We were just fixing to head them home." Wes smiles coldly. "To our home."

"Those cattle belong to me, mister." The man pulls a paper from his vest-pocket. "Here's my bill of sale."

Wes' face hardens. "Is that a fact? These are Sandigras cattle, carrying the big S brand. I sure didn't sell them to you. My signature isn't on that paper. So, that makes you a liar mister and a cattle thief."

"Those are mighty harsh words." The man tenses. "I paid good money for them hides."

"Money is just money." Wes smiles coldly. "Don't add your life."

"You ain't taking them cattle, mister."

"It's your call fat man." The slight blink of the man's eyes as his hand goes into action is all it takes as Wes pulls his own weapon. The forty four, belches fire and lead, catching the man twice in the chest. A blank look comes into his eyes as he collapses slowly into the dusty street. The big man's weapon never cleared its holster.

"Anybody else want to claim those cattle?" Not a word is spoken as the men look down at the blood spreading around their fallen leader. Wes holsters his pistol and motions for Pole to do the same.

"We're just hired hands, mister, not gun hands." The oldest of the group raises his hands and backs slowly away. "We don't want any trouble."

"I'm Wes Tobin of the Sandigras. If any of my cattle find their way here again, I'll track down and kill whoever sells them, and whoever I find with them."

"What about the men who sold them to us?" A younger man whines. "We thought they owned them cows."

"You're young, but you ain't that stupid." Wes hooks his thumbs in the gunbelt. "You knew they were stolen. Why else would you meet way off down here to take possession of them?"

"Nobody calls me a liar." The youngster drops his hand to cover his pistol butt.

Pole shakes his head sadly. "Don't be a fool kid. He'll kill you before you blink."

"Let it go, Billy." One of the other men plead with the hotheaded rider.

"I didn't call you a liar, youngster." Wes tenses, not wanting to kill the kid unless he is forced to. "I'm sorry."

"You're sorry alright." The big pistol belches flame as the youngster fires, then falls backward as the heavy slug from Wes' pistol knocks him into the dirt.

"You, boys pass the word. There will be no more cattle stolen from the Sandigras." Wes steps closer to the men. "I'll personally hang or shoot every cow thief I find driving our beef."

One man frowns, looking down at the two dead men. "When word gets out about this, I figure you just cured that problem, for good?"

Pole holsters his pistol and points down at the dead men. "Just for the record, who were these fellows?"

"Amos Powell, foreman of the Flying S, south of Tucson, and Billy Mitchell."

"You tell your boss, if I catch anymore Flying S hands, driving Sandigras cattle, I'll come pay him a personal visit." Wes stares hard at the three drovers. "You understand me?"

"We understand."

Ramone looks to where Rusty stands, staring across at Pole and Wes. "Your new friends are hard men, señorita. Their hearts are cold."

"Then they should fit in fine out here, Ramone."

"Let's head for home." Wes starts for the corrals. "You helping, Ramone?"

"No señor, I will see the señorita gets home safe to her father."

"Ramone, I'm riding in with Pole."

"No, señorita." The Mexican looks across at Wes. "If your father finds you with these men, there could be big trouble."

"I don't want to leave him."

"Do you want your father or brothers killed niña?" Ramone hands her the reins to the horse. "That one is a bad hombre. He is a diablo, the devil. He kills without sorrow. No one can stand against him, not even Señor Flannery. Little one, you must ride with me, away from this place, now."

Rusty hugs Pole before mounting her horse, and looks over at Wes like she has never seen him before. Leaning down, she touches Pole's cheek. "I will be waiting for you."

"I'll be riding the canyons." Pole holds her hand. "Thanks for coming after me."

"Did you see the way she looked at me, old hoss?" Wes opens the corral gate, letting the cattle out. "Like she'd never seen me before."

"I 'spect she hasn't, old friend." Pole looks away embarrassed for Wes. "Not really."

Boston Flannery, flanked by his sons and several others, sits across the road, waiting, as the herd moves slowly toward them. The redheaded Rowdy Flannery, pulls his pistol several times, returning it to the low-slung holster.

"That'll be enough of that, boy."

"I'm just limbering up, Pa. Just in case she's been abused."

"You hush that kind of talk against your sister." The older Flannery glares over at the redhead. "You hear me, boy?"

"I hear you."

Despite the dust boiling up around the herd, Wes and Pole can plainly see the riders waiting ahead. The trail leading down to the Sandigras Canyons is only a couple miles further. Wes is surprised, as he figures the Flannerys would have been waiting further south.

"We got ourselves some company." Pole shakes his head.

"Looks like your father-in-law to be." Wes gazes through the cloud of dust.

"Yeah." Pole reaches across and pulls in on the gelding Wes rides. "They're her blood, pard, I can't lose her. Let's ride easy on her folks."

"It's their call, Pole. Why don't you pull back, out of the way?"

The tall man shakes his head and looks to where the Flannerys wait. "You know better than that, all I said was let's go easy on them."

"I'll try my best." Wes unhooks his tie down.

Pole looks down at the holster, then back up at Wes' face. He knows the cold, hard look that covers the face. Trouble is only seconds ahead of them, trouble he didn't want any part of, because of the girl. He has sided Wes too many times in the past, an old habit that's hard to break, one he won't break, not even for the girl.

Wes lets the cattle drift by themselves to the north, pulling at the sparse grass lining the trail. Reining his gelding to a stop, before the Flannery's matriarch, the two strong willed men stare at each other as the cattle drift around them.

"Where is she?" The question comes out hard and crisp. "Where's Sarah Ann?"

Wes ignores the question. Reaching into his shirt pocket, he pulls out the makings and rolls a smoke. Locking eyes with Flannery, he strikes a sulphur, lighting the cigarette. "You mind elaborating a little on that, Mister Flannery."

"My daughter, you know who I'm talking about."

"No, I don't."

Rowdy Flannery kicks his horse forward. "You're lying, Tobin."

"Call off your pup, Mister Flannery, or there's liable to be some bad trouble right here."

"You're a little outnumbered, gunfighter." Rowdy's hand hovers over his pistol grip.

Wes smiles. "Not the way I figure it."

"How's that?"

"When the dance starts, Rowdy, I aim to kill your father first, then you big mouth. After that, it won't matter much now, does it?"

"You think you're that good?" Rowdy Flannery sneers.

"You know I am, boy."

"You shut up now, Rowdy." Flannery looks over at the redhead, placing both hands on the horn. "Where's Rusty, Mister Tobin?"

"Probably home by now," Wes relaxes. "Ramone said he would see her there safe."

"You telling the truth?" Flannery studies Wes' face. "She's with Ramone Ortega?"

"I don't lie, Mister Flannery."

"Tell me Tobin, why would she ride off like that to help you find a complete stranger?"

"I 'spect you'll have to ask her about that."

Flannery looks across where Pole is rolling himself a smoke. "She sweet on you, tall man?"

"I don't talk about a lady, Mister Flannery. You'll have to ask her." Pole smiles slightly.

"I will, when I see her, but right now, I'm asking you." The big man blusters.

Pole looks calmly across at Flannery, but says nothing. Minutes seem to tick away, before Boston Flannery turns his horse back to the north, veering off down the rough trail, leading to their ranch. Rowdy Flannery is the last to turn back, the green eyes glaring coldly at Wes and Pole.

Looking over to where Pole sits, Wes winks. "You should have introduced yourself to your new family."

"I'm in no hurry to get to know them," Pole grins. "I expect, before this is over, I'll get well enough acquainted with those boys."

A week passed since the cattle returned to the Sandigras range. The fence was repaired good as new, with one exception. A five-strand, eight foot wide gate, big enough to let any size herd of cattle pass through, was built into the fence. Wes never asked where Pole was keeping himself these days, but since their return, the tall man prefers spending most of his time riding the far-flung valleys alone. Pole rode the Flannery's horse to check the canyons one morning and returned riding Wes' gelding. Wes doesn't have to ask, he knows.

Monte keeps the rest of the hands busy with preparations for the oncoming winter months. The Sandigras valleys are quiet, but Wes and Pole still ride out every day, passing up and down the range, ever vigilant for rustlers or fence cutters.

Noise, from several fast traveling horses, sound on the hardpan soil coming across the lower valley, closing in behind Wes as he rides alone, checking the fence lines. Turning in the saddle, he pulls the gelding in. Behind him, jerking their little mustangs to a sliding stop, sit several Apache warriors across the trail. Wes recognizes the half-breed Martine in front of the warriors.

"Do not look surprised white man. You asked to speak with Suttero." Martine turns to a warrior beside him. "This one is Chief Suttero. He speaks broken English."

Wes nods. "Some say I do too."

"I have told Suttero of you and your wish to talk with him." The warrior looks across at Wes. "He will speak with you, but he promises nothing."

"I am in your debt, Martine."

"I told the chief that you are a great warrior and how you shoot your gun so fast." Martine looks over at the rider beside him. "He has heard of the two men you killed to the south."

Wes was amazed. How did the Apache find out about the shootout in Mexico so quickly? "I am not a great warrior, my young friend."

"The soldiers at the fort know of you. They say you have killed many men." Martine argues.

"The Mexican bandito, Ramone says you are a devil, a man who thirsts for blood."

"Something I am not proud of."

Martine shrugs. "Why are you not? An Apache would be proud. You should be proud."

The stocky older warrior, sitting beside Martine, motions at the pistol on Wes' hip, then mutters something in Apache.

"Suttero wishes for you to show him how you shoot gun. Chief want you to shoot your gun like you did at your rancho."

"Why does he wish me to do this?"

"Do it white man; empty your weapon. This is the way to show the warriors you trust them." Martine frowns. "They do not believe my words that you wish to be a friend to the Apache."

"Trust them." Only the whisper of a breath passes as Wes unlimbers his pistol and fires, putting five clean holes through a cactus at thirty yards, holes a man could cover with the palm of his hand. "I trust the Apache."

Martine looks over at Wes as the Chief speaks again. "Suttero says you only fired five shots."

"Tell the Chief, I load my pistol with only five shells." Wes reloads. "Tell him, I am not a devil."

Hearing the words, Suttero laughs and nimbly, dismounts, finding a smooth rock to sit on. "What do you want of the Apache?"

"Peace here on the Sandigras. No more Apache raiding Sandigras cattle, or killing our people."

All the Apache warriors whirl suddenly, slipping silently into the surrounding rocks. Wes is curious as he doesn't hear or see anything to cause their alarm.

Martine and Suttero leap to their feet, as Pole is dragged forcibly from behind some trees by several warriors. Martine holds up his hand when he recognizes the tall figure. "This is one of the whites from the white rancho."

"They jumped me at the base of the canyon, Wes." Pole shrugs the dark hands from his arms. "There's at least fifty of the red sons down there."

"Trust?" Wes turns on Martine and Suttero. "You speak of trust, yet you bring so many warriors with you?"

Suttero raises his hands. "In the past, white man, my people have trusted the words of the whites, and we have suffered greatly."

"Everyone lies, red and white."

"I do not lie." Suttero rises to his full height. "No Apache lies."

Wes nods. "I believe Chief Suttero, now we will speak of peace between my people and the Apache."

"Why should we want peace? We raid. We take what we want from the whites to feed our families." A stocky warrior speaks up.

"You lose warriors when you raid the whites." Wes glances around at the frowning warriors. "If you raid the Sandigras, many of these young men will die."

The Chief looks at the gathered warriors. "These warriors are not afraid of death, it has always been this way. Our women and children must eat."

"The Sandigras will give you cattle to feed your people when the game is scarce?"

"And the other whites here?" The Chief questions. "What will they give?"

"I can only speak for the Sandigras and the men who ride for me." Wes looks over at the Chief. "We will not fire on the Apache, providing we can have peace here in these canyons."

"I also cannot speak for the other tribes, the White Mountain, Chiricahua, Mescalero, Coyoteros or the Membranos."

"I cannot speak for the other whites." Wes looks around him. "Your people Suttero, are the closest. The rest of the tribes have to pass through your lands to get to these valleys."

"I cannot stop them if they wish to raid here in this place."

"I want your word Chief, that your people will not raid this ranch any longer."

"Why do you want peace with us white man?"

Wes looks across at Pole. "My men are good fighters, but they are few, and we have many enemies."

"White enemies?"

"Yes, white enemies." Wes shrugs. "If your people do not make war on the Sandigras, I will give you cattle, to stave off the hungry times."

"Weapons, whiskey?"

"Cattle, blankets, medicine, and clothing," Wes shakes his head. "No whiskey, no weapons."

"Do you speak with a straight tongue white man?"

"I too, do not lie."

"You are a brave man, maybe it will be peace. We will see in time."

"How much time?" Wes looks about at the curious warriors. "We have many enemies."

Suttero walks toward the surrounding warriors and turns to face Wes. "You bring our gifts, then we will speak more of this treaty you wish."

"We must ride into the white man's town to get your supplies. We will meet here at this place in ten sleeps."

Suttero nods at Martine. "It is good, but we will meet further west. I will send word with this one where we are to meet."

Wes looks across at the younger man and smiles. "We are in your debt Martine. What can I bring you for your services?"

"I would like a white man's smoke."

Wes and Pole both laugh as they pull out their Bull Durham sacks and start rolling cigarettes for all the warriors, until they run out of tobacco and papers.

Monte sits at the head of the table as a platter of sausage and bacon make the rounds. The gathered men eat hungrily as Ellen places hot biscuits and gravy on the table. Suddenly, from outside, the loud baying of the two hounds, Wes has brought back from Tucson, break the silence.

Looking through the window, Pole lets out with a whoop, "Old Jenks is back."

Forgetting breakfast, everyone rushes outside as four riders pull to a stop at the back door. "Are we in time for breakfast?"

"You're in time." Wes steps down and shakes hands with Jenks. "It's good to see you."

"It was a long trip."

"Where's Jacob?" Wade looks about the yard and over at the corrals for the young rider.

"Dead, we were jumped north of here two days ago." Jenks looks at the upturned faces. "Ambushed, we had to fight our way out. He didn't make it."

"Apaches?" Pole looks across at Jenks.

"Couldn't rightly tell, but I believe they were white men using those new repeating Winchesters," Jenks shrugs.

"You see them, Jenks?" Wes looks sharply at the rider. "Was it the Running H bunch?"

"No, I didn't see anyone, I just had a hunch they were white men." Jenks shrugs. "They didn't fight like Apache, hollering and calling to one another."

"You bury him?" Monte steps closer to Jenks.

"Best we could." Jenks shrugs. "They were still taking shots at us from the ridge."

Wade turns on Jenks, his eyes blazing. "Seems funny, one of my men gets killed and you four don't get a scratch."

"Are you calling me a liar, Sam Wade?" Jenks tosses a leather, wrapped bundle over to Wes. "Your money boss, more than I expected."

Wes looks at the four men and nods. "You boys earned a bonus come payday."

Jenks shrugs. "No, sir, we were just doing our job."

"Unsaddle and feed your horses, then y'all come in and have some breakfast. Ellen will have it on the table." Monte steps between the two men, his huge presence making itself known.

Later, after breakfast, Monte and Wes stroll slowly through the yard, making the rounds of the barns and corrals. In the past, the two cousins and partners enjoyed both a warm and stormy relationship. Now, the future and prosperity of the Sandigras Ranch depends on their ability to work together.

"I'll be riding into Tucson tomorrow."

"Supplies for the Apache?"

"Maybe things are settling down, Monte." Wes nods absently. "We've made a shaky peace with Suttero and his Apaches. I believe Boston Flannery and his clan just want to be left alone."

"Are you saying we're out of the woods?" Monte kicks at the soft dirt, "that we can live here in peace?"

"No, there's still Halleck and probably an occasional rustler to deal with." Wes builds himself a smoke. "Halleck and his Running H riders are now our main concern."

"Not the cow thieves?"

"They'll always be rustling on any range, Cousin." Wes blows smoke into the cool morning air. "When we catch men stealing from us, we hang them."

"Simple as that, no trial?"

"I've given fair warning, Monte, I'll hang the first man I catch with a running iron or our cattle."

"It's hard to believe, this basin is ours." Monte looks across the canyon floor, smiling happily.

"It's ours Monte, and we're gonna keep it no matter who rides against us."

"We've got a big crew now, more than we need." Monte looks over at the bunkhouse. "Maybe we should let a few of them go."

"Our cattle brought a good price up north." Wes places a foot on the lower corral rail. "With the money I have and what Jenks brought back, we've got enough money to keep us running for at least two, maybe three years."

"In three years, we'll have enough cattle for another drive north." Monte nods. "If we don't get rustled blind."

"We'll have plenty of grown stuff by then, alright." Wes flips the burned-out smoke away. "I say we keep all the hands and take a herd north again in the spring."

"This spring?" Monte looks sharply at Wes.

"Jenks made a profitable drive this time, why not?"

"We won't have the heavy stock to trail that soon." Monte looks over at Wes. "What we got left are just yearling's, we need full-grown steers."

"We'll buy from the other ranches to the south."

"You mean Flannery?"

"And others." Wes turns. "The following year, we'll have plenty of two year olds of our own to ship."

"Longhorns take up to seven or eight years to mature enough for market." Monte rubs his chin thoughtfully. "You know that, Wes."

"Ain't talking about longhorn cattle, Cousin. I'm talking about Herefords, the cattle I'm bringing in come spring." Wes points at the valley floor. "In a couple years, red and white cattle, plus a few mixed breeds, will cover the Sandigras."

"You're right. I've seen them new Herefords in Texas. They'll mature in two or three years for market," Monte smiles. "Hopefully, we're in business, Cousin."

Both men whirl, as the noise of a fight sounds behind the bunkhouse. Tossing their smokes, they hurry toward the racket of loud voices and cheering. The sound of the struggle and excited voices grows louder as they turn the corner of the building to find Jenks and Sam Wade locked together in combat. Rolling around on the ground, punching, gouging, and kicking, as both men are covered in dust and dirt.

As Monte starts forward to break up the fight, Wes catches his arm and pulls him back. "Let 'em blow off some steam. They might settle the air around here a bit."

"You sure?"

"Yeah, I'm sure. It always helped me and you get our problems lined out, didn't it?"

Monte rubs his jaw and smiles. "Most times I reckon it did at that."

Pole walks over from the doorway of the barn and observes the fight. "Pretty good set-to, if you ask me."

"Yeah, you stay here and help me make sure it don't get out of hand."

"I was just fixing to ride out." Pole frowns.

"She'll wait, you break them up before they get beat up so bad they can't work." Wes watches as Jenks lands a hard right to Wade's face.

"Then I'm riding."

"Kinda early to be riding ain't it?"

Pole grins. "You ever heard the early bird gets the worm? It's never too early to ride and listen to the early morning creatures, and smell the dew on the grass."

"You do that compadre, and while you're smelling the dew and seeing Miss Flannery, tell her you won't be meeting with her tomorrow."

Pole cuts his eyes at Wes. "Just why not?"

"Cause we're heading for Tucson come daylight."

Nodding, Pole starts toward the circle of men and the fight. "I'll tell her. She'll just love that. You know she ain't real fond of you anyway."

"Imagine that, and here I thought we were good friends."

"Yeah." Pole grins. "I sure wouldn't bet on it."

"You've seen a lot of her lately." Wes calls out to the tall man.

Pole turns and looks back at Wes and Monte. "It ain't interfering with my work, so I expect it's none of y'alls concern."

"That's not what I'm worrying about."

"What then?"

"That redheaded brother of hers, that's what," Wes speaks up. "He's a killer. I've seen it in his eyes, and I figure him for a back shooter unless he's got the deadwood on a man."

"You mean the one they call Rowdy?"

"Yep, old Boston Flannery's oldest." Wes nods. "Don't let your feelings for the girl get you killed."

"She's my business, Wes. She's gonna be my wife, if she'll have me."

"Yes, sir." Wes backs off and drops the subject. Pole is easy going as most, but where the girl was concerned, he has a closed mind. Motioning to Monte, the two cousins start back toward the house.

"I'll be careful, old friend," Pole calls out. "I'll meet you at the west canyon about midafternoon."

"You do that." Wes watches as Pole steps between the two combatants.

"He's fixing to ride clear across the Sandigras just to see a girl?" Monte shakes his head.

"What can I say?" Wes grins. "He's in love."

"What would a woman ever see in that beanpole of a man?" Monte shakes his head. "I know Pole's your best friend, but he's downright homely."

"Ain't you heard? Love's blind Monte, she loves him." Wes watches as Pole breaks up the fight. "I wouldn't let Rusty Flannery hear you talk about her man like that."

"She must be smitten with love, or half blind."

"Like I said, looks ain't everything to a woman, cousin."

"I've heard she's something to behold."

"She's a real looker alright." Wes grins as he watches Pole separate the two fighters. "She's got that Flannery temper so it ought to be interesting."

"Well, I'm fixing to have me another cup of coffee."

"I'll be saddling up."

Monte nods. "Oh, by the way, I think me and the misses are going to accompany you to town tomorrow."

# CHAPTER 9

The morning air is cool, putting a chill in the air as the sun hasn't risen enough to heat up the desert sand. The wagon bounces over the bumpy road, jarring its passengers unmercifully. With the iron wheels and no springs, the huge work wagon catches the small of some of the passenger's backs with every pothole or rock it happens upon.

Wes and Pole bring Sam Wade and the youngster, Charlie Mack, along in case Apaches or Mexican bandits appear on the closely watched trails leading into Tucson. Most travelers use the roads at their own peril and only the ones with heavy army escorts are safe.

Pole looks over at the bruised and battered face of Wade and grins. "Was it worth the bruises, Sam?"

Cutting his eyes at the tall man, Wade smiles stiffly, and nods. "It was, every one of them."

Fifteen miles into Tucson is rough enough without throwing in the scorching sun's midday heat. By the time Tucson comes into view at noon, with the larger buildings looming in the distance, the sun comes out blaring down with a vengeance on the travelers.

Despite the heat and jarring of the wagon, nothing bothers Ellen. She looks forward to her first trip into Tucson since moving onto the Sandigras. A beaming smile never leaves her face, as she's happy to be going anywhere, to break the day-to-day monotony of the ranch. "Is it a big place, Monte?"

"We weren't here long enough last time we came through, I can't remember." Monte shrugs, he's only been to Tucson one time when they recorded their deed. "Afraid you'll have to ask Wes, I don't know for sure."

"It's big enough, Miss Ellen." Pole looks over at her. "Most anything a man wants is waiting just ahead in that little old town."

Ellen smiles and looks over at Pole sweetly. "Does the town have what a woman wants, Mister Nichols?"

Pole clears his throat, blushing beat red, then looking toward Tucson. "Yes, ma'am, of course the town will have all the latest fandangle and frills a lady could want."

"That's great, Pole. In that case, I'm gonna buy the makings to fix you boys a big chocolate cake when we get home." She laughs, "Maybe it'll put a little meat on your bones."

"Good luck doing that," Wes smiles. "With all the riding and exercising, he's been doing lately, it'll be hard."

Pole's face turns redder as he hears the hidden jibe from Wes. Meeting Rusty back in the canyons, whenever she could slip away from her pa, was impossible to keep from the sharp-eyed Wes.


The mercantile is full of shoppers as Monte and Wes follow Ellen inside the cool, well-stocked store. She marvels at the rows of can goods, rolled fabric, china, everything she needs or wants. Smiling and speaking to the women she walks by, Ellen starts filling up the long counter with different items.

Hardly twenty minutes have passed before Charlie comes busting through the door, making the small bell sound noisily. "You better hurry boss."

"What's wrong?"

"Pole and Sam are into it with the Running H crew." The youngster starts for the door. "I think there's gonna be gunplay."

The muffled sound, like thunder, causes Wes to break for the saloon at a dead run. Again, the sound of a shot rings as Wes, with Charlie right on his heels, crash through the swinging doors. Wes lunges sideways, pulling his pistol, as Pole whirls on him, ready to fire.

"It's me Pole." Wes looks about the smoke-filled room. "The rest of you people hold still, real still."

Sam Wade is down, rolling in the sawdust, trying to reach his pistol. Two of the Running H riders lie prone on the bloodstained floor. The rest of Halleck's men back up against the long bar with their hands plainly visible.

A city deputy pushes through the wide doors, surveying the room, taking in the downed men. Kneeling beside the dead cowboys, he feels their chests for any sign of a heartbeat and then stands to his feet. "They're both dead." He looks over at Pole. "Who did the shooting?"

"I did." Pole holsters his weapon.

The deputy looks down at Sam first, then over to where Wes stands. "I saw you and the boy run in here after the gunshots."

"These two men work for me." Wes nods down at Wade.

"What about you." The deputy picks up Sam's pistol, rotating the cylinder as another man rushes through the doors. "You do any shooting?"

"I told you, deputy, I killed them both after they shot Sam here in the leg." Pole speaks up again, watching as the man checks the loads in the pistol.

"Are you that good, boy?" The tall City Marshall takes over the questioning. "It's well known in these parts that these boys of Halleck's were handy with a pistol."

Pole doesn't bother to answer, just watches as the new arrival makes his own inspection of the bodies and their weapons. The shots came so quickly, they sounded like one to Wes, from across the street.

"Is that what happened, Harry?" The Marshall looks over at the bar owner.

"Yeah, the Halleck riders started the ruckus and pulled first, but I say it was still murder." The barkeep points at Pole. "That one there is pure poison with a shooter."

"Who are you, mister?" The Marshal turns his attention on Pole. "Where you from?"

"He works for me." Wes steps forward.

"I didn't ask you, I asked this man." The tall Marshall looks Pole up and down.

"My name's Pole Nichols, from Texas."

The cold black eyes of the lawman turn fully on Pole, then shift around the room. "You're lucky, Mister Nichols, that Mister Halleck or Waco Grange isn't here."

"I am?" Pole sneers in the man's face. "You're scaring me plumb to death with them names, Marshall."

"Harry here vouched for you. I'm letting you ride out of Tucson. If I were you, I wouldn't be showing my face in Tucson again." The Marshall motions toward the swinging doors. "Now get, before I change my mind."

"That'll be hard to do lawman, as I own part of the Sandigras Ranch and aim to buy my supplies here regularly." Pole grins over at the saloon owner, "Also my liquor, Mister Harry the barman, I'm a heavy drinker."

"You heard me, Nichols." The Marshall pulls his pistol threateningly.

"We'll leave as soon as I get Mister Wade doctored on, Marshall."

Wes steps between Pole and the Marshall. "You do have a doctor in this town?"

"I said get out now, all of you." The Marshall turns the pistol, pointing it dead center at Wes. Normally a good-natured person, Pole is now mad clear through, as he is angry enough to take on the town law and Wes knows it. Looking the lawman in the eyes, Wes lets his hand drop to his side.

"We're gonna get help for my rider Marshall. We haven't broken any laws, I know of, so don't push it."

The hardness goes slowly out of the man's face as he looks at Wes. "I'm just trying to prevent more killing. If Mister Halleck rides into town, it could get bad."

"We'll ride out as soon as he sees the doctor," Pole speaks up. "Don't make a mistake, Marshall. Ain't nobody here scared of Mister Halleck, or you either."


Monte stands at the swinging doors of the saloon, looking curiously at Wes, as he and Pole carry Wade from the saloon to the waiting wagon. "Well, you got the supplies for the Apache Cousin, were they worth it?"

Wes nods. "If a hundred dollars in blankets, food, and clothes will save us one life Monte, it was worth it."

"I was referring to the two dead men lying there on the floor."

"Like I said, Cousin, it was worth it." Wes glares at the big man. "Their carcasses weren't worth a hundred to me."

"They're still men, Wes."

"Were they Monte?" Wes frowns. "If they were faster, we'd be burying Pole and Sam right now. They bit off more than they could chew in my book."

Wade lies in the back of the rumbling wagon, with bundles of blankets, clothes and boxes of supplies for the ranch and the Apaches. His leg is rests lightly on a pile of blankets with a white bandage the doctor applied.

Pulling across a small creek, Wes raises his hand for a halt. "How you doing, Sam?" Wes offers the wounded man a smoke.

"It ain't hurting none right now." He takes the smoking cigarette and nods. "Thank you, kindly."

"You were lucky it didn't hit anything vital or break a bone." Pole leans from his horse and grins. "That old, sawbones put enough laudanum in you to put a grizzly bear to sleep for the winter."

"You ain't never been hit by hot lead I see." Wade laughs. "Thank you for pulling my chestnuts out of the fire, and getting the doctor for me."

"What happened back there?" Monte turns on the wagon seat and looks down at the man. "What started the fight?"

Pole looks over at the big man. "We were having a cool beer and Halleck's men started hooraying us something awful."

"Is that it?"

"Pretty much." Wade looks up at Pole and winks. "We were purely innocent of anything."

"You two? Shucks, I doubt you've been innocent since the day you were born." Monte slaps the team with the check lines.

Wes can see the red, rise in Pole's neck, and changes the subject. "I'm out of smokes Pole, bring me some back here."

"He's your cousin, Wes, but I swear, one of these days."

"He's a caution Pole, but have patience." Wes looks about him. "We've got ourselves a good thing here. We can't be bickering among ourselves."

It's two hours past dark, when the wagon finally rolls into the ranch house of the Sandigras. Most of the hands are on the porch, taking in the evening quiet as the wagon creaks to a halt. Seeing Wade all bandaged up, the questions start flying. Monte raises his hands to stop the talk as everyone goes to work, helping unload.

"You men had supper?" Ellen takes Monte's arms as he lifts her bodily from the wagon.

Jenks removes his sweat stained hat and smiles. "Don't fret yourself, Miss Ellen, we'll make do tonight. You've had a long trip."

"Nonsense Jenks, you men get Sam inside, then unload the wagon. I'll round us up a bite to eat." She smiles tiredly. "We haven't had anything either."


All the men resume their seats on the porch, waiting expectantly for Pole to fill them in on what happened. Charlie Mack can hardly restrain himself as he waits for the story to be told. He wants to tell it himself, but it was not his story to tell.

"Well… and that's what happened," Pole finishes the tale, looking over to Wade, resting comfortably on a cot.

"You boys ought to have seen it." Charlie expands his chest. "Old Pole did them boys in for good."

"Halleck ain't gonna be happy about this." One of the new hands, Luke Wilson, speaks up. "Did you happen to catch the dead men's names?"

"Wilson, do you know Halleck?" Pole looks at the rider.

"Yeah, I rode for him for five years."

"Why'd you quit?"

Wilson looks sharply at Pole, then over at Jenks. "You questioning my loyalty?"

"I'm asking you a simple question. Why did you quit?" Pole's voice becomes hard. "It's a plain question."

The rider's eyes drop. "I didn't like their rules."

Pole drops the subject as Ellen calls them into dinner. "We'll finish this later." As Pole disappears through the kitchen door, Charlie looks around at the hands. "I'd of never believed it."

Luke Wilson looks over at the youngster, "What wouldn't you believe?"

"I wouldn't have believed that tall beanpole could be as rough as he is." Charlie beams. "He's cat quick with that hog leg of his."

"Is he or was he just lucky?" Wilson tosses his burned down smoke.

Charlie stands up, starting toward the door, then stops and looks back at Wilson. "You try him Luke, find out for yourself."

"Maybe I will at that." Wilson glares at the grinning Charlie. "Those boys were friends of mine."

As the hands head for the bunkhouse after supper, Pole waits outside on the porch. Wes can tell, by the way the tall man is puffing on his smoke and fidgeting, he has something on his mind.

"You coming to bed, old hoss?" Wes stands beside Pole and strikes a sulphur against the door frame.

"I'll be along directly. I figure I'll hang around here a minute."

"We've had trouble enough for one day." Wes looks back through the door where Monte is still having coffee at the table while Ellen cleans up. "We've sure had enough fighting among ourselves to last awhile."

"Go to bed, Wes, I have to settle this. There won't be any gunplay." Pole cuts his eyes coldly. "You ain't wanted here, right now."

Nodding, Wes tosses his unfinished smoke into the yard and walks away. Tapping lightly on the doorsill, Pole gets Monte's attention and motions him outside, without attracting Ellen's attention.

"Yeah, what do you want?" Monte steps heavily onto the porch.

"We've got a sick horse in the barn, he needs your attention."

Pole lights the two lanterns hanging in the alleyway of the large barn and turns to where Monte stands waiting. Unbuckling his gun belt, he hangs it from a peg and removes his hat.

Monte looks about the barn and back at Pole. "I didn't figure there was a sick horse out here."

"No, Monte, just a sick overbearing lout of a man."

"You sure this is what you want?"

"I'm sure." Pole moves toward the big man, who stands waiting, straddle legged. "Ain't never been surer of anything."

Curious glances are cast around the table, but not a word or question was asked about the dark bruises and torn knuckles on Pole and Monte. Everyone at the table is wondering who won the fight, knowing they probably missed the fight of their lives. With the quiet nature of these two men, they figure they will never find out.

Pole rides out, after breakfast, heading south. He hardly reaches the flats across from the ranch when Wes hails him. Loping up beside the tall man, Wes pulls his gelding down to a walk, falling in beside the other horse.

"You keep your eyes open out there today." Wes motions out across the flat valley. "Halleck lost two men and there's still that red headed Flannery boy."

"I aim too." Pole wraps his leg lazily around the saddle horn. "You figuring they'll hit us, ain't you?"

Wes nods. "We took this valley away from him. We killed one of his top guns and now the two in Tucson. I doubt Halleck will take it lying down"

"I'll be on the west side." Pole clucks to his gelding. "If you get lost, let out a holler."

"You feel better now, old friend?"

"Yeah I do, a lot better." Pole feels of his swollen face. "I'll say one thing; he's a tough nut to crack."

"Yep, I can vouch to that." Wes grins and nods his head. "Tell Miss Rusty I said howdy."

Pole smiles at the remark and lopes off toward the far canyons. Wes watches him disappear, then turns to the eastern most side of the canyon floor. Except for yesterday, everything has been quiet on the Sandigras Range. He shrugs, maybe Halleck hasn't figured on trying to get the canyons back, but now with two of his men dead, things would surely change. A proud man like Halleck has to make a move against them as he has a reputation to uphold.

Two hours later, Wes is near the far canyon that leads off from the main grasslands, when his horse pricks his ears. Only seconds pass, when Wes picks up the sound of a hard running horse, far out in the brush. By the sound of the pounding hooves, the horse is in a full-out run, coming his way fast. Releasing his pistol tie down, Wes rides the gelding into the brush, waiting for a glimpse of the approaching rider.

"Rusty!" Wes spurs his horse forward, shouting at the girl. "Hold up, what's your hurry?" Pulling her heaving horse to a sliding stop, feet from him, she slides to the ground.

"You're here, thank goodness."

Wes dismounts and grabs the shaking red head before she crumples to the ground. "What's wrong, Rusty?"

"It's Pole, he's been shot."

"How bad?"

"He's hit hard. He sent me to get you and then he passed out." Rusty pushes his hands away and turns to her horse. "We have to hurry before he bleeds to death."

Helping her back on her blowing horse, he follows her at a lope, back to the south.


Pole regains consciousness and drags himself into a sitting position against a small cottonwood. His shirt and the ground beneath him are drenched in blood.

"Are you hurt bad?" Wes yells out as he jerks his plunging gelding to a sliding halt and rushes to the wounded man. "Where were you hit?"

The pain racked eyes blink open, trying to focus. "Bad enough I reckon, old hoss, and it feels like all over."

Wes pulls the bloody shirt back and examines the wound. Pole has been shot in the lower back, the bullet making a nasty exit wound through his left side. Rusty bandaged the wound the best she could, trying to stop the bleeding before riding for help.

Wes cusses as he removes the blood soaked shirttail, she used. "I told you to be careful."

"I tried, pard, I just don't have eyes in the back of my head."

"I know."

"How bad does it look?" Pole feels Rusty take his hand. "Give it to me straight."

Wes looks over at Rusty then drops his eyes. "You'll be alright."

Wrapping the wound again, with some fresh cloth from his saddlebags, Wes looks out across the flats and back at the girl. "He can't ride. We've got to get a wagon."

"Our place is closer, but we can't get a wagon down the canyon trail from this end."

"You'll have to ride to the Sandigras and bring help." Wes looks at her. "Can you do that?"

"Pole's horse is run out. I'll have to take yours."

Wes didn't notice before, she has been riding one of the Sandigras horses. "What became of your horse?"

"We were sitting under this tree when Pole was shot. My horse was on the other side of the fence. I climbed through the wire instead of opening the gate. The shot must have spooked him."

"Take mine and don't let the grass grow under your feet." Wes grabs his horse. "Hurry, Rusty."

"I'll hurry." Rusty kisses Pole and starts for the horse. "You keep him alive Wes, please."

Wes watches her mount. "Tell someone at the ranch to go for the doctor."

Wetting his kerchief, Wes mops the face of the sweating man and rolls a cigarette. Riding at a steady lope, it will take the girl at least two or three hours to reach the ranch headquarters. Then, there was the return ride in the rough wagon. Wes looks down at the pain-racked face of Pole and shakes his head. Wounded like he is, and the severe loss of blood he has sustained, Wes doubts Pole will last until they get him back to the ranch.

"How bad is he hurt?"

Wes whirls, his pistol streaking from his holster. Boston Flannery and his redheaded son Rowdy, stand ten feet away. In his concern for his friend, Wes didn't hear them approach.

Lowering the pistol, Wes looks toward the redhead. "He's lost a lot of blood, could be lung-shot."

"Let me take a look." Flannery kneels down and pulls back the bloody bandages. "Rusty's horse came home. We tracked him back here."

"Where is she?" Rowdy Flannery speaks up, looking about the canyon.

"She rode to the Sandigras for help."

Flannery stands up and rubs sand on his bloody hands. "He'll never make it back to your headquarters."

"What choice do we have?" Wes studies the men. "We can't leave him here."

"Rowdy, cut over the split and ride into town. Bring Doc Harper back here with you. Tell him this man is shot hard."

"Pa, he's an outsider," the red head argues.

"I know what he is boy, now do as I say and ride, ride hard."

"You aim on doctoring him out here?"

"The doctor will be here in half the time. Soon as he arrives, we'll bring in a tent and blankets." Flannery looks over at Wes. "There's no other way if you want him to live. He ain't hit in the lungs, the bullet's to low down, but he's hit mighty hard just the same."

"What can I do?"

"Pray, Wes Tobin, pray hard."

"Are you a religious man, Mister Flannery?"

"I try to be when folks will let me." The big man looks down at Pole. "Praying, never hurt anyone, just maybe it'll help."

"You got any idea who shot him?" Wes looks at the departing back of Rowdy Flannery.

"It wasn't a Flannery, if that's what you're asking."


Doc Harper rides in with Rowdy at almost the same time Rusty and several men from the Sandigras pull up with the wagon. Carrying a black doctor's bag in his hand, the small, dark complected, doctor hurriedly approaches Boston and Wes.

"This is going to be highly unusual." The doctor makes a quick assessment of Pole's condition. "Mister Flannery is correct, if we move him, he'll surely expire."

Boston looks over to where Rowdy sits smoking. "Head for the ranch boy and bring back a tent and supplies."


For almost two hours, Wes paces while Doctor Harper works on Pole. He expects at any moment to hear the worst, but the little doctor keeps working feverishly beside his patient. Standing up, he wipes his spectacles and closes his bag.

"Doc?" Wes and Rusty step forward.

Doc Harper looks up into their worrying faces. "Right now folks, it's even money, one way or the other."

"That's your best guess?"

"That's it, were I you, I'd thank Mister Flannery here, he might just have saved this man's life."

"We know that, Doc?" Wes looks down at the pale face. "We're indebted to him."

"He did some mighty good doctoring before I got here. If you people tried to haul him back eight miles in that wagon, he'd be a goner for sure."

"We're all in debt to Mister Flannery." Wes nods. "We'll always be thankful to him."


Rowdy and several of his brothers ride up, leading a pack mule, several sacks of grub, and cooking utensils. Boston Flannery puts the men to work stretching the large tent over the unconscious man.

"I need to be getting back to town." Harper picks up his coat. "Mrs. Ferguson is ready to have her baby."

"What about Pole?" Wes steps forward. "Won't he be needing you?"

"I've done all I can do for now. Keep him warm and still, and don't try to move him."

"When will you be back?" Rusty takes the doctor's arm, looking down at Pole concerned.

"Soon as the baby's born."

Wes nods. "Three of you boys ride back to Tucson with the good Doctor."

Handing Wes his bag, the little man mounts awkwardly and looks down. "Remember, keep Mister Nichols still. Don't move him and for Pete's sake, keep the cigarettes and whiskey away from him."

Wes hands two gold pieces and the bag, to the doctor. "I hope this is enough. If it isn't, sing out."

Looking at the money, Harper smiles, "It's too much. I'll see you tomorrow."

"For that man's life Doc, nothing is too much."

Boston Flannery watches the riders disappear toward the canyon rim and smiles. "Well, I reckon our secret passage into these valleys is no longer a secret."

Wes knows he is referring to what he called the slit, a trail Monte and his crew overlooked. "It doesn't matter now, Boston, there won't be any more fences between the Sandigras Range and the Flannerys."

"That's good Wes Tobin, real good." Flannery smiles and turns to where his boys wait. "Rusty you and the boys mount up. We've done all we can here."

"I won't be going yet, Pa." Rusty sits beside Pole, holding his hand.

The green eyes of the rancher, narrow as he looks at his daughter. "It's that way, is it?"

"When Pole gets on his feet, he'll tell you himself proper." Rusty takes her father's big hand. "For now, I hope you'll understand. I can't leave him."

Rowdy steps forward, threateningly. "You ain't staying here alone with strangers."

"I'm a big girl now brother, I'll do as I please."

"Leave it be, Rowdy." Boston Flannery starts for his horse. "Let's ride."

"We'll see after her, Mister Flannery, just like she was one of our own." Wes walks after the big man.

"I know that, or I wouldn't be letting her stay here. Anyway, peers to me she may be one of yours soon." The horse groans as the big man mounts. "You never did tell me where you got them panther tracks across your face."

Rowdy walks forward, his shoulders bunched, the dark eyes smoldering. "It'll be the talk of the country, a Flannery, my sister, staying out in the woods alone with strange men. I won't have it."

Only a hard slap is heard, sounding like a limb breaking, before the redhead flies through the air, landing on his back. "I'm still running the Flannerys, boy, now get mounted!"

# CHAPTER 10

For a week, Wes rides the canyons, looking for any sign of the man that back shot Pole, but to no avail. The ground is just too dry and rocky. Whoever did the shooting, apparently has a grudge against the man or against the Sandigras. It has to be the Running H because Rowdy Flannery has an alibi, there is no one else who could possibly have a reason to shoot him. Wes figures it has something to do with the killings of the two Running H riders in Tucson.

Two men were left to guard Pole and the girl while he regains his strength. On several occasions, Wes tries to get her to return to her home. Even though Pole is gaining his color back and eating better, his pleas fall on deaf ears, she won't budge an inch.

Dismounting in front of the tent, Wes clears his throat and ducks under the flap. Rusty has Pole propped up on a pillow, spooning beef stew down him. He has to smile, Pole is weak, but he sure is enjoying the baby-sitting, attention, and tender care he is getting.

"We thought you got lost," Pole speaks weakly as Wes enters the tent, "I ain't seen you in a spell."

"Been riding, how you feeling?" Wes pulls himself up a stool and sits down.

"About as helpless as a newborn calf."

"I'll bet you ain't enjoying yourself at all."

Pole smiles at the girl. "I didn't say that."

"You feel strong enough to move to the ranch?" Wes strikes a match, staring through the smoke as he lights up. "Looks like rain could be moving in and it could turn cold."

"Sounds like I don't have a choice." Pole looks at the cigarette. "Sure could use one of those."

"Nope, doctor's orders, no smoking or drinking," Wes shakes his head. "Don't worry, I had a couple beers just for you and several cigarettes."

Pole cusses, "Shucks, I ain't dead, but if you two keep torturing me this way, I could turn up my toes."

"No, you ain't dead Pole Nichols and you ain't about to get that way." Rusty touches his forehead. "Missing a few smokes and a couple beers won't kill you."

"It could," Pole grumbles under his breath.

"We need to move you to the ranch," Wes insists.

"It won't rain for a couple days yet." Rusty sets down the bowl. "Give him that time to regain a little more strength."

"Alright Rusty, two more days, that's it, then the wagon will be here." Wes takes one look at the two and exits the tent. Charlie Mack and a rider named Nate Newhouse stand waiting beside his horse.

"You boys need anything?"

"Yeah, some work to do." Newhouse looks at the tent. "This ain't the kind of work I hired out for."

Wes studies the men coldly. "What about you Charlie, you bored too?"

The young rider laughs, in a good-natured way. "Watching that tent just tickles me plumb pink, boss."

"Well Newhouse, if you want work, ride to the ranch and draw your pay, then go find you some."

"Shucks Mister Tobin, I didn't say I was quitting."

"Alright then," Wes starts to mount his horse. Changing his mind, he turns and enters the tent again.

"Forget something?" Pole glances up from the cot.

"Tell me Pole, did you see who shot you?"

"I seen him." Pole nods. "He wasn't but about twenty feet right out there."

Wes looks back at the flat ground. "How'd he get behind you, there's nothing to hide him there?"

"I had my attention on something else." Pole smiles up at Rusty. "Just didn't hear him ride up."

"Uh huh, who was it?"

Pole looks up and shakes his head. "Told you already, it's my business."

Wes removes his hat and runs his hand through his dark hair. "Why didn't you tell me, you seen who it was? Sure would have saved me a lot of tracking."

"Ain't none of your business, that's why!" Pole rises slightly from the bed. "None, you leave it alone."

"I happen to run the Sandigras. Everything that happens in these canyons is my business."

"I run it too, and I'm telling you this ain't your affair."

"You know, he's bound to know by now, that you're still alive?" Wes argues. "He could try for you again."

"That's why you've got me guarded day and night for, ain't it?"

"Tell me."

"Nope, I ain't." Pole is hard headed. "I'll take care of this gent myself, when I get out of this bed."

"What about you Miss Flannery, did you see anything?"

"I seen it." She looks over at Pole. "He done told you, it's his business to tend to, not yours."

Wes stalks outside, slapping his hat against his leather chaps. He knows it is useless. Pole is set in his ways. When he said no, he meant it. Well, he can't blame him for wanting to get the man that almost killed him. Who wouldn't?


The morning is still young, not a bird can be heard singing as the clouds begin to bank deep, converging together in a sickly grey to black color. Sam Wade takes a worried look at the dark sky as he pulls the wagon to a stop before the tent, just as the first light rain starts splattering against the canvas. Four Sandigras riders, hurriedly carry the cot, Pole lies on, to the back of the wagon. They lift the cot onto the oak floor, pushing the cot beneath the protection of the heavy canvas tarp that covers the wagon bed.

"Dang it, I can walk." Pole pushes at the hands trying to hold him down on the small cot. "Leave me be."

Rusty gently lays her hand on his shoulder and pushes him back onto the pillow. "Let them carry you."

While Pole is generally a good-natured citizen, there are times though his temper can be like a hair-trigger, touchy. It amazes Wes, the slightest of words, the girl can calm him with her soft, gentle voice and touch. Feeling the healing scratches on his face still, he shakes his head. She sure didn't treat him that way when they were having their tussle back in the canyon.

Only minutes pass before the storm hits with a howling fury, cold blowing rain pelting the riders. Wes cusses his stupidity. Why did he let Pole and the girl persuade him to wait the extra days before sending out the wagon? The four riders with him quickly slip on their rain slickers and pull their hats down as the rain comes down even harder.

The wagon barely travels two miles toward the ranch when the rain starts forming small waterways that they will have to cross. Looking in through the tailgate, Wes can see Pole and the girl are staying snug and dry, despite the deluge of water cascading down, lashing at the canvas.

Already the temperature has dropped considerably. Sleet and hail start mixing in with the rain as it turns colder. Despite his wounded leg, Sam Wade insisted on driving the wagon to bring Pole in. Grinning mischievously, from under his felt hat, as he notices the miserable pinched look on the men's faces as they ride horseback, he can't help himself from making sport of them.

"You boys wet yet?" He laughs, giving them a hard time from his perch beneath the tarp. "Nice and dry up here."

He slipped behind the driver's seat, under the canvas covering, trying to keep the dressing on his wounded leg dry. Watching the storm lash out its fury on the riders and horses, he laughs when the horses lunge forward and kick up, as large pieces of hail lands with a bite against their rump. Bowing their heads against the rain and wind, the horses pick up their pace, knowing they were heading for home.

"Payback is hell, Sam." Newhouse and Charlie yell back at the same time. "When that leg mends, we'll have our turn."

"Yeah, it sure is boys, y'all remember the last time you tied the outhouse door closed with me inside." Wade laughs louder. "Yes siree Bob, payback is hell. Come on rain."

Listening to the men banter with one another, even in this weather, Wes only shakes his head and marvels. Cowboys fight over a bottle or a woman, they argue who has the fastest or meanest horse in the remuda, or who has the ugliest dog. Even in conditions like this, they laugh and joke with one another like the sun was shining.

So far, the heavy slicker that hangs below his stirrups is turning the water, at least for the time being. He is still dry, but he knows, as all horsemen do, the rain will soon find its way under the slicker. Lightning strikes like the crack of a whip, hitting the ground, seemingly close by; close enough to make the hair tingle on a man's arm. Then, comes a heavy roll of thunder, as the heavy rains lash down at them, without letup. Wes looks up as another lightning strike lights up the dark sky. Shaking his head, as he takes in the low ceiling of thick clouds, he knows they are in for a long, dangerous ride to the ranch and the warm safety of its buildings. With lightning striking as it is, riding shod horses with metal bits in their mouths, metal cinch rings, and other metal on their rigging, can be dangerous; it sure isn't smart.

They are still at least five miles from the ranch house, with several small creeks to cross. Normally the creeks are all shallow and easy to cross. However, now with rain coming down in buckets, Wes figures they could get out of banks quick, possibly making it impossible for the wagon to cross. Pole is still in no shape to ride a horse. His wound could tear open, so that's out of the question. If the wagon can't cross, then they will have to wait out the storm where they are.

Pushing ahead of the wagon, he spurs his gelding hard, forcing him into the middle of the next stream he comes to, so he can check it's depth. Splashing through the fast running water, Wes sits the gelding on the other side and watches as the wagon splashes across. Wes is thankful he chose the horse he rides. Despite the banging thunder and lightning, the lashing cold rain, plus hail striking his head and rump, the grulla gelding remains calm, responding to every touch of the reins.

So far, the water has risen only halfway or a little better to the wagon bed, but Wes knows, with the way the rain is coming down, the next crossing could be far worse. Motioning for Wade to pull the team to a stop, Wes quickly dismounts and starts tying down the wagon bed to the frame so it can't float up and off its axles. Despite his leg, Wade bails out and helps with the other side.

"We've only got one real dangerous stream to cross, between here and home, boss." Wade climbs back to the driver's seat. "It could be a booger bear."

"Let's go, when we get to it, I'll cross first. You wait and I'll see how deep it is." Wes remounts and watches as Wade shakes out the lines on the team. "Don't cross until I give you the okay."

"Yes, sir, but you be careful, those small creeks will be hard running and their bottoms slick as a peeled onion.

A mile ahead, and less than that from the ranch buildings, Wes reins in on a small crest, looking down at the surging water. Limbs, brush, and debris of all kinds, floats down the fast surging, muddy stream. The small slough isn't that wide, but the banks leading down into the water, are steep and muddy.

"You boys tie on to the wagon with your ropes and don't let it run over the team." Wes screams above the storm as he takes the lead rope of one of the leaders. "We can't wait to check it; she's rising way too fast. Let's hit it hard."

Wade looks at the muddy water and then turns to look behind him where Rusty is holding Pole. "You two lovebirds take a deep breath and get a good hold onto each other. This could get a little rough."

"Let's go Sam, whip 'em up." Snubbing the lead rope to his saddle horn, Wes takes several wraps then rakes the gelding hard with his spurs, forcing the horse into the fast water before he can balk.

Lightning flashes again and comes with the heavy rolling thunder. Heavy rain lashes their faces, halfway blinding them, as Wade stands in the bed of the wagon cussing and yelling at the frightened team. Slipping and sliding down the steep bank, the horses set back hard against the harness britching, trying to hold back the heavy wagon. Three riders with their horses tied fast to the rear of the wagon, pull back hard on their reins. They force their fractious geldings to help hold back the rain-soaked wagon as it slides down the slick bank. No one can tell whether the horses are holding the wagon or if the wagon is sliding them down the muddy incline.

The churning, muddy water rises quickly above the wagon bed, causing it to lift momentarily from the gravelly bottom of the stream. Standing tall in the bed, Wade whips the horses hard with the wet lines as the leaders pull the wagon into chest deep water.

Again, comes the wild cussing from Wade as the check lines strike out, above the straining and scared horses. Wes is trying his best to hold the leaders straight, as the far bank nears. The rear of the wagon raises up, floating clear, swinging downstream with the surge of the water.

Young Charlie's gelding lunges in fright as the weight of the wagon, plus the pull of the water, pulls him sideways, making the horse lose his footing and roll sideways in the torrent. Wade looks back as the leaders touch bottom and start scrambling from the dangerous creek, pulling the soaked wagon behind them. Hearing a scream, he turns as Charlie's horse rolls in the water, causing the youngster to lose his grip on the wet saddle.

Stripping out of his boots and coat, Wade dives from the wagon as its wheels touch bottom. He only gets a glimpse of the boy one time as the fierce rolling creek pulls him downstream. Charlie is still clad in his rain slicker, chaps and boots. Wade knows he doesn't stand a chance of swimming out of the hard current without help.

Stroking hard, Wade grabs for the youngster as he floats behind the wagon. He feels the weight of the sodden garments and the undertow of the water. Stroking with all his might, Wade knows it is a losing battle. He is pulled under as he hasn't fully regained his strength from his leg wound. Still, with the tenacity of a bulldog, he hangs on; he has to, the youngster's life depends on it.

With his death grip on Charlie's collar, Wade feels himself being pulled under the water, as his back collides roughly against the gravel bottom. With his mouth and throat full of muddy water, he knows he has to turn the boy loose or chance drowning himself. Like a dream, he feels his body getting jerked backward and submerges again, but still he hangs on.

Wes backs the gelding from the water, dragging both men from the surging stream, up onto the muddy banks. He was extremely lucky to catch Wade's upper shoulders in his loop. If he would have missed, he wouldn't have gotten a second chance. It was the rope pulling that Wade was feeling as he was pulled backward.

Wade coughs several times, looking over to where Wes is pounding on young Charlie's back, trying to force water from the blue lips.

"Did he drown or is he alive?" Wade tries to rise but his wounded leg is too weak from the beating it has taken from the gravel bottom.

"Little of both I expect, but thanks to you I think he'll make it." Wes pulls the coughing boy to a sitting position. "I thought you'd strangle him, before we finally got you to turn him loose. You boys help me; let's get him in the wagon."

"Anybody see his horse?" Newhouse tries to spot the gelding.

"Never mind the horse, let's get out of this mess." Wes points the soaked freezing riders toward the corrals. "If he makes it out, he'll come into the corrals on his own."

"He better make it, Charlie's got a brand-new, thirty dollar mail order saddle, cinched to his back."

With the wagon and all hands safely sitting across the raging stream, the storm seems to pass as quickly as it started. Everyone takes one final look at the surging water and follows Wes to the corrals.

"That's my last bath for the year." Charlie speaks weakly from the rear of the wagon. "I'll never get dried out."

Newhouse looks to where he is sitting and grins. "Your brand-new saddle is across that little slip of water. You going after it?"

Only a dark glare comes from the youngster as he leans back in the wagon. "Don't reckon any of you boys has a dry smoke or match on you?"

"If I did, I'd be smoking the blame thing." Nate Newhouse growls.

Ellen has the coffee boiling with steaming hot biscuits and syrup on the table as the wet riders make their way slowly through the door. The cot containing Pole is passed from man to man, until it reaches the stove where everyone wants to shake Pole's hand and pat him on the shoulder. Even Monte pushes forward, insisting on helping Pole into a comfortable position beside the stove.

"Whoee, what a frog floater," Jenks laughs, as he looks around at the near drowned men. "It must have rained a foot before it finally quit."

Charlie walks around the table and extends his hand toward Wade. "I'm forever in your debt, Sam Wade."

"Forget it lad, you'd have done the same for me." Wade takes the outstretched hand as Ellen wraps his leg. "I know you would."

"I dunno Sam, that water sure looked dangerous." Charlie shakes his head. "I dunno."

"You would have." Wade slaps the youngster on his back. "I don't doubt that for a moment."

With the coming morning and the bright new sun, Wes finds the storm did little damage. Only the puddles around the yard and corrals, plus the dripping water from the eaves show any signs there was a storm at all. A few down limbs lay strewn about the yard, but little other damage shows the storm's fury touched the ranch buildings.

Monte holds the men in close, shoeing horses and oiling up the wet harness and saddles from the soaking they received the day before. Charlie's bay gelding found his way to the barn about sun up, no worse for the near drowning and drenching he underwent. Charlie is relieved to see him alive and unharmed, not to mention the thirty dollar, double rigged, Texas saddle that he spent near two months wages on.

"You might ought to teach that nag to swim, Charlie boy," Newhouse laughs.

"I will do that before we try crossing another flood like that one."

"We were lucky last night, boys." Wes walks up and hears the last remarks. "I want to give my thanks to a brave man."

Wade is surprised as he takes the extended hand. "Well, thank you, boss."

"Next time we're in town, I'm gonna stand you to the biggest steak and all the beer you can drink."

Wade grins from ear to ear. He has never seen the softer side of Wes Tobin, only the hard core owner of the Sandigras.

Two weeks later, Pole is up and walking around the ranch yard with Rusty's assistance. Not nearly recovered to his full strength, most of the time he is content to sit in a rocking chair on the front porch, looking off across the flats, puffing on his old corncob pipe. Between helping Ellen with the cooking and washing, Rusty watches after Pole like a mother hen.

The men just sit down to their Sunday dinner when a loud banging breaks the early, afternoon stillness. Newhouse bangs the steel bar against the dinner bell. "We got trouble, everybody get out here!"

Wes races from the kitchen, strapping on his pistol as several wagons and horsemen appear far out on the canyon floor. Monte and Jenks appear at the back door, still chewing on Ellen's fried chicken.

"What is it, a raid?" Monte squints, as he tries to see across the flat grassland.

Jenks swallows hard. "Beats me, there's enough of them to start a war."

"You men, break out the rifles and ammunition." Monte turns, looking for the women. "You two, get behind something solid and stay there."

"Hold up a minute, Cousin." Wes raises his hand. "If I ain't mistaken, that's Boston Flannery with some of his clan coming in."

Jenks swears, "Yeah, but coming in for what?"

As the riders and wagons near, they recognize their occupants and it becomes clear, Wes was right. Several of the wagons and outriders belong to the Flannery Clan, but some were from Tucson as well. He recognizes Doc Harper riding in a spring buggy with another well-dressed older man, while Boston Flannery leads the procession, riding his big buckskin gelding.

Recognizing the man with the doctor, Jenks laughs. "Guess what boys, whatever they're a wanting, it'll be peaceable enough. They've got the preacher man with them."

Monte is still skeptical, curious why so many people are riding into the Sandigras. Wes, on the other hand, has a sneaky suspicion. Jenks announcing the preacher is with them, kinda cinches the idea. Looking around for Pole and Rusty, he sees the worried expression on their faces and figures he is right.

"You better let me handle this Monte, unless you want a full-blown war on your hands." Wes steps from the porch into the wide yard as Boston Flannery rides up.

"Have at it, with my blessings, Cousin." Monte bows and waves his hand at the newcomers.

Wes puts on his best smile as he approaches the big buckskin. "Welcome to the Sandigras, Boston. Get down and meet the family."

Flannery gives a scowl as he looks down at Wes. "You know why we're here, Wes Tobin."

Wes lets his eyes stray to the preacher and drift over the rest of the gathering. Men, women, and children are stacked like cordwood into every wagon and everyone has a mischievous smile on their face.

"Right offhand, I'd have to answer no, but I have my suspicions." Wes smiles. "Light down and give that nag a breather while we have a drink and talk over whatever you got on your mind."

"Well, I'm a telling you plain out." Flannery sticks out his enormous chin, making no move to dismount. "Me and my boys are here for one of two things."

"Which are?"

"My girl Rusty has been living in sin with that arrogant thimble legged hand of yours, the one you call Pole Nichols."

Wes nods, here it comes. "Well, sir, she's been living here, but not in sin."

"You're saying so, don't make it so." Flannery doesn't back up a bit. "What will folks hereabouts think of us Flannerys?"

"I doubt they'll think anything, Boston."

"Me neither!" The chin seems to peek out more. "Cause we're here to have a wedding or a killing. Which will it be?"

"One or the other, huh?" Wes is about to break out into a smile. He knows the big man is bluffing, putting on a show for the spectators.

"Speak up man, which will it be?" Flannery repeats.

"First of all, Pole Nichols is part owner of the Sandigras, not my hired hand." Wes looks around for Pole. "Second, I reckon it's up to him and your daughter, if or when they get married."

"No, it ain't. I've done fetched the preacher and a band all the way out here. Now we're fixing to have ourselves a wedding, then a shindig with all the trimmings." Flannery stops in mid-stride. "Did you say he was part owner of this spread?"

"He is."

"Well, now, then we're for sure enough gonna have us a wedding."

Wes looks around to find Jenks grinning like a treed possum. "Get Pole and Miss Rusty out here."

"Yes, sir boss."

Pole, with Rusty's assistance, slowly hobbles into the yard, stopping face to face with Boston Flannery. The big matriarch of the Flannerys slowly lets his gaze wander up and down the skinny frame of his about to be son-in-law, and then dismounts.

"Well, you seem to be doing a little better since I seen you last, young feller."

Pole looks over at Wes curiously, then nods. "Yes, sir, I understand I've got you to thank for that."

"I'll come straight to the point, little man." Flannery steps closer. "You either make an honest woman of my baby girl or we're fixing to have a burying right here."

"We're aiming on getting married for sure." Pole straightens and pushes Rusty a little to the side. "But, I ain't about to stand here and be threatened into it by you, Flannery."

"I don't threaten, boy." Flannery points behind him. "When you've got your strength back, you'll have every one of her brothers to whoop."

Pole looks contemptuously over at the brothers and smiles. "That don't look like too much of a job from here."

Flannery nods. "That settles it then. Let's have a wedding."

"I ain't even asked her yet, for Pete's sake, Mister Flannery." Pole shakes his head. "I haven't asked you're permission either."

"You've got it my boy."

"Great, but I still haven't asked your daughter."

"Asked her?" Flannery shakes his head. "Ask her what? You think she's gonna tend someone as downright ugly as you, unless she is in love? Dang man, are you daft or something?"

"Mister Flannery, you're soon to be my relations and I sure don't want it, but me and you are fixing to butt heads right here and now."

"Shot up like you are, how are you gonna fight?"

Pole steps forward. "One more word old man, and we're fixing to have at it."

Flannery stands there with a shocked look on his face, and then starts laughing. Stepping forward, he sticks out his huge hand. "You'll do boy, you'll do to marry into our clan."

The wagons empty quickly. Tables are set up, a huge fire pit is dug, and a half beef is put on the spit. Kegs of beer appear miraculously on the back of two wagons, which immediately draws the attention of almost every man present, and the ire of the preacher, who's frowning, shames some of the men away.

Dishes of potatoes, corn, green beans, and squash, line the table. Cakes and pies of every kind sit on a separate table, catching the eyes of every kid present, making their mouth water with expectation. Boston Flannery has planned out a real slam bang of a wedding party for his only daughter, and by the looks of things, he is gonna have it.

The dinner bell summons everyone present to gather in front of the house. Flannery speaks a few words to the preacher and steps back. Smiling, the man removes his hat and asks for quiet as he recites the Lord's Prayer with every head bowed.

As the Reverend finishes, with a loud Amen, all eyes turn as Rusty appears in the doorway, dressed in a snow-white dress and veil. Boston Flannery didn't forget to bring along the wedding dress Rusty's mother wore on her wedding day. Wes looks at Mrs. Flannery, standing next to her daughter, and wonders how she ever fit into the dress. The woman is a perfect match for Boston Flannery, almost as tall and definitely much bigger around.

Pole waits on the porch in a broad cloth suit of black, with his hair slicked back and his boots shined. His blue eyes bug out as Rusty exits the house in the wedding dress, letting him behold her true beauty in a woman's attire for the first time.

Wes watches from the edge of the crowd as his friend and Rusty are formally married then turns toward the barn. Ellen watches him walk away and follows him a few steps. "You're not staying for the dance and festivities?"

"I'll be here. I'm just going to check on my horse." Wes smiles sadly at her, turning and walking away.

Ellen nods. "That's good, it would be poor manners to leave your company, but your horse is probably in need of attention."

Wes stops and draws on his burned down smoke, not turning to face her. "I'll be back."

Nodding, she walks back to where the plates of food are being filled as the hungry people pass the long table, smiling and shaking hands with the newlyweds. Stopping, she looks back, as Wes disappears inside the barn.

"What's eating at him?" Monte steps up beside her.

"I don't know, he seems down." Ellen shrugs. "He looks sad to me."

"Maybe it is the girl."

"Rusty, no I don't believe so."

"No, I didn't mean Rusty." Monte shakes his head. "Someone from a long time ago, bad memories I suspect."

Ellen looks up at Monte in curiosity. "What girl, and how long ago?"

"Back in Texas, down along the Brazos River." Monte stares toward the horse barn where Wes has disappeared. "He had him a girl back there many years ago. He sure thought a lot of her."

"I really can't imagine Wes Tobin in love."

"Before the war Ellen, he was different."

"What happened to her?"

"She promised to wait for him until he came back from the war."

"And?"

"Him and Pole rode off to war. While they were gone, Comanches raided deep into Texas."

"And the girl?"

"She was taken captive."

"Is she dead?" Ellen shudders and looks up at Monte.

"We never found out." Monte shakes his head. "Wes was gone five years. When he returned, me, him, and Pole did a lot of riding and asking at all the forts in Oklahoma and Texas."

"And?"

Monte shakes his head. "We buried a lot of Comanche bucks, looking for that girl; a lot."

"And Wes?"

"I think that's what turned him like he is." Monte wraps his arm around the small woman. "I mean, Wes was always wild, but the war and coming home to find the girl taken captive, seemed to make him cold and hard."

"How sad, I've never heard him speak of her."

"He wouldn't, not Wes. He buried her many years ago." Monte looks down at the little woman and smiles. "Come Misses Belton, we have guests to entertain."

"Yes, Mister Belton."

# CHAPTER 11

Wes drives the team while Jenks rides shotgun beside him. The foreman's sharp blue eyes scan the valleys and canyons they cross, as they leave the Sandigras range. Following the rough wagon road up, over the rim, they intersect the sandy road leading west toward Tucson.

Veering off to the south, loaded with the supplies, as Wes promised Suttero and his people, the wagon makes its way southwest, toward the rough mountain terrain of the Dragoon Mountains. The country they pass across is dotted with saguaro cactus, prickly pear, and runty cedar trees. As the midday sun rises slowly overhead, heating up the dry land, sweat drips from the bellies of the work team.

"Martine said to send up a signal as soon as we pass Rock Springs. Well, there it is." Jenks points a bony finger at a rock outcropping two days later.

Wes pulls up close to a small pool of water and stops the wagon at the base of the rocks. "Scratch a fire together while I water the team."

Stepping down from the wagon, Jenks looks around nervously. "You know when I light this fire, we're gonna be covered up to our eyeballs in Injuns, Apache Injuns."

"Thought you trusted Martine?" Wes unhooks the trace chains from the team. "After all, he is half white."

"I trust him. It's some of the others that gives me the shakes." Jenks starts gathering what pieces of wood he can find. "And we're a long way from help."

Wes laughs. "Light it. I don't know about Martine, but I do trust Suttero."

"An Apache is an Apache boss, they're an unpredictable breed." Jenks strikes a sulphur to his smoke and lights the shavings he placed under the firewood. "What makes Suttero special?"

"I trust him is all," Wes shrugs.

"Wes you sure this is gonna work?" Jenks starts piling more small sticks on the blaze, grumbling all the while. "Suttero is apt to take these supplies, cut our throats, and then start raiding the canyons like he always has."

Wes shakes his head and looks at the far-off mountains. "He may be an Apache and whatever else you say, but I trust the man, red or white."

"Well, hoss it's your hair, and maybe mine, when those bucks get here," Jenks argues. "What does he have to gain making peace with just the Sandigras?"

"Build up the fire Jenks. Where's your sense of adventure?"

"There's a difference between adventure and suicide, if you haven't noticed." Jenks looks around at the mounds of dirt and rock. "A big difference."

"It'll work out," Wes smiles. "Suttero knows, as well as I do, the day of the free roaming and raiding Apache is finished."


The smoke drifts heavily, like a dark cloud across the sky, making it visible for miles in every direction. Sitting alongside the wagon, Wes and Jenks watch the surrounding terrain closely. The day passes slowly as the men alternate between smoking and sipping on their canteens. Not a cloud shows in the clear blue sky as the day wears on. The only noise, besides the blue jay's occasional sharp cry, is the horses' switching tails and stomping feet, as they try to rid themselves of the swarming flies on their backs and legs.

Jenks blinks and sits up, as several warriors seem to rise from the ground like ghosts, as they suddenly surround the wagon and men. Thirty warriors brandishing rifles, some with streaks of war paint across their faces, stand silently facing them.

"You still trust these heathens?" He looks over to where Wes slowly stands up. "These bucks are painted for a fight."

"I 'spect, we're a fixing to find out pretty quick."

With a tall warrior following beside him, Martine walks forward and stops near the wagon where Wes and Jenks wait. "Suttero said you would come, white man, I and this one did not think so."

"I gave him my word." Wes shrugs and studies the other Apache. The straight and proud carriage of the man shows him to be a man of importance. "The same as he gave me his word."

"This one is called Naiche." Martine nods at the warrior. "He is the son of Cochise, of the Chiricahua Apache."

"Cochise!" Jenks looks at the warrior. "Holy cow, if that is Naiche, we're goners for sure."

"Why does the Chiricahua come here?" Wes looks about him calmly. "Why have you brought so many armed warriors to face only two whites?"

"His wife is sister to Suttero's woman." Martine shrugs. "He bring wife to Rancheria to visit. When he found out a white man is brave enough to come to Apache land, he came with us. He wants to see if a white has the nerve to come here alone, and if he would keep his word."

"And the warriors?"

"We have heard this is a wild and terrible land, with whites killing defenseless Indians so we brought protection with us." Martine smirks.

"White's killing defenseless Indians." Jenks sneers at the halfhearted joke.

Wes looks over at the tall warrior. "I am here and I have brought the gifts as I promised. Where is Suttero?"

"He is in another stronghold." Martine motions at Naiche. "He sends this one to speak for him."

Naiche studies Wes for several moments without speaking. No sound is made as he looks calmly into the white man's eyes, trying to read something in them. He was only a child when his father Cochise, went on the warpath after the Bascombe affair. The war with the whites had given him very few chances to speak with a white man or to learn their ways. Neither man blinks as each stare at the other. Finally, Naiche speaks and when he does, it is with a surprisingly soft, guttural voice.

Martine smiles, "He says you are indeed, a brave man."

"I am not so brave, Suttero gave his word. I believe him to be a great chief, who will keep it." Wes shrugs indifferently. "Tell him, I will be friends with all the Apache."

"He wants to know why. The whites take whatever they want from the Indian anyway. Why do you need to be friends with the Apache?"

"To take what is not mine, is not my way. I do not steal what belongs to another."

"Enju." The lone word is all that needs saying.

"I don't believe it, but I think you made a friend in that Apache." Jenks nods at Naiche. "I have heard of him before and he is a white hater."

Wes looks over at Martine and points at the wagon. "Tell Suttero I have kept my word. Now, I expect the same from him."

"He will keep peace with the Sandigras people. Suttero is a man of honor."

"Good, tell him also, if he needs meat for his people, to come to the ranch, and we will cut him out some cattle."

"All this just to keep peace, white man?" Martine looks over at the wagon. "I do not believe it."

"It's cheaper than keeping men ready to fight the year round."

"Some of these warrior's think you are afraid. They think you want to buy your safety."

"What does Martine think?"

"I know why you want peace with the Apache. I have heard words at the Fort." Martine shrugs. "You are a smart man. You divide your enemies so now you have only the whites to fight."

"The Apache were never my enemies, but now we are truly at peace."

"And the white's, are they your enemies?"

"Some, not all."

A powerful warrior, sturdier built than the others, steps in front of Wes and scowls bitterly. Wes slaps the brown hand away as it reaches for his pistol. Glaring, the warrior grabs for the hilt of his knife.

"This white is at peace with Suttero." Martine steps between the two men. "Harm him and you will die."

The words from the warrior are guttural and deep. Wes looks over at Martine and shrugs. "What did he say?"

"It is better, white man that you don't know."

"What?"

"He says you are a woman. You hide behind the Apache like a woman."

Wes nods slowly and unbuckles his gun belt. Pulling his skinning knife, he points it at the warrior. "Tell this warrior I am not a woman. I'm ready when he is."

"He is a great knife fighter, he has killed many." Martine shakes his head and motions at the warrior. "The scars across his body show this."

"Whites are not weak, we will fight."

"If you are killed, Suttero will be mad."

"I don't aim to be killed. It is he who will die." Wes motions for the warrior to fight.

"This is Suttero's nephew, his sister's only son." Martine smiles. "His father was killed in a raid down in Mexico. I think Suttero will be a little upset if he is killed. Perhaps if he dies, you won't have peace with the Apache."

"Great, that's just great." Jenks shakes his head.

Naiche steps forward and places his hand on the warrior's arm, pushing it down. Shaking loose, the coal black eyes of the young warrior glare hard at Wes before he stalks away. The soft words of the chief speak again.

Martine expels a long sigh of relief. "Naiche says he is young and his heart is bad. His blood runs hot toward all whites."

"With that disposition, he may not get a lot older." Wes picks up his gun belt. "Thank Naiche for me."

"It is not over white man." Martine watches the warrior mount his horse. "His name is Torio. Someday, he will try to kill you."

"Why?" Wes can't understand the warrior's hate for him. "This one hates all whites, but he hates you even more." Martine looks at Wes. "He thinks you have made Suttero lose face with the other Apache tribes. If you are dead, Suttero will go back to raiding both sides of the border."

"I am alive and I plan on staying that way."

Martine grins. "For now, you are alive, white man."

"Tell him, if he wishes, we will settle this now as warriors, not sneaking around in the dark later."

"Not now, Wes Tobin."

Wes and Jenks watch as they load the trade goods onto spare horses. They breathe a sigh of relief as the warrior's ride off, yelling and yipping their strange war cry.

Jenks lets out with a low whistle as the last of the Apache disappear. Rolling a smoke with shaking hands, he shakes his head. "That's a lot of goods to give away just for peace."

"No Jenks, you're dead wrong." Wes raises his hand to wave. "I think the Sandigras can now live in peace. A few supplies are a cheap price to pay."

"We'll, I don't mind telling you, boss," he lights the smoke and exhales. "Apaches are enough to make a man give up drinking and that young nephew of Suttero's makes a man think about getting religion."

Wes laughs easily. "They are something at that."

"Did you see the way they came in on us, not a sound, smell, nothing?" Jenks shakes his head. "Nothing, gives a man the shakes like they do."


Two days later, Wes pulls the tired team into the corrals and tosses the lines to Charlie. He is tired, not use to riding on a hard seat, atop a jarring wagon. His back is hurting and sore, from his toes to his ears.

Jenks slowly climbs down from the high seat and stretches his arms. The Sandigras seems almost deserted, no hands in sight, no horses.

"Where is everybody?" Jenks looks over as Charlie unhitches the team.

"South, Monte has every hand we have left, gathering hay and bringing it into the barn for the winter."

"What do you mean, every hand we have left?" Wes turns and looks at the young hand. The way the remark was worded, makes him curious. "What's happened?"

"Just that." Charlie shrugs. "Most of the new hands Monte hired up and quit. They lit out for town two days ago."

"Sam Wade?"

"Gone."

"Wilson and Grant."

"They're gone too. Only Newhouse and the ones of us, you hired on with Jenks are still here."

"Why, what happened?"

"You'll have to ask Monte that, Mister Tobin. I don't rightly think it's my place to say."

"Since when have you taken to calling me, Mister Tobin?"

"Around here anymore, I don't know who to call what."

"Pretty bad was it?"

"Yes sir." Charlie shrugs his shoulder. "Pretty bad."

"Where is he?"

"They were headed for the south canyon this morning when they pulled out." Charlie looks over at Jenks. "Like I told Jenks, they have been hauling hay for two days now. I was left behind to watch over the place and the women."

"Saddle my blaze faced sorrel." Wes turns for the house.

"You want me to ride with you?" Jenks asks.

"No, you rest up." Walking through the back door, Wes almost collides with Rusty, who is carrying a bundle of blankets outside to the clothesline. Apologizing, he holds the screen door and lets her pass.

"Pole is on the front porch."

"Thank you," Wes smiles. She seems to read his mind. She is one of the few people he can't figure out. He never knew what the girl was thinking. Turning his attention back to the house, he finds Ellen studying him.

"Are you hungry, Wes?"

"I am, but I need to see Pole first, before I eat."

"I'll have it ready for you."


Pole sits in the high-backed rocker, looking off toward the far canyons as Wes opens the screen door, leading out on the front porch. He seems even skinnier than ever as he rocks back and forth, engrossed in his thoughts.

"Pole, you asleep?"

"Shucks, no pard, just sitting here thinking is all." The ever-present smile slowly spreads across his face. "This old rocking chair and me have become good friends of late."

"How are you feeling?"

"Weak as a kitten, that's how," Pole cusses. "I just can't regain my strength."

"Well, you sure ain't gonna do it in less than three weeks, that's for sure."

"I see you didn't get scalped." Pole reaches for the makings. "How was your encounter with the noble red man?"

"Long and bumpy, but other than that we had a good trip, going and coming."

"We were worried, Rusty, especially."

Wes looks over at the rocker. "I doubt that, you know the way she feels about me."

"She was for a fact. I reckon, seeing how she was raised out here, she knows how treacherous the Apache can be." Pole puffs away happily. "She sure don't cotton to Apaches, one little bit."

"What happened with the men while I was gone?"

Pole takes the pipe from his mouth and studies it. "Just Monte being Monte is all."

"What happened, Pole?" Wes is in no mood for beating around the bush. "Tell me the strait of it."

"I reckon Monte got out of bed on the wrong side a couple days ago. Anyway, he stomped a mud hole in Jim Cole for no reason, other than being downright ornery." Pole takes a puff on his pipe. "Wade jumped in and Monte decked him, then all hell broke loose. When it was over, they all left out madder than wet hens."

"Monte whip them all?" Wes shakes his head.

"He was trying when Ellen broke it up with a broom." Pole cackles aloud. "It was quite a little set-to for a few minutes, I'm telling you."

Wes shakes his head. "I don't see anything funny in losing half our crew."

"Well, we sure lost half of them, that's a fact," Pole shakes his head, "Actually more than half."

"Why didn't you stop it, for crying out loud, Pole?"

"I'm crippled or have you forgotten." Pole shrugs laughing again. "Sure was a show, though."

"Pole this is me you're talking to," Wes frowns. "Crippled or not, you could have stopped it."

Pole becomes serious. "I could have, but Monte was long overdue for his comeuppance. Trouble is, he was the one who came out on top, mostly anyway."

"By the looks of him a few weeks back, you gave him what for." Wes straddles the front porch rail. "I thought you and him had become friends."

"Ain't got a thing to do with the way he treats me. No, sir, old Monte started in on the boys for no reason at all."

Shaking his head, Wes turns and starts to enter the house. "I hope you enjoyed the show."

"I did, I surely did." Pole grins. "Where you headed?"

"To find Monte, to try and work this mess out."

"Why bother, you rode a long way already today. He'll be along soon enough."

"No, I better go now."

"Well, good luck old pardner, you're gonna need it." Pole nods. "Monte can be downright hardheaded."

Sunday breaks, bright and sunny, not much different from any other fall day in Tucson, except for one thing, the man riding a big black horse straight down the middle of the street. Two low-slung guns, hang from the man's waist. Even the greenest of bystanders would have no difficulty recognizing this one.

Dressed almost completely in black, from his felt hat to his boots, the man puts off an air of arrogance the minute his dark eyes focus on a man. Reining in at the saloon, he dismounts easily, letting his cold eyes survey the street across the swell of the saddle. Turning, he climbs the steps slowly, taking plenty of time to let the town people see him and wonder why he is in their fair city.

Several men standing at the long bar, back out of his way, giving him plenty of room as he enters the saloon and approaches the bar. Focusing a long, mean look on the room, as he props his feet on the foot rail and turns to face the men, he gives them all a case of the chills.

Not a word is spoken by the stranger, none are needed. Here is a gunfighter. They have never seen him in Tucson before today, but they know exactly who he is. The dark clothes, two tied down guns and the arrogant posture, clearly identify the man. Brock Leland stands before them in the flesh, his cold black eyes squinting at them as if he is looking plumb through every man.

"I'm looking for Rowland Halleck." The cold eyes glance around the room. "Anybody know his whereabouts?"

Not a sound comes from the bystanders. Only a large mantel clock's ticking, sitting behind the bar, can be heard in the saloon. The hard face settles on a lone cowboy, standing at the end of the bar. With a sudden swing of his arm, Leland sends a beer glass sliding along the bar, hitting the man's arm.

"What did you do that for, mister?" The cowboy faces Leland.

"I asked you a question."

"I heard what you said." The cowboy glares at Leland. "You sure didn't ask me anything."

"Careful Frank, that's Brock Leland." The barkeep whispers to the cowboy.

Straight white teeth show as Leland draws his lips back in a smile, reminding the men in the saloon more of a lobo wolf than a man. "I won't ask you again, boy."

"He's got a ranch about ten miles southeast." The cowboy turns back to the bar and picks up his beer mug. Slapping his hand against the bar, Leland points at the bartender. Reaching with his left hand, he picks the full mug up as the barman places it before him. Turning his attention back to the room, he sips the beer slowly, letting his eyes pass along the faces, finally settling on Wade. "You there, is that about right, ten miles?"

"Give or take a mile." Wade looks at the man easily.

"Who do you ride for?" Leland takes a sip of his beer, looking over the brim of the mug.

"Myself, if it's any of your business."

"My friend, I make things my business, one way or the other." Leland looks at Wade and smiles. "Now, do any of you brave gentlemen ride for the Sandigras Ranch?"

Not a word comes from the room, as the men present know he is just baiting them. They know he wants one man to say something. Before them, stands a killer and he wants blood. Every man turns his back on the gunfighter. Nodding, Leland walks cockily from the saloon, a swagger in his step. Sighs of relief come from the men, watching as he rides out of town. Not one would admit it, but the gunfighter made every man in the room nervous. Scared is a better description of how they felt.

Wade walks to the swinging doors and stares at the back of the gunfighter. He is ashamed, as this is the first time in his life, he actually tasted fear come up in his throat. He couldn't help it, Leland has the coldest eyes he has ever looked into. Yes, he is ashamed, but he is alive, alive only because he swallowed his pride and kept quiet, not admitting to working for the Sandigras. He has always heard, pride goes before a fall. Well, he lost his pride but he is still alive. Wade isn't stupid. He knows he is no match for Leland in a standup gunfight.

Only one thing brings Brock Leland into a town. He is here either to kill a man or to put the scare in one. Wade is curious since Leland asked for Halleck. Was he here to kill the man, or go to work for him?

"I seen him kill Tom Dollar in Abilene, about a year ago." A short teamster named Knowles picks up his beer. "He's fast, real fast; quicker than a greased pig."

"Yeah and if the stories about him are true, he's meaner than a riled bobcat," another speaks up. "They say he loves to kill and really enjoys it."

"That's a pure fact. Did you see his eyes?" The teamster nods. "After he gunned Dollar, he stood over him and smiled. I'll never forget that look."

Harry the barkeep, looks over where Wade stands. "I'll lay you odds, he's come here after your ex-boss, Wes Tobin."

"You think Halleck sent for him?" Wade walks back to the bar. "He's already got a gun hand, Waco Grange."

"Yeah, he's got Grange. Maybe he wants a little more insurance on his side." The barman picks up Leland's empty mug. "The way Tobin went through Les Bodine, maybe Halleck doesn't have faith in Grange to do any better."

"Maybe," Wade nods, walking out onto the sidewalk as he mumbles, "Well, he's sure got plenty of insurance in that one."


Smoke drifts from the stovepipe as Ellen and Rusty prepare supper. Wes just walked out to the corrals after his sorrel when Monte pulls the wagon into the yard. Newhouse and Harley Raper pile out of the back and start unharnessing.

"Good to see you back, Cousin."

Wes leans on the wagon bed. "Good to be back."

Monte sees the look on Wes' face. "I reckon Charlie told you that Wade and several of the others quit us."

"He did, I was just fixing to ride out and meet you." Wes watches his cousin's face. "Why did they quit the Sandigras?"

Monte shrugs. "We had a little difference of opinion day before yesterday, next thing I knew, they saddled up and rode off."

"Just like that, they just rode out?"

"That's right, just like that."

"I heard y'all had quite a set-to, before they left."

Monte turns on Wes with his feet squared, "I already told you, we had a little problem. You're making a mountain out of a molehill, Wes."

"We needed those men. I told you, we needed them." Wes shakes his head, looking at his cousin. "You've been prodding them hard lately."

Every man present, within earshot, is listening and waiting for one of the cousins to throw the first punch. They all know, in the past, there has been bad blood between the two men. Why, they do not know, but they are aware both men are strong-willed and quick-tempered.

"Rider coming in, Monte." Charlie points toward the canyons, breaking the standoff. "It looks like Sam Wade, too far to make out his face, but by the way he sits his horse, I'd say its old Sam."

The horse comes at a slow lope across the flat valley floor, his rider sitting smooth and relaxed in the saddle. Reining up, yards from the wagon, he walks the horse forward, into the barnyard.

"Howdy, boys."

"Mister Wade." Wes studies the man. "Light down, supper will be ready pretty quick."

"Wasn't sure I'd be welcome." Wade steps down.

Charlie reaches for the reins. "Let me take care of your horse, Sam."

"Thank you, Charlie boy."

Pole hobbles outside, waiting to see the explosion, he figures is coming.

"Why wouldn't you be welcome, Sam?" Wes offers the rider a smoke.

Wade thanks Wes as he takes the offered cigarette. "Quitting you like we did, without warning, I just wasn't sure I would be."

"I've already forgotten our little disagreement, Sam." Monte shrugs. "What brought you back?"

Rubbing his jaw, Wade grins awkwardly. "I ain't forgotten it."

"Me neither, my ribs will be sore for a while to come, I had it coming." Monte laughs and smiles as he shakes hands with Wade.

Wes and Pole almost faint. In their lives, they have never once known Monte to apologize, or even give an offhanded apology like he just did.

"I'm afraid I got bad news, boys. I figured I owed it to y'all to come out here and warn you."

"Spill it, what's happened?" Wes steps closer to the rider.

"Nothing yet, but I'm afraid Halleck hired another gun hand."

"Who?" Wade exhales the smoke. "Brock Leland."

"You sure?" Wes stiffens and looks hard at Wade. "You sure it's Leland?"

Wade looks over toward the barn, "The old mule skinner, Billy Knowles, told us who he is. He seen him gun a man once, some of the others recognized him too."

"Tall man with dark, hard eyes, dressed in black?"

"Down to his toes." Wade flips the burned stub. "Black as the ace of spades with eyes to match."

"Leland!" Monte rubs his chin. "I've heard of him. He's a bad one, for sure."

"You say he asked where Halleck's ranch is located?"

"Yep, that's what he asked, then he tried to push a cowboy into a fight."

"What happened then?"

"Nothing, when the fella wouldn't fight, he just got on his horse and rode out."

Wade looks at the faces surrounding him. "I'm telling you boys, I never thought of myself as a coward, but that man scares the by gollies out of me."

Wes nods. "You ain't alone Sam, any man that ain't afraid of Brock Leland is loco. He's the worst kind of sidewinder. He's a crazed, cold blooded killer."


The dinner bell rings, drawing their attention from the subject of Leland and over to the house. Charlie and Jenks are already long legging it toward the back porch and washbasin.

"You hungry Sam?" Monte starts toward the house.

"Starved." Wade pats his stomach. "You reckon Miss Ellen would feed me after running us off with a broom the way she did?"

"What are we waiting for?" Monte slaps him on the back. "She was hitting me same as you, let's eat."

Wade takes hold of Wes' arm as Monte walks away. "I figure he's been hired by Halleck to kill you."

Wes drops his smoke and looks off toward the canyon. "I reckon we'll find out soon enough."

"Will he come at you straight on or try for your back?" Wade puts out his own smoke.

"Leland's arrogant, full of himself." Wes starts for the porch. "He'll call me out straight on, that's his way. He's got to prove he's the best and he wants everyone to know it."

"What makes a man that mean?"

Wes ignores the question. "Tell me Sam, why did you and the others quit the Sandigras?"

"Monte's a hard man to work for, is all."

"I know he is. Anytime you and the boys want your jobs back, they'll be waiting." Wes starts for the kitchen. "Let's eat."

"I'll tell them," Wade nods. "We'll be back."


The man in black, Brock Leland, rides up to the wide veranda of the Running H and dismounts. The huge silhouette of Rowland Halleck appears in the doorway. Stepping out onto the porch, he studies the man as he ties off his horse.

"I reckon you're Leland?"

"I'm Leland."

Nodding, Halleck motions to the door. "I'm Rowland Halleck, come in out of the sun."

Waco Grange walks through the back door of the ranch house as Halleck is ushering Leland into his sitting room. Grange already heard the gunfighter was coming. He resents that Halleck doesn't believe he is capable of handling the Sandigras problem alone. Seeing the gunman ride in, he has to listen.

He knows the fiasco at Corrales, when Tobin killed the Big W foreman Amos Powell, is what provoked Halleck into sending for the deadly gunfighter from Wichita. Grange is beside himself since he knows the men on the ranch were talking, mostly about his inability to kill or run Tobin from the Sandigras.

The canyon range is vital. Halleck has to have the grass it carries for the two herds of hot cattle he has coming from Mexico. Down in the canyons, the grass is abundant. Up higher on the flats, it has already been grazed down, almost to the ground. Even in a good year, the upper plateau will only graze a few head over several acres.

Fences on the Sandigras have been cut, cattle stolen or run off. Even Pole Nichols, Tobin's friend, was almost killed and still, the Sandigras carries on business as usual. Grange is a hired killer and he isn't afraid to face Tobin, but the opportunity hasn't presented itself. Tobin hasn't taken the bait to come into Tucson with his men for a showdown, and so far, Halleck refuses to let the Running H riders attack the Sandigras. Grange wants to ride against the Sandigras as they outnumber the riders from the canyon, better than three to one. Nevertheless, Halleck wants to kill Tobin off first, then he figures the rest will abandon the canyons without a fight.

Listening to Halleck talking with Leland, through the thin walls, Grange knows he has to act fast. If Leland kills Tobin, he knows Halleck would have no further use for his services. No longer would he be able to earn the extra pay he demanded as a troubleshooter for the Running H. Grange is not getting any younger. The thought of moving on and looking for another job like this one doesn't interest him in the least.

He listens quietly, undiscovered by the private meeting between the gunfighter and the rancher. Watching from the kitchen window, as Leland leaves the ranch in a lope, Grange swears softly. Grange has to admit, the man looks formidable, in both appearance and demeanor. He has never been afraid of any man, but just the looks of Leland, affects him differently. Something about him, his confidence, arrogance, the meanness coming forth from the cruel eyes and lips, something makes him very uncomfortable. Grange wonders, would he be able to walk out into a street and face the man? He is no coward. Many times, he has looked death in the face. In his line of work and with his reputation, he's been called out many times. Never once has he been afraid or doubted himself.

Walking into Halleck's office, he finds the Running H owner watching the disappearing rider from the window. "You trust him, Mister Halleck?"

"Trust him, no, but I need him." Halleck looks over at Grange. "You haven't done me any good."

"Mister Halleck, I can kill Tobin." Grange argues, "You've not let me ride into Tucson and call him out."

"He'll kill you Waco. Is that what you want?"

"I live by my gun; if he kills me, then Leland can try." Grange shrugs. "Word gets round I'm scared of Tobin, I'm as good as dead anyway."

"Let Leland take care of Tobin." Halleck pours them a glass of brandy. "You'll always have a job with the Running H."

"No, sir. I can't do that." Grange takes the glass. "I take your pay, I have to try."

"Don't let your pride get you killed, Waco."

"All a man like me and Tobin has is our pride, Mister Halleck." Grange seems to plead with his eyes. "Let me try."

Halleck turns and takes one last look at the disappearing back of Leland, turning back to where Grange stands. "Alright Waco, I owe you that much. You find Leland. Tell him I said to let you try your luck first."

"Thank you, Mister Halleck." Grange hurriedly turns from the room. "Thank you."

Halleck watches the man exit the room and shakes his head, whispering quietly. "Thanks for what you dang fool, getting you killed?"

Walking out on the ranch porch, as Grange rides off to catch Leland, the Running H owner waves at a ranch hand passing by. "Tell Bacon I want to see him."

"Yes, sir, Mister Halleck."


The old cowhand limps slowly up to the ranch house and climbs the steps. "You wanted to see me, boss?"

"How old are you Bacon?" The rancher takes in the bowlegged stooped man standing before him.

"Shucks Rowland, I ain't rightly sure." Bacon scratches his grey hair. "Maybe a little past sixty."

"You rode for my Pa when I was a lad."

"Yes, sir, I gave you your first horse and your first drink of whiskey," the cowhand smiles. "You're old pappy, bless his soul, picked me up when I was just a lad and gave me a job."

Halleck laughs. "Yeah, the horse bucked me off every day for a solid week, and the whiskey gave me the bellyache."

"Made a man out of you, didn't it?"

"Bacon, I need the Sandigras range." Halleck shoves a chair toward the old-timer. "You know how it is."

"I know, but you should have bid higher than you did."

"Don't tell me what I should have done."

"You're the boss." The old man shrugs. "You figured no one else would dare bid on that grass."

Halleck nods, aggravated with himself. "I figured wrong."

"What can I do, Rowland?"

"Wes Tobin is the only thing holding the Sandigras crew together." Halleck looks out across the range. "I hired Brock Leland to kill him, and I still got Waco."

"You may be wrong there." Bacon shakes his head. "There's still the tall drink of water that sides him."

"You mean, Pole Nichols? Is he that salty?"

"I seen him draw when Tobin killed Les. Yes, sir, he's that fast." Bacon nods, "Now he's married into the Flannery clan."

"He what?" Halleck's jaw drops. "Who did that string bean marry?"

"Rusty Flannery, and from what I've heard, she dotes on him."

"Rusty Flannery?" The name comes out as a question.

"Yep, and you know what old Boston thinks of that daughter of his."

"We can't afford an all-out range war with Boston Flannery." Halleck swears.

"You think it could come to that?"

"Depends, Tobin won't matter much to Flannery." Bacon looks at the big man. "I'd sure leave the skinny one alone."

"I've still got a job for you to do, Bacon."

"Yes, sir."

"I want you to ride into Tucson, hang around and let me know what happens."

"That's it?"

"Keep an eye on Leland and Grange. I need Tobin dead, Bacon. I've got to have those canyons back."

"Rowland, you're a rich man already. Just turn those cattle around that you're bringing in and pull in your horns."

"No!" Halleck's eyes turn red. "This is my land. I'm not letting a Johnny-come-lately, take it away from me."

"It's not your land. Tobin has the deed," Bacon argues. "You're beating a dead horse."

Exasperated, Halleck glares across at the old cowboy. "If you're riding for the Running H, just do as you're told."

"Yes, sir, Mister Halleck, I'm heading for Tucson."


Monte sharpens a match with his knife as he follows Wes and Pole from the breakfast table. Two weeks have passed since the meeting with Suttero and his warriors. In the canyons' isolation, time seems to pass quickly.

Pole's wound is mending and his strength is returning fast. Monte has given him and Rusty a room of their own in the attic. The little redhead is ecstatic as she furnishes the small room with curtains and a large bureau.

"Ellen says we're needing supplies." Monte tosses the handmade toothpick on the ground. "We're almost out of everything."

Wes nods. "Alright, I'll ride in tomorrow."

"Ellen wants to go into town."

"I'm going too." Pole speaks up, turning to walk away.

"You up to it?" Wes calls out to the tall man.

"I'm going." Pole starts forward again. "Quit worrying; I'm fine."

"Rusty going?"

"No!" Pole walks away, making Wes look at him curiously. He doesn't know what, but he knows Pole and something is on his friend's mind.

"You know Monte, if Leland is in town, there's liable to be trouble." Wes turns, heading for the bunkhouse.

"We have to have supplies, Cousin."

"I was thinking of Ellen." Wes nods. "Tomorrow then, we'll leave early."

# CHAPTER 12

Tucson remains the same. Wes notices it hasn't changed at all, as he rides into town ahead of the wagon, while Pole follows. Monte, with Ellen sitting beside him, drives the team slowly down the middle of the street.

Sam Wade stands in the door of the Oxbow Saloon, watching the procession curiously. Looking back over his shoulder, where Waco Grange is playing cards, he steps quickly through the door. Halleck's gun hand has been in town for a whole week, making no secret of the fact he is here waiting on someone from the Sandigras to ride into Tucson.

Now, all three Sandigras owners pull up across the street at the mercantile store. Brock Leland is also in town, staying in the Desert Hotel during the day, then playing cards at the Oxbow every night until midnight.

It's late morning, too early for him to get out of bed and put in an appearance. So far, since returning from the Running H, the gunfighter has kept to himself, except for the card games. Surprisingly, he plays an honest poker game and hasn't caused any trouble. Something is amiss, but Wade can't figure what it is.

Stepping aside, as one of the Running H riders hurries through the swinging doors, Wade watches the cowboy. There isn't much doubt where he is heading. All week, Grange put out the word around town that Tobin or any of the Sandigras riders are dead men, the minute they show up in Tucson. Wade knows Grange; the man isn't bluffing. He would kill the first Sandigras rider he finds in town. He wants Tobin, and killing a Sandigras rider, would surely bring him to Tucson.

Weak and giving out from the long ride to town, Pole takes a seat in front of the mercantile, watching, as Wade hurriedly crosses the street and steps on the porch beside him.

"Pole, how are you?"

Smoke drifts from the tall man's makings, as he studies Wade. "I'm doing good Sam, stronger than I was when I seen you two weeks ago. How are you?"

"I need a job, Pole." The cowman looks shamefaced at the sidewalk. "I know we quit the ranch cold, but there just ain't any work here and it's coming on winter."

"Monte's still running the day-to-day ranch work," Pole looks up at the man. "You heard Wes, he said you could have your jobs back anytime."

"We'll get along with Monte, we have to, if we want to eat."

"You boys are good hands Sam, the best." Pole tosses the burned stub into the street and looks up at Wade. "You've got it; go get your possibles."

"What about Monte?" Wade looks across the street. "He gonna let you hire me back on?"

Pole shakes his head. "Catch up your gear; you'll ride out with us."

"I'm a thanking you." Wade looks shamefaced. "We had it coming, but now I'm dead broke."

"Tell the other boys, same goes for them, providing they can take orders from Monte." Pole looks hard at Wade. "No back sass and no grumbling."

"There's one other thing Pole, Waco Grange is over in the saloon talking tough."

"Talking tough is he?" Pole frowns. "Well, that's fine, they say he's a mighty tough man."

"Yes, sir, anyway, he's talking mighty tough 'bout what he's gonna do to the first Sandigras rider that shows himself in Tucson."

"Why would he do something, just because a man rides for the Sandigras?"

"I'm only guessing, mind you, but I figure he'll do something to pull Wes into Tucson where he can get to him."

"Well, Wes is here, what about Leland?"

"Haven't seen him today," Wade shrugs. "Ain't showed his ugly face all day, but that's normal for him."

"Wilson?"

"He's over there with Grange, drinking and talking tough." Wade nods at the saloon.

"I came into town especially, to see Mister Wilson." Pole pulls his sidearm, rotating the cylinder. "Go over there and tell him I'm waiting out here, would you Sam?"

"Luke Wilson, why Pole?" Wade looks curiously toward the saloon. "He's a mean one, fast with his handgun too."

"Just tell him, you'll find out when he does." Pole slips the pistol back into the well-oiled holster. "Do this for me Sam then get clear."

"I told you, Grange is over there, is Tobin gonna back you?"

"I don't need help, Mister Wade." Pole frowns. "Remember, no back sass."

Shrugging, Wade makes his way slowly across the street, looking back only once, hoping Pole would change his mind and call him back. Pole watches as the man disappears inside the swinging doors of the saloon. Standing stiffly, he positions his pistol, stepping out into the street as Wade reappears and nods, before moving sideways, away from the swinging doors.

Wilson's face appears in the doorway first, looking over the doors, before exiting the saloon. He finds Pole, standing alone in front of the mercantile. His eyes turn, making a complete survey of the dusty street. Smiling nervously, Wilson crosses the sidewalk and steps down into the street waiting, standing spraddle-legged in the dirt. He heard Pole Nichols survived the shooting, but he can't believe the man is standing here in the street, facing him.

"Heard you were looking for me, Pole?" Wilson calls out. "I'm glad to see you pulled through alright."

"I'm not looking for you anymore Wilson, I've found you." Pole pulls the half-smoked stub from his mouth and lets it dangle from his fingers, "You back shooting skunk."

Wilson never saw the hard side of Pole Nichols. He sure never saw the skinny man look as hard as he does now.

"What do you mean by that?"

"In one minute Wilson, I aim to kill you or die trying." Pole flips the smoke. "Make your peace with your maker, then pull your shooter."

"You mind telling me what I've done?"

"Not at all, you're the polecat that shot me in the back." Pole's eyes narrow. "I seen you that day, plain as I'm seeing you now."

"I say you're lying Nichols." Wilson's courage returns. "I never back shot you or anybody else for that matter."

"Make your play, now."

Both pistols roar, as smoke and lead billows from their barrels. A shocked look crosses Wilson's face as he begins to crumble, then Pole fires again. Wes charges through the door of the mercantile, as the second shot sounds off, just in time to see Wilson fall.

"You hit?" Wes is trying to look at Pole and watch the door of the saloon at the same time. "You okay?"

"Nah, he missed me clean." Pole reloads his pistol. "He was a mite faster than I figured though."

Waco Grange steps through the swinging doors and looks down at the body of Wilson. "It took two of you to take him down."

"You're lying Waco and you know it." Wade speaks from where he stands. "You were watching it from the window."

Glancing sideways quickly, to where Wade is standing, Grange spits into the street. "I'll take care of your big mouth later."

Wade laughs, "Mister Grange, you've been bragging about what you're gonna do to the first Sandigras rider you see. Well, there they stand."

"Waco, you can have Mister Wade, but you got to go through me first." Wes steps sideways, away from Pole.

"That'll be my pleasure, Tobin." Grange flips the thong from his pistol.

"No, he's mine." Pole starts forward. "I started this dance, I'll finish it."

"Not this time Pole. Grange came after my scalp, it's my fight." Wes places his hand on the tall man's arm and pushes him back. "You've done what you came here to do."

Shrugging, Pole climbs back onto the mercantile porch, out of the line of fire, as the two men circle each other slowly. Monte pulls Ellen from the doorway, back into the store. Nothing stirs along the street, as many eyes watch the grim dance being played out. The minutes seem to tick by, but it is actually only seconds, before the deadly sound of gunfire erupts once again on the street.

Marshall Linder runs up the street, just in time to see the two men draw. Then came the fatal roar and smoke of gunfire. Grange barely clears his holster when Wes pumps, two shots into him. Staggering forward, he looks into Wes' eyes dumbfounded, and drops slowly to his knees, falling face down into the street.

"I'll have that gun, Tobin." The Marshall's gun barrel points direct at Wes. "I thought I ran you and your Sandigras killers out of Tucson a month ago?"

"You asked us to leave, Marshall." Wes turns on the lawman, a deadly expression on his face. "No one's ever run me outta any place I wanted to be."

"I said I'll have that gun." Linder steps forward, his left hand outstretched, the pistol cocked in his right.

Wes looks down at the butt of his pistol for only a second, then looks into the Marshall's eyes. "If you feel lucky Mister Lawman, take it."

"It was a fair fight Marshall, Grange pulled first."

All eyes turn to where Brock Leland sits calmly in front of the saloon. No one saw him appear on the street or sit down. The lean gunfighter stands slowly, deliberately, stretches and then steps into the street. The man reminds Pole of a stalking cat, walking down his prey, coiled and ready to spring.

"You see it, Mister Leland?" The Marshall seems relieved. He had seen the deadly look in Tobin's face.

"I seen it, along with fifty others standing about here, Marshal." Leland stares hard at Wes.

"Who else seen it?" Linder looks about him. "Who else?"

"We did, Marshal." Monte speaks up as he and Ellen, with the store man, walk from the store.

"What about Wilson lying there, who killed him?"

"I did." Pole steps forward. "I killed Wilson."

"Anybody see it?"

"Again, only about fifty of us," Leland frowns, repeating himself.

Linder looks over at Leland curiously, knowing the gunfighter is a hired hand of Halleck's. Why has he put in with Tobin and saved Tobin from being arrested and hauled to jail? He's helping the man Halleck wants dead.

Holstering his pistol, the marshal looks over to where Wes and Pole stand. "You can thank Leland here for speaking up for you, or I'd run you in right now."

"We'll do that Mister Marshall." Wes nods disgustedly.

"You'll do something else, Tobin." Linder frowns as he looks around the street. "Get your people, and leave town, now."

"Is that an order, or are you just asking?"

"I don't want any more shootings in my town today."

"There won't be." Wes looks across at Leland. "We'll pull out as soon as we load our supplies."

"Not a second longer."

"Seems to me, you're always asking us to leave your fair city, Marshall."

"Your trouble Tobin, you and your whole Sandigras bunch are trouble I don't need." Linder looks over at Monte and Pole.

Wes turns sideways and looks hard at the city Marshal. "I said we're leaving, don't push it."

His jaw biting down hard and bunching up, Linder wants to say something more, but the wild look in Wes' eyes makes him pause and walk away.

Walking to within a few feet of Leland, Wes stops, "Thanks."

Leland smiles crookedly. "Why you're welcome Mister Tobin, but you know I can hardly earn my pay with you sitting in jail, now can I? Besides, it's only professional courtesy for one hired killer to help out another."

"I'm not in jail now."

"You're fast Mister Tobin and so is your friend there." Leland nods at Pole. "The question is, are you fast enough?"

"Like I said gunfighter, now's a good time to find out." Wes feels like Pole now, in a killing mood, his fighting blood aroused.

Leland stands less than ten feet away from him. Wes knows, without him, Halleck would be finished.

"Yes, it is, but it'll have to wait for a spell, Mister Halleck's orders." Leland turns with a laugh and strolls away.

"I'm calling you Leland, right now." Wes waits, his right hand resting over his pistol.

Laughing out loud, Leland saunters away without a backward glance. He knows Wes wouldn't shoot him in the back.


Wade and the rehired Sandigras riders, join the small group as they turn from town and head down the east road. The street crowds with bystanders and gawkers as they pass slowly out of Tucson. Leland nods at Wes as they pass in front of the saloon, then saunters back inside. Pole studies both the gunfighter and the Oxbow Saloon, then wipes his mouth. Seldom has he ever left a town completely dry. One beer would have sure tasted wonderful.

Near the outskirts of town, Monte looks over at Sam Wade and the other riders curiously, but he never questions the men's presence. Pole smiles, as he figures Monte would argue, and is shocked when the big man never utters a word.

Looking across at Wes, he shrugs, rolls a cigarette absently and mutters. "I hired Sam and the boys back on."

"You own a third of the Sandigras, you hire whoever you want."

Striking a sulphur on his saddle, Pole blows smoke, then shakes his head. "Wilson shot me in the back, like a coward, but I'll say this for him, he died game."

"He did for a fact. You know you've got a little blood showing on your shirt." Wes noticed Pole wince when he mounted his horse.

"Yeah, reckon I do at that." Pole looks to where the bullet had torn a hole in his plaid shirt. "He nicked me a mite; reckon I'm leaking a little."

"Why didn't you tell me back in town?"

Shrugging, Pole looks back at Ellen. "Miss Ellen was white as a sheet back there, weren't no reason to worry her none."

"You knew you were going after Wilson, that's why Rusty wasn't allowed to come into town."

"I reckon." Pole nods. "I didn't want her to watch. Anyway it's finished now."

"I hope so, but both of us know it's not over." Wes looks back at the riders following him. "Halleck still has Leland and they'll try something soon."

Marshal Linder watches as the wagon and outriders pass his office, then turns back to his desk. He saw Tobin outdraw Waco Grange. Yesterday he wouldn't have believed it was possible for any man to kill Grange. Linder has been a Marshal for many years. He witnessed many gunfights and knows many bad men. For Grange to go down in front of Tobin's gun, without firing a shot, is hard to believe. He saw Leland back away from a showdown with Tobin. Was it fear? Linder doubts it, as Leland makes his living with a gun. The man is arrogant and his reputation wouldn't let him back down from any man. To do so, would invite every gun hand in hearing distance to come looking for him, looking to earn a reputation. It must be Halleck holding the man back. Linder knows Leland heard him order Tobin, there would be no more gunplay in his town. He also knows Leland paid him no heed. He is in the Marshall's office, only because he was placed there by Halleck. Everyone in Tucson knows he is Halleck's puppet, just as Leland is his hired killer.

Every eye is on the Sandigras riders as they ride slowly out of Tucson. No one pays attention to the hard running horse that Bacon Hollister is leaving town on.

"Wonder why Leland didn't push you into a fight today?" Pole rolls himself a smoke. "I could see it in his eyes, he wanted to alright."

Wes shakes his head and takes the cigarette from Pole. "You heard Marshal Linder tell us no more shooting in the town limits?"

"Yeah, I heard alright," Pole grins. "Leland would have that Marshall for dinner if Halleck said for him to. No, that wasn't the reason."

"What then?"

"That I don't know." Pole squints into the afternoon sun. "There is a reason, I'll guarantee that."

Behind them, on the wagon seat, Ellen shivers uncontrollably despite the stifling heat from the desert floor. Placing his huge arm around her small shoulders, Monte draws her close. "I told you, he is a hard man."

Nodding slowly, she studies Wes' back. "He didn't even flinch when he shot that man."

Wes unharnesses the team, as the other hands help Monte carry the supplies into the house. Rusty helps Pole from his horse and toward the house.

Looking at the blood and his torn shirt, she frowns up at the tall man. "What happened?"

"Just a little difference of opinion is all." Pole winces as he steps onto the porch. "I ain't hurt bad, it's just a scratch."

"A scratch, another inch over and I'd be a widow." She looks over to where Wes stands. "He was the cause of this trouble, wasn't he?"

"No, Rusty, he wasn't." Pole follows her eyes. "He's my friend."

"I'm your wife Pole Nichols, you promised me thirty years." She glares again at Wes. "A fine friend, he is."

"Wilson shot me in the back wife, you know he did." Pole takes her by the arm. "I had to call him out, before he got another chance at me."

"Promise me Pole, you'll stay out of gunfights from now on, please." Rusty touches his pale face. "You're already shot to pieces. You've got more bullet holes in you than Pa's underwear."

Pole looks softly down at the girl. "You're a Flannery woman, Rusty, you know a man has to rear up on his hind legs now and then, if he's a man."

Nodding slowly, she smiles up at him and helps him through the door. "Yes, I'm a Flannery woman, and I'll be beside you always, but I don't have to like it."

"I know you'll be there for me, little lady."

Halleck paces back and forth, across the backroom of the Desert Hotel, glaring occasionally over to where Leland sits smoking a cigar.

Waco Grange, his number one troubleshooter, is dead. He knows by now, the Running H and its owner, are the laughingstock of Tucson. For years, Rowland Halleck and his men have run roughshod over every small rancher and business owner in Tucson. He owns the Marshall's office and the town council, or he once did. Now he is getting paid back in full, and Halleck is furious. Word will quickly get out the Running H has become weak. Men he wronged over the years, men who hated him, will come out of the woodwork, looking to even the score.

"I watched the old man ride out of here like his rear was on fire." Leland laughs cruelly. "Reckon he brought you the word of Waco's failure."

"Why didn't you take Tobin yesterday?" Halleck is furious. "Why, he was right in front of you."

"There were two reasons Mister Halleck." Leland is sarcastic. "One, there were three or four of them against me. The second, before that fool Grange met his demise, he said you wanted me to hold off until you gave the word."

"I need the Sandigras range and I need it now." Halleck stops pacing and looks out the door. "I've got cattle coming in, lots of cattle."

"You'll have it, the next time Tobin crosses paths with me," Leland smiles.

"It better be soon." Halleck downs his whiskey. "You kill Tobin, then we'll ride against the rest of that bunch."

"I'll kill him."

Halleck looks around at Leland. "I don't care how you do it, just get Tobin out of the way, the rest will be easy."

"I don't know so much about that." Leland brushes a piece of lint from his black hat. "I watched that string bean partner of his take out your man Wilson without breaking a sweat."

"I'm giving you three days, Mister Leland." Halleck turns toward the front desk. "You get the job done by then, there will be an extra thousand in it for you."

"Three days?"

"In less than two weeks there will be five hundred head of young stuff arriving here." Halleck looks back. "Three days, Mister Leland."

Halleck looks back at his new hired gunfighter and swears under his breath. Slapping the felt hat against his leg, he leaves the room and slowly climbs the stairs to his room.

Leland smiles slightly, pulling a cheroot from his breast pocket. It was always the same. The man doing the hiring always wants the job done quick, whereas the one doing the killing always wants to take his time. He deliberately delayed his confrontation with Tobin. Now, it has paid off.

With Waco Grange dead, the deadly game completely changed. Now it is only Brock Leland left to face the Sandigras and its owners. Leland smiles cruelly. He now carries the entire load on his shoulders, a fact that is going to cost Mister Halleck considerably more than they had agreed on. He knows Halleck wouldn't like it, but he has no choice, unless he wants to lead his riders personally onto the Sandigras Range, and do his own fighting. A mere extra thousand isn't nearly enough.

Exiting the hotel, Leland heads across the street toward the saloon. He needs information and the local drunks are the best place to obtain it. Stepping through the swinging doors, he takes in the vacant tables, crossing to one, as he pulls out a chair and sits down.

Rowdy Flannery watches the gunfighter curiously as the man's eyes study each man in the room for several minutes. A half-empty bottle of rye sits on the table in front of the redhead. Rowdy knows better than to drink, especially on Boston Flannery's money, but tonight he feels mean and the rotgut whiskey makes him feel even meaner. With the fiery liquor fogging his brain, tonight he isn't afraid of anything, not even Brock Leland.

The older Flannery sent him and two of his brothers into Tucson to pick up salt for the ranch. His two younger siblings, Lee and Billy, are loading the pack mules while Rowdy loads his insides with rotgut whiskey.

Leland's eyes settle on the half-drunk redhead as the youngster's eyes lock on his. Neither man blinks, as each studies the other. Kicking back a chair, Rowdy waves the half empty bottle, motioning for Leland to join him.

"You inviting me cowboy?" Leland motions at the empty chair Rowdy pushed toward him.

"Come on over and sit yourself down, Mister Leland."

"You know me, huh?" The cold eyes lock onto Rowdy's face.

Rowdy nods, lifting the glass to his lips. Sipping the fiery liquid slowly, he studies the hard face of the gunman across the lip of the glass. "Yes, sir, I know you."

"You don't seem too impressed."

"Should I be, Mister Leland?" Rowdy sneers, "You let that Sandigras bunch kill two of your men right outside and you didn't lift a finger."

"Words like that could get you killed, youngster." Leland starts to rise from the chair then relaxes. "But, tonight's your lucky night, boy. I'm in a peaceful mood."

"Maybe they could get me killed, then maybe they could work to my advantage."

"How's that?" The gunfighter settles back into the chair, curious about what's prodding the young Flannery.

Rowdy twirls the glass in his long fingers and smiles. "I figure you and me want the same thing, Mister Leland. Maybe we could work together."

Leland leans forward, closer to the redhead. "I'm listening."

"It's simple, you want Tobin dead. I want that skinny sidekick of his dead."

"Why?"

"He made a fool out of us Flannery's by marrying up with my sister." The whiskey glass slams down hard on the table. "I want her to be a widow and the sooner the better."

"Way I heard it, your own pa approved of the wedding." Leland studies the youngster.

"Pa's an old man, too old to run the Flannery clan anymore." Rowdy looks into the dark liquid, sitting before him. "When a man gets too old and starts to make mistakes, he should get himself a rocking chair and step aside."

"So you're planning on taking over?"

"He's dug his spurs into me one too many times, and for Pole Nichols, my brother-in-law, I want him dead." The whiskey glass flies across the saloon and smashes against the back wall.

"That'll be enough of that Rowdy Flannery." The barkeep walks from behind the bar with a wooden club. "That'll cost you exactly two bits extra."

Pulling some silver from his pocket, the youngster flings it at the bar. "Buy yourself a dozen, Harry."

"You're drunk, boy. Your pa is gonna skin you alive when you get home." The small barman shakes his head.

"How about you, Harry?" The forty five appears from under the table. "Why don't you skin me alive?"

Leland lays his slender hand across the pistol and pushes it down. "Not him Mister Flannery, we've got other fish to fry and things to talk over."

Nodding drunkenly, Rowdy uncocks the pistol and returns it to his lap. "Bring us some more glasses, little man."

Leland smiles crookedly. Here in front of him, sits the answer to his problem, exactly what he had come into the Oxbow looking for. The youngster is loaded with hate, for some reason, enough hate to help him get rid of Wes Tobin. Pole Nichols doesn't matter. When Tobin is dead, they will finish off the rest of the Sandigras outfit.

The two younger Flannerys enter the saloon to find Rowdy and Brock Leland at one of the tables, their heads close together, whispering quietly. Pulling up vacant chairs, they stop short when Rowdy cusses and waves them away. Looking disgustedly at their whiskey sodden older brother, they shakes their heads and move to another table.

"We'll have to sober up Rowdy before Pa gets downwind of him."

"Why?" The smaller of the two shakes his head. "I say let Pa see his oldest son drunk as old Caesar."

"Caesar was an old man, he's earned the right to get drunk."

"Maybe Caesar has, but Rowdy hasn't. All he wants to do is beat on us and make us do all the work."

"He does do that for a fact." Lee frowns, looking over to where Rowdy sits talking.

"I say let's haul his carcass home passed out, slung over his horse, and reeking of whiskey."

"You know what would happen to us when he sobers up, Billy." Lee shakes his head. "No sir, I like living."

"Then let's ride over to the Sandigras and hit our new brother-in-law up for a job."

"And leave Pa?"

"I didn't think of that." The younger one called Billy relaxes back in his chair. "I reckon we can't do that to Pa."

"You know we're gonna do like always, sober Rowdy up and haul his sorry carcass home."

Billy nods sadly. "I reckon you're right."

Rowdy stands up shakily and nods down at Leland. "See you in a couple days."

"I'll be here." Leland nods. "Remember, we only got three days."

"Be here, and don't forget the money."

"I said, I'll be here." Leland doesn't like the redhead, but he needs him. Sometimes a man has to crawl in bed with a rattlesnake to get a job done. He wondered, coming into the saloon, how he was gonna get rid of Tobin quick. Not now, Rowdy Flannery has given him the answer, with Pole Nichols thrown in to boot. Leland smiles, two days from now, the job will be finished and he could head back for Kansas and civilization with Halleck's money. Neither man reckoned on the blinding winter blizzard, fixing to descend on Arizona, temporarily putting their plans on hold.

# CHAPTER 13

A powdering of fresh snow blankets the ranch yard, greeting Wes as he steps from the bunkhouse. Pulling his blanket lined coat, tighter against the sharp wind, he angles toward the house and a hot cup of Ellen's coffee. Looking up at the thickening clouds, he picks up his pace. Before entering the warm kitchen, Wes looks across the flats, surprised at the change in the weather. He heard the weather in this part of the country could change drastically overnight, now he is witnessing the quick change. If he isn't guessing wrong, there will be a foot of snow in the canyons before sundown.

Monte and Pole meet him on the porch. "We're in for an early storm, looks like."

"A blizzard is more like it." Pole put in. "I'd bet my bay horse on it. Those clouds are sure banking up."

Monte pushes his hands deeper into the large pockets and nods. "Let's get the boys fed, then we better start pushing every cow we can find, closer, into the small canyon. We'll put out hay and keep them watered just in case."

"Half our young stuff is fixing to drop their calves," Pole swears. "This cold is gonna bring them calves sooner."

Wes pats the lean belly of Pole and laughs. "Well, my friend, you need something to do. You're getting fat around the middle."

"I am?" Pole looks down at his baggy pants. Shucks, I thought I was just about right."

"Ring the bell, Pole. Let's get the boys out of their warm beds and on their feet." Wes pushes on into the warm kitchen and looks over where Ellen and Rusty are busy cooking breakfast for the men.

"Morning, Wes, sit down," Ellen smiles, as he removes his hat and coat."

"Good morning to you Miss Ellen and Miss Rusty." Wes pulls out a chair as Rusty hands him a steaming cup of coffee. "Thankee kindly, ma'am, whatever you're cooking sure smells good."

"Flapjacks and eggs," Rusty speaks up, looking over at Wes coolly. She hasn't forgiven him for getting Pole shot in Tucson, nor did she intend to.

She knows as long as Pole shadows Wes, he would be in danger, and for that, she despises Wes Tobin. No, despise is the wrong word, she just wants him out of their lives. Maybe it's fear or jealousy of the man. Whatever it is, she wants it to stop. She wants Pole all to herself, safe. Rusty Flannery lived with danger and death, her entire young life. Now, she has Pole. Now, all she wants is peace and quiet.


Grumbling and complaining, as most cowhands usually do early in the morning, they troop into the warm kitchen and find their seats around the long table. Two coal oil lamps dimly light the kitchen as Rusty sets the steaming platters of hot food in front of the men.

"If you want to eat breakfast Nate Newhouse, you get uncovered and be quick about it." Ellen points at the rider and his covered head. "And don't make me tell you again."

"Yes, Miss Ellen, sorry I forgot." Newhouse removes his hat and hangs it on the back of his chair, "Sorry."

Smoke drifts lazily across the room as the men finish their breakfast and light up. Wes swallows a mouthful of coffee, waiting for Monte to issue out the jobs. He can hear the storm outside blowing and howling as the wind pick up.

"We're moving cattle today boys, all of them." Monte looks down the long table. "Push as many as you can find into the main canyon, then we'll meet and herd them this way."

"It's fixing to break loose out there, Monte." Jenks leans over his coffee. "She's gonna blow hard, and that'll sure make the temperature fall fast."

"Then we better get to it." Wes stands up. "You boys split up and work in pairs."

"Dress warm." Pole looks over at the women. "Throw the men together some biscuits and side meat, will you Rusty?"

Jenks worriedly gazes out the window. "Boys, it could get bad; y'all be careful."

"Don't get lost out there." Wes reaches for his coat. "When she starts to snow so hard you can't see, come in. Leave the cattle wherever you manage to get them."

"Pole you stay here and string a tight line from here to the bunkhouse then over to the barn and corrals. When you finish, load the sleds with hay." Wes turns for the door.

"I can ride," Pole protests, "I feel just fine."

"Yes you can, but I want you here." Wes looks over at the women and nods.

Monte stares unbelievingly out the window as snow swirls around the yard. "We'll be needing firewood brought in."

Ellen turns from the stove, shaking a spoon at him. "You worry about your cows, Monte Beldon. Me and Rusty will take care of the kitchen and house."

"Yes, ma'am." Monte smiles.

Wrapping his bony hand around the door latch, Jenks hesitates before opening it. "Some of you boys ain't use to this type of storm. You do like the boss said. When it hits, you better be home, 'cause it don't show mercy to anyone who gets lost out there, whether it be man or beast."

"How long you figure we got, Jenks?" Charlie is tugging at a stocking, pulling it down over his ears.

Shaking his head, Jenks opens the door and looks up at the darkening sky. "Not long, maybe four, five hours before the main storm hits, then the wind will howl as fierce as a Comanche Indian for days, driving the cattle before it. You ride with me, Charlie boy."

Wes nods, as he knows the foreman wants the younger, less experienced rider with him for his safety. Jenks witnessed storms that blew in like this one, on several occasions. He knows the cold can freeze a man to death if he gets turned around or caught in it. Everyone stands about the kitchen, pulling on their heavy coats, dreading the cold winds and freezing rain they are fixing to ride in. They are cowmen and the cattle come first, and their own comforts come last.

The horses are humped up in the corral, their rumps to the north wind as the riders rope out the animal they want. Today is not the day to be astride a broncy or spooky horse. Wes ropes an older, grulla gelding, one he rode through the last storm, one he knows to be steady and foolproof. On a hot still day, a man could ride the buck out of a bad horse, but cold like it is today, that would take some time.

Watching, as Sam Wade swings up, on a sorrel horse, that immediately breaks loose, pitching across the corral through the loose remuda, Wes starts to laugh despite the cold wind and blowing snow.

Loping their horses to the south canyons, Wes already feels the cold biting through his chaps, chilling his legs to the bone. Wade's sorrel is still trying to crow hop as he lopes along. Today is a day that will try the metal of all the riders, separating the men from the boys. The sharp stinging wind causes his eyes to water constantly, in spite of the wool scarf he wrapped several times around his face. Looking over to where Wade lopes along beside him, he shakes his head. This is gonna be one miserable day to get through, especially mounted on a horse like the sorrel, but Sam Wade is a Texas cowboy, he likes the rough ones. Wes heard him remark several times, if a horse doesn't have a little fire and buck in him, he isn't worth his salt.

The cattle will bunch up not wanting to untrack, especially moving due north, straight into the hard blowing wind. Animals, except for buffalo, have a bad habit of turning their tails to the wind and drifting. As Jenks said in the kitchen, he has heard of cattle drifting before a storm clear across miles of open prairie.

Wade yells through his scarf, the words come out muffled. "Boss the wind is getting worse. These cattle are gonna be hard to drive into it."

"All we can do is try." Wes looks down at the dog that followed them. "Maybe he'll help us a little."

"That mangy cur, he don't know come here from sic 'em about cattle." Wade laughs. "Now if they were biscuits, I expect he'd work 'em."

Wes bought the big dog in Tucson, when he bought the hounds. He was hoping the dog would keep near the house and help run the coyotes and varmints out of Ellen's chickens. He always made the dog stay at the ranch when he tried to follow him out on the range. Today, with the howling winds and blowing snow, he didn't notice the dog following them until they were too far out to send him back.

"Now don't go selling him short Sam, he might just surprise you." Wes remembers the man he purchased the dog from saying the reason he was getting rid of him was the big dog chased his neighbor's milk cow.

"I'll bet you my new Stetson he won't untrack when we find them cows."

Wes grins, looking down at the dog. "Against what?"

"If he don't help work them cows, you have to buy me a new rope and horse blanket."

Shaking his head, Wes laughs. He can't believe two grown men are out in the middle of a snowstorm, arguing over whether a cur dog will run cattle. At least the dog has taken their minds off the cold for a short spell. He did see the dog tackle a full-grown wolf, so he knows the animal has grit. The previous owner said the dog caused his neighbor's milk cow to go dry, chasing her.

"It's a bet."

"What size head you got?"

"About two sizes smaller than it was when we left the house."

"Yeah, it's cold enough to shrink rawhide."


An hour later, they split up as the fence comes into sight near the end of the farthest canyon. Both riders start pushing cattle out of the cedar trees, where they found some shelter from the blowing snow and wind. Wes rides the grulla into the first cattle he finds, driving them from the trees, only to have the cows run around the clump of trees and reenter the woods from the far side.

Riding to where Wade is having the same problem, both men run at the cattle, whipping them with their lariats, until they finally start back toward the ranch. Going a short ways, the cattle turn away from the freezing wind, making a break for the end of the canyon and the sheltering cedars.

Wes is about to call Wade back and head for home when the big brown dog lights into the cattle like a cyclone. Baying and snapping at their heels, he has the small herd quickly moving at a trot for the ranch. Spreading out again, the riders push the cattle north, picking up cattle as they ride.

Once he finds out what Wes wants and he isn't gonna get yelled at for chasing the herd, the dog is a natural. Wes grins as the dog nips at a heel or snaps at a tender nose when a cow tries to turn back. The big dog is everywhere, lunging through the snow, driving the stubborn cattle forward, toward the distant ranch.

"What size hat did you say the Stetson was Mister Wade?"

"I didn't, but it's worth losing to get out of this cold." Wade tries to laugh despite the freezing wind. "That no account pot licker sure is worth his weight in gold."

"He is for a fact." Wes only shakes his head as the dog stays after the cattle, pushing them on relentlessly, racing from one side of the herd to the other, never tiring.

The small herd grows, as other cattle, seeing the larger bunch heading north, fall in with them with little urging from the riders. A mile from the ranch house, Wes motions for Wade to turn them into the small side canyon that Monte designated as the holding place for all the cattle they bring in. The wind picks up again with the snow already blanketing the trees and ground.

Ahead, Wes can see the bunched shape of other cows that were already in the canyon. Jenks and Charlie ride up, out of the blowing snow and halt. Both men are covered in snow, but grinning happily.

"We've got most of them." Jenks screams above the wind. "We've been waiting on you two and guarding the gate."

"Has everybody reported in?"

"You boys are the last."

Wes waves his arm. "Head in, we'll close the gate."

"You ain't got to tell us twice." Jenks yells and turns his snow-covered gelding for home. "Let's git, Charlie boy."

Wes and Sam dismount and pull the poles into place, closing off the entrance. Monte has built the gate to hold yearlings for market, now the bottle necked canyon is just the place to feed the mother cows while the storm blows out on the flats. The canyon's steep sides and the trees growing along the small creek will provide some shelter for the cattle.

As Wes dismounts, he looks down at the ground in front of the horse barn. Already the snow covers the ground at least a foot deep and he knows more is coming. The worst of the storm is starting to hit as they unsaddle and put their tired horses inside the warm barn, out of the wind. Petting the big dog, he brags on him as the dog looks up at him.

"I ain't ever seen you pet him before, boss." Wade lights himself a smoke. "Don't reckon he expected it."

"He deserves it Sam. If it weren't for him, we'd never have driven them cattle in. We probably would have lost every one of them."

"Yep, and I wouldn't have lost my hat either."

"You keep your hat; it wouldn't fit me, no how."

"Well, thank you, Wes."

"We'll feed the horses and let them cool out, then we'll turn 'em back out under the lean-to."

Wes slaps the snow from his coat and hat. "They've earned their corn today."

"I can smell Ellen's coffee from here." Wade knocks snow from his saddle. "Leastways I think I can. Man my hands are pert near frozen. Sure hope my nose ain't."

"Warm 'em up a bit, then we'll go get some of that coffee you smell." Wes ties a short rope around Wade's waist then around his. "This is just in case your froze nose don't lead us in the right direction."

"I'm ready." Wade pulls his heavy gloves back on. "We headed for the bunkhouse or main house?"

"Let's go for the coffee." Wes pulls at the heavy barn door, forcing it open enough for them to pass through. The wind is blowing in gales with the snow blowing so hard they cannot see the house or the coal oil lamp placed in the window, beckoning to them, calling them home.

Grabbing the taut rope, Pole had strung, Wes snaps the ropes, he tied around their waists onto the rope. Close together, for support, both men turn from the barn, fighting their way along the rope, hanging on with both hands, warding off the pull of the wind. Only a few feet remain between them and the house before the light becomes visible, then they stumble onto the porch. Hearing their boots stomping against the boards, Monte opens the door and pulls the half frozen, snow covered men, inside.

Helping them off with their heavy overcoats, Monte pushes them up behind the red-hot cookstove. Ellen places steaming hot coffee cups into their shaking hands.

"Man, what a blow." Wade tries to talk through his chattering teeth. "I ain't ever seen anything like it."

"How many you figure we got in?" Monte returns to his seat at the table, looking across at Jenks.

Jenks shakes his head. "Ain't no way of telling. Maybe half our herd, maybe a few more."

"I didn't think it snowed like this in Arizona." Pole shakes his head and looks at Rusty. "The land is supposed to be desert."

Pouring coffee, she winks at him. "I've seen it do this a few times down here, but this is the worst blow I've ever seen."

"How long do these storms last?" Monte makes the rope chair groan as he rocks back in it.

"The worst I ever seen lasted long enough to kill off half our stock and we're better protected back in the breaks than you are here in the canyons." Rusty returns to the stove. "Any of you gentlemen want to go bring in some more water for coffee?"

"I ain't that thirsty Miss Rusty, but I'll go fetch you some water." Charlie laughs.

"You be sure to tie that rope onto your scrawny little self before you head for the well," Jenks laughs. "That north wind will blow you clear to Mexico if you don't."

Pulling on his heavy sheepskin coat, Charlie grins and pulls down his hat. "At least it's warm down there."

"We'll take the sleds in the morning and put out hay." Monte sips on his coffee as Charlie leaves the room. "Maybe we can troll in a few more head."

"You might, but I doubt it." Jenks walks to the window and looks out at the blowing snow where Charlie is pulling on the frozen well rope. "Snow's gonna be awfully deep in drifts all along the valley, if it don't stop blowing."

"I ain't gonna let them cows starve," Monte swears. "Not a one, if I can get hay to them."

"Me either boss, but I sure don't aim on killing myself or any of the boys plunging out into this mess." Jenks returns to his coffee as Charlie reenters the kitchen.

Wes walks from behind the stove and pulls out a chair. "We'll just see what tomorrow brings. Maybe it'll blow over by daylight."

"I seen this kinda storm come up once, up in Montana," Wade speaks up. "The storm lasted a solid week before it quit blowing."

"Where's Newhouse and Harley?" Wade notices they aren't in the room.

"They went to the bunkhouse, said they weren't about to fight this storm both ways," Jenks laughs.

"They gonna miss supper?"

"They'll be along, if I know them." Jenks fumbles with paper and tobacco. "Those two don't miss a meal, unless they're drunk."

"Better get it on the table, Ellen." Monte looks over at her. "Let these boys eat and get some rest."

"I aint in no hurry, Miss Ellen," Jenks looks out the window. "It's a long walk down that rope to the bunkhouse."

"They'll have us a warm fire going over there." Wade walks from behind the stove. "Leastways they better have."

Ellen waves a wooden spoon at the table. "Yes, and you boys are going to take them some supper if they don't show up."

Plates are barely to the table, before the sound of stomping feet and mumbling voices, carry from the porch. Harley Raper and Newhouse push open the door, letting the wind and snow carry into the room.

"I told you boys, those two ain't about to miss a hot meal," Jenks laughs, slapping Newhouse on the back.

"Hope you two got us a hot fire going over there?" Wade looks over at the snow-covered men.

"We do, and a pot full of coffee sitting astride it," Harley smiles.

"How was the walk over here?" Jenks asks.

Newhouse takes the coffee Rusty poured and looks over at the foreman. "Why, like a Sunday stroll in the dark with your favorite girl."

"How's that?" Ellen has to hear this one.

"Stormy and dangerous, ma'am."

Jenks and Rusty were right, come morning, the storm still rages and the blowing drifts are halfway up the north walls of every building on the Sandigras. The wind finally dies down, but the snowflakes still fall hard. The snow is deep, making it difficult for the men to pass between the bunkhouse, corrals, and house.

Monte fashions a pair of rough homemade snowshoes and breaks trails between the buildings, stomping down the snow so the men can walk back and forth with the help of the ropes. At least in the daylight, when the wind stops, they can see the ranch house across the yard.

Despite Jenk's warning about the danger of the storm blowing in again, Monte is dead set on taking out the loaded sleds. He listened to the foreman about the danger, but Monte is bound and determined to haul hay to the hungry cattle.

After breakfast, Monte pulls Wes aside and looks out across the valley. "We've got to get the cattle some feed. If we don't, we're liable to lose them all."

"The sleds are already loaded; let's give it a try." Wes nods. "The sleds aren't that heavy. The deep drifts and creek crossings will give us the most trouble."

"It's only a little over a mile to the canyon." Monte nods. "We'll make it."

"Let's harness up the teams."

"We'll hitch up four horses to the lead sled," Monte starts for the barn, "Just a single team to the second.

"That ought to work. It'll just take the two of us," Monte hesitates. "Ain't no need for the others to get out in this mess."

"It's always been the two of us and Pole, Cousin."

"You worry more about him than you do me," Monte laughs.

"You ain't just been shot." Wes adds, "Twice."


The snow varies. In places, the drifts are deep, and in others, the wind has blown the ground almost bare. Monte drives the lead sled and angles around the deeper snow when possible. Wes follows and stays in the broken trail. Snowflakes still fall heavily across the valley, but for the moment, the stinging ice and wind cease.

The cattle smell the hay and come floundering through the deep snow as soon as the big sleds pull through the gate, pushing greedily against the sleds. Despite the freezing air, Wes manages to work up a sweat in his heavy sheepskin lined coat, while forking hay from the sled to the hungry cattle. Monte drives the sled in a small circle while Wes feeds the herd. Frozen steam comes from his mouth as ice forms on the wool scarf he wears.

"These cows are already drawn badly, Monte." Wes leans on his pitchfork, catching his breath. "The ones we didn't pick up will soon be in real trouble."

"You're right, it's over seven miles from here to the back fence and I figure, if they drifted before the storm, some will be bunched up against it." Monte shakes the lines. "There's nothing we can do for them. It's just too far in this weather."

"Seven miles of deep snow and drifts," Wes corrects Monte, lighting a smoke and looking down at the hungry cattle. "How many you figure are in this bunch?"

Monte peers out, over the feeding cows and starts counting. "Maybe a hundred and fifty, give or take a few."

"That means we could have another fifty to seventy five still out there, and some of them might drop calves in this mess."

"Storms do that alright. Seems as if the bad weather causes them to calve right in the middle of it." Monte declines the smoke Wes offers.

"What are you thinking?"

"I say we unload the other sled, go back and have the boys get them reloaded and ready for an early start tomorrow morning."

"Just me and you?"

"Like the good old days, Cousin. Just me and you against the world." Wes smiles. "You remember the Duncan boys and that little set-to down on Wolf Creek?"

"Remember?" Monte shakes his head, "It took us two weeks to get over that little disagreement."

"Yep, those were the good old days alright."

"You know Cousin, I never have figured out what was good about getting your head kicked in."

"Considering the odds, we didn't do so bad."

"Those Duncan boys were a tough lot."

"They did have us outnumbered a little." Monte shakes his head again. "I swear Wes, tell the truth. We got the crap kicked out of us."

"Yeah, reckon we did at that, but it sure was a good fight, while it lasted."

"Which wasn't long."

Wes looks up, as the wind picks up again and nods. "We get caught seven miles from home, things could get just as rough as that fight."

"They're our cows, let's go get them come morning." Wes tosses another fork full of hay. "They won't last out this cold."

Monte nods, "You're thinking they'll follow the sled back here, once they smell the hay."

"This bunch came right to it; they're hungry. If we can manage to drag a sled that far back, they'll follow it out."

"Let's get to her." Monte reaches for the fork. "Better let me do that Cousin, you look a little peaked."

"You're welcome to it." Wes hands over the fork. "We'll have the boys come up and bust holes in the ice so they can get water."


Except for the noise of silverware, not a sound emits from the hands as they eat their supper. Occasionally, someone would look over at Monte and Wes and shake their heads.

Pole looks down the table and points his fork at Wes. "If you're crazy enough to try pulling them sleds all the way across this range, I'll be going with you."

Rusty pivots on the bench and looks at him. "Pole you're in no shape."

"I'll be going." A glare from Pole stops her, and he looks across at Wes. "Am I part owner of this spread or ain't I?"

"This is gonna be a cold trip pard, but you are a part owner." Wes nods.

"Then I'll be going with you come daylight."

"It'll be earlier than that old buddy." Wes looks across the table. "We'll need a couple lanterns to light the way until daybreak."

"I'll get 'em ready for you, Wes."

"Thank you, Charlie." Monte sips on his coffee. "We're just hauling one sled all the way. We'll drop the other one off at the holding canyon."

"I'd like to come with you." Wade looks down the table.

"It's only a two-man job Sam, now we have three, that'll be plenty." Wes returns to eating. "Thanks for offering."

"You boys take shifts at keeping holes open in the creek." Monte looks around the table. "Any questions?"

"It just don't seem right." Jenks looks across the table at Wes.

"What's that?"

"You three are the bosses of this spread, we're the working end." Jenks picks up his cup. "We, hired hands, should be going out after them cattle."

"Normally you would be, but I ain't about to send you out in this weather, no sir." Monte looks around the room. "I ain't about to have you men go out there while I sit here warm and comfortable."

Jenks looks across the table at Monte, as if he has never seen the man before. "Yes, sir."

"You boys take care of things around here and break ice for the herd."

# CHAPTER 14

The horse teams are hitched and ready, as hot breath blows from their nostrils. They stand outside the barn waiting, where snow falls steadily across the barnyard and corrals. The hands hastily nail side rails to the sleds, to permit higher piles of hay.

Rusty places a basket, plumb full of biscuits and side meat, in the front of the sled. Looking to where Pole is lighting the lanterns, she shakes her head. "He has no business going. He's still too weak," she whispers to Wes.

Wes pulls on his gloves and nods. "No, he doesn't Rusty, but he's a proud man, doing what he thinks he should. I ain't about to tell him not to go."

"I know."

"Then smile, wish him well, and don't let him see you worrying."

"That would be a lie, Wes." Rusty looks over at Pole. "I can't lie to him."

"Yes, it would, but right now he needs to know you believe in him."

"You know I do and so does he." Rusty touches Wes arm. "You bring him back to me, please."

"I'll bring him back, Miss Nichols." Wes climbs aboard the sled. "Let's go, gentlemen."

"We're crazy men, you know that Cousin?" Monte's breath floats on the cold air. "Crazy."

"What would we do today if we stayed here?"

"Nothing much; stay warm, eat good, and play some cards, I reckon." Pole grins. "Shucks, that ain't no fun. Let's go."

Whistling at the brown dog, Wes jumps him up on the sled beside Monte.

"You think a lot of that hound don't you, Cousin."

"You'll see if we need him." Wes pats the dog. "He's worth several riders in this weather."


Monte holds the sled in the same tracks they made on their run yesterday. The horses don't have to pull hard now, but they will, once they run out of trail and need to break new track. Normally, the sled isn't heavy for four horses, but dragging it across deep snow makes the sled harder to pull. Pole takes charge of the lines on the second team and will not relinquish them to Wes.

The lanterns put out an eerie light, reflecting across the snow covered land. Flakes hiss as they settle on the hot globe. In the front sled, Wes settles back snugly in the hay, wrapped in wool blankets, while Monte drives the team. Passing the cattle pen in the canyon, Monte draws in the horses and looks toward the pole gate. Not a single cow is in sight.

Wading through the deep snow, Monte stops beside the sled Pole drives. "How you doing, Pole?"

"Well, to tell the truth Monte, I'm tired, cold, and sore." Pole leans back against the hay.

"We'll leave this sled here." Monte starts unhitching the team as Wes transfers blankets and food to the front sled. "Make yourself a snug place and bundle up, me and Wes will do the driving."

"Sounds good to me, I may have bit off more than I can chew." Pole wades weakly up to the front sled.


Wes rides the extra team and breaks trail as Monte follows with the sled. The small creeks cause most of the problems. The wind filled the washes full of heavy snow. Wes' horses lunge through the first deep wash, packing down the soft snow. Turning the team, he recrosses the stream several times before Monte clucks to his four horse hitch and starts across.

Pole wraps two heavy wool blankets around him as he burrows down in the hay. With the big dog lying across his feet, he's as snug as ten toes in a sock. The snow continues to fall as daylight breaks as they cross the canyon.

Wes stops the team he is riding and slides stiffly to the ground, holding onto the hames until his legs can hold his weight. Looking back, where Monte is stepping from the sled, he shakes his head and laughs. "Well, Cousin, we're halfway, it's all or nothing now."

Monte grins stiffly. "That's a fact. The fats in the fire for sure if that storm hits us again."

"We'll make it. How's Pole?"

"Why don't you ask me, I'm right here?" Pole laughs, as Wes looks to where the tall man stands with the dog.

"Shucks, I thought you and that hound were still hibernating in your soft bed."

"I'm feeling better." Pole rolls himself and Wes a smoke. "I'll ride for a spell and let one of you warm up a bit."

"You got another one of those?" Monte points at Pole's smoke.

Pole quickly rolls another cigarette. "Wish I had a cup of coffee to go with it."

"We've got the girl's food." Wes looks at the rolled up food. "You boys hungry?"

Monte looks east as the sun appears and shakes his head. "It'll wait; blow out the lanterns and let's get moving."

Not a track or a creature show anywhere in the snow blanketed valley floor as the sled runners slide smoothly along the hard crusted ice. Large flakes fall quietly to earth as the trace chains jingle like they are keeping time with the snow.

Pole is astride the lead horses, while Wes drives the sled team and Monte snuggles in the hay. The miles roll by under the sled, as the horses trot to the south. The look of the landscape has changed completely, now covered under the heavy blanket of snow. Only an occasional stand of cedar or a lone tree, steer Pole toward the end of the canyon.

Monte rises from his blankets and looks around the canyon. "I'll tell you, Cousin, if it snows like this more than once a year, I'd look for greener pastures, but it sure is a beautiful sight."

"Ain't that the truth?" Wes blows into his gloves, trying to warm his cold hands. "Rusty and Jenks said they haven't seen anything like this storm, only once or twice in their lives."

"How much farther to the back fence?"

"Can't say for sure, maybe an hour or so."

"We're making good time, but the horses are tired." Monte reaches for the lines. "Crawl in there and warm up a bit."

"The return trip will be easier on them." Wes wraps himself in the blankets and settles in the hay, with the dog for company.

"Pole, you okay up there?" Monte can see the snowflakes falling on the tall man's slumped shoulders.

"I'm okay. One thing's certain, though."

"What's that?"

"I know what a polar bear feels like now."

Wes laughs. "It's all in the mind. If you don't mind, it don't matter."

"Uh huh, well, whoever said that wasn't sitting astride a bareback horse in the middle of nowhere, and in the midst of a blizzard."

"A cup of Ellen's hot cocoa would sure taste good right about now." Seeing Pole look back at him in disgust, Monte grins.

"Talking about anything hot ain't helping matters."

They guessed right, cattle stand humped up against the fence and gate that shut off the Sandigras from the Flannery passes. Looking up from their ice covered faces, the hungry cattle bawl as they watch the sled approach and get themselves a smell of the hay. Struggling to walk, with their half frozen legs, the cows start clumsily toward the loaded sled.

Wes tosses off his blankets and forks a few handfuls of hay down to them. "We'll give them just enough to get them to follow the sled, then we'll head back."

"Let's eat, give the horses a little hay, and let them rest for a spell." Monte swings the team in a circle, facing north, and pulls them up.

"How you doing, Pole?"

"I'm still alive Monte, ain't froze solid yet."

"That's a relief. We'll switch out the lead team with yours. They'll be fresher."

"Boys, y'all better look off to the north." Wes and Monte both turn their attention back, toward the ranch and look up at the ever-darkening sky. "We're here and I ain't leaving without these cows." Wes quickly helps Pole switch out the teams.

"Man, I thought it was over with." Monte shakes his head. "We better hurry."

Pole takes a biscuit and meat from Monte and studies the clouds. "If I don't miss my guess, we're fixing to grab the elephant by the tail."

"Let's go." Wes mounts one of the geldings and hands Monte the halter rope of the other one. "Let Pole drive the sled and kick out enough hay to keep them coming. We've got to make time."

"If they'll follow." Pole clucks to the team then sprinkles a little hay out to the side of the sled.

Wes and Monte, with the brown dog, push the hungry cattle from behind. They smile at each other as the cows fall in beside the sled, fighting and pushing at the small amount of hay Pole forks to them.

Monte quickly counts the herd and shakes his head. "We're still short a few, but we ain't got time to look for them." Monte pushes the workhorse into the rear of the cattle.

"Here come a few more." Wes nods off to the west as five cows and a newborn calf trot toward the sled.

"We better catch that calf and put him on the sled if we want to save him." Monte uncoils his lariat and tosses it on the small calf.

"Stay put, I'll load him." Wes slips from his horse and catches the baby. "Here's you some company Mister Nichols, almost as pretty as Rusty."

"Almost." Pole takes the calf and deposits it beside him on the running board.

The north wind starts picking up again as they follow the well-broke trail, back toward the Sandigras. Wes feels the temperature dropping and the stinging particles of ice as the snow once again starts to turn into heavy sleet.

With their wide brim hats pulled down low and the wool scarves hiding the men's faces, only their eyes show as they push into the cattle hard, making them stay close to the sled. The cattle plod on, to the north, even though their natural instinct is to turn their faces from the wind and ice. Their hunger, plus the nipping dog, forces them to follow the sled.

"This storm picks up anymore, they're gonna be hard to drive, even with the hay." Monte hollers over the moaning wind.

"We've only got another three or four miles to the canyon." Wes wipes at the ice on his scarf. "Whip 'em hard, use that rope."

One by one, the cattle start to turn out of the storm, away from the icy blast. Pole pushes more hay from the sled, but even that doesn't pull the hungry cattle as it first did. Wes yells above the roar of the wind, urging the big dog after the stragglers.

"We're gonna lose them," Monte swears, as he swings the heavy lariat.

"If they break, they're goners for sure. There won't be no turning them back," Wes cusses at the stragglers.

The wind blasts everything in its path, as the cold penetrates through the heavy coats and leather chaps. As Pole stops momentarily, to light the lanterns, the cattle bunch up around the sled, as they try to get more hay.

Monte rides up close to Wes and leans over his horse. "We better let 'em go and try to make it to the ranch before we freeze."

"It's not far now, let's push them hard."

"It's a gamble, our lives against theirs."

"I'm taking them in, if I can." Wes pulls his hat down and ties it tighter with the stampede string. "The dog will bring 'em in."

"Lead on Cousin, I'm behind you."

Wes can't believe it. Never has he seen anything like the wind and ice that beats at him unmercifully. For some reason, the cattle sense the danger of leaving the sled or they are just hungry. Either way, they stop trying to turn back to the south and stay bunched up near the sled, grabbing hungrily at the hay Pole forks down.

It's an ongoing battle as Wes hits a cow, breaking her into a trot. She goes a few feet and the dog nips at her heels, forcing her on, into the eye of the storm. He is thankful, at least they haven't sulled up on them or tried to turn as a group, if that happens, he knows they will lose control of the herd.

Suddenly, the sled stops moving ahead of them. Wes and Monte think they hear Pole yelling. Wes looks over at Monte. "Ride up and see what the problem is."

Monte starts to turn his workhorse around the cattle, when four riders come into view, appearing like ghosts out of the storm. Both men let out raspy cheers as Rusty, Wade, Jenks, and Charlie ride up to them. Wasting no time greeting one another, the men push the cattle toward the canyon and home.

Staring across the brim of a hot cup of coffee, Wes looks around the kitchen at the gathered riders. "Y'all sure were a welcome sight, I'll say that."

Wade smiles sheepishly. "We were out chopping ice for the cows when Rusty rode up."

"Yeah, she said another storm is coming and wouldn't stop fussing until we agreed to go bring y'all in."

"Well boys, we're thankful you did." Monte walks away from the warm stove. "We saved most of our cattle and there will be a bonus in it for you."

Jenks clears his throat. "We were just doing what we get paid for. You don't owe us nothing extra."

"Monte is right, if you hadn't come, we'd of lost the cows and maybe our own necks too." Wes nods his thanks to Ellen as she pours him another cup of coffee. "You've all earned a bonus."

Rusty wraps a wool blanket around Pole's thin shoulders, sitting down close to him. Smiling, she pats his hand, leaning her redhead against his shoulder.

"You give Rusty the bonus Monte. She fussed and fumed like a sitting hen until we agreed to go. Then she led us straight to you and those cows," Wade laughs. "She's quite a woman."

"I've got my bonus, Sam Wade." She hugs Pole and scoots closer to him. "I don't need anything else. Besides, all I did was follow the sled tracks, straight to you."

Pole slaps his hand on the table. "It's done; we're here, safe now, and the cattle are in the canyon, a little cold, but they're alive."

For a solid week, the men break ice, shovel snow, and haul hay out to the canyon. Finally, the sun peeks through the clouds and the snow starts to melt away, letting the cattle get to the short grass underneath.

"I'm sending Wade and Newhouse into Tucson tomorrow for supplies." Monte walks to where Wes is shoeing his horse. "You need anything?"

"Tobacco will do."

"Our cattle will start drifting back across the canyons. I hope this will be the last storm we see like this for a while." Monte stares out across the flats. "We can't hold them in the canyon. We don't have the hay to keep them fed."

"No guarantees about the weather, Cousin." Wes rasps a foot flat and picks up a shoe. "You're right, we don't have near enough hay put up to feed them another two weeks, so we'll just have to let them drift."

"Next year, I intend to build another barn just for hay and fill it plumb full."

"With hay?"

"Yes, sir. We won't get caught with our britches down again." Monte looks about the yard. "If another storm hits us this year, we'll lose some cattle."

"We were lucky alright," Wes agrees. "Where are you gonna get enough grass to fill a barn that big?"

"We'll close off the sandstone canyon and save the grass for the barn." Monte points across from the corral. "We'll put it right there."

"You gonna haul sawed lumber in, same as the house and barn?"

"I am, soon as we get time. I'll get a sawmill so we can start sawing." Monte nods.

# CHAPTER 15

Wade pulls the team alongside the mercantile and steps down from the wagon. Tying the horses off, he follows Newhouse into the store. Grabbing a handful of crackers and a slab of cheese, both men back up to the potbelly stove to warm their backsides. It's still early morning, but with the storm and cold winds, the store has very few customers.

"Sam Wade, Nate Newhouse, what are you boys doing so far from home in weather like this?" Joe Donner, the store man, greets them.

"Mister Belton sent us in for supplies." Wade munches on his dinner. "Here's Misses Belton's list."

"Was the Sandigras hit hard?"

"It snowed and blew us dang near bald headed. Then it tried to freeze us, but we came out alright." Wade laughs. "This is sure enough good cheese."

Donner nods. "Y'all were protected some down in them canyons, but the Running H and many others didn't fare so well."

"Lose cattle did they?" Newhouse asks as he munches contentedly on his cheese. "How many?"

"From what I heard, quite a few."

"That's too bad, it couldn't have happened to a better man," Newhouse smiles.

"Yeah," Donner looks down the list, "Mister Halleck ain't too happy. He's fit to be tied."

"I figure he is, any cowman losing cattle would be." Wade lights a smoke.

"He's blaming Wes Tobin and the Sandigras for his losses."

"For a fact?" Wade walks to the front window and looks out. "Now, why would he do that?"

"Just tell Tobin, he's on the prod, and that hired killer of his, Leland, has been making threats."

"What kind of threats, Mister Donner?"

"Now boys, don't get riled at me." Donner steps back behind the counter as he takes supplies, Ellen ordered, from the shelves. "It's Brock Leland making all the threats."

"What's he saying?"

"Nothing much, 'cept any Sandigras punchers riding into Tucson are dead the minute he sees them."

"Talk's cheap." Newhouse finishes his crackers.

"Don't sell Brock Leland short, boys. He's a cold-blooded killer; you tell Tobin that." Donner looks across the counter. "You boys take my advice and ride out of Tucson soon as you're loaded."

"We'll tell Mister Tobin." Wade nods, ignoring the man's warning. "Fill that order and we'll be back to load her."


The saloon is crowded, as Wade and Newhouse belly up to the bar. Ordering beer, they are greeted by some of their friends as they stand enjoying the warmth of the saloon. The cool beer really hits the spot, even with the cold temperatures.

"Sandigras scum!" The words come harsh and cold as the weather outside.

Turning, Wade watches the path between him and the voice, clear, as the bystanders step back quickly. Leland stands spraddle legged in the middle of the room, his coat pulled back to reveal the two guns he wears.

"We're Sandigras riders, but we're not scum, Leland." Wade speaks softly, turning back to the bar. The sound of two shots, reverberate across the room, as Leland draws and fires without warning. Wade and Newhouse are flung backward as the heavy slugs rip into them. Walking forward, Leland fires two more shots into the prone men.

Turning, Leland looks coldly around the room. "Self-defense is the way I saw it. What about you boys?"

Many eyes look to the undrawn pistols on the dead men, but none dare speak against the crazed hired gun of Halleck. Grinning wickedly, Leland glares one more time at the watching men, retreating out the double doors.

"Cold-blooded murder is what it was." The barkeep looks down at the two dead men. "Cold-blooded murder."

"Wade and Newhouse were good men, not gunfighters," another speaks up. "He killed them boys in cold-blood."

"Somebody better get the Marshall."

"He's gone over to Bisbee to pick up a prisoner." The barkeep looks up as Donner, the store man, enters. "He's Halleck's man. He wouldn't do anything if he were here."

"I was just coming to tell them their order is ready." The store man runs his hand across his face. "I warned them to leave town. What happened?"

"It was Leland. He shot them boys down, without warning. Sam Wade got it in the back."

"Let's wrap them in some blankets and put them in the wagon. I'll need someone to take them out to the Sandigras."

"Leland would probably kill anybody that tries that."

Donner pulls a double eagle from his pocket and holds it up. "No, that's what he wants. This is for any man that'll step up and take them home."

Not a man moves in the room. Their eyes lock on to the money, but not one offer comes to take the job. Finally, the money returns to Donner's pocket as he turns to leave.

"I'll do it. I'll drive the wagon."

All eyes focus on the old cowboy they all know rides for the Running H. The man's eyes look down at the dead men as he rises from the table and walks toward the bar.

"You, Bacon?" The barkeep shakes his head. "But you ride for Halleck."

"I'll do it, said I would, didn't I?"

Donner looks doubtfully at the old man. "You sure you'll be welcome on Sandigras range?"

Looking around the bar at the gathered men, the old man shakes his grey head. "It don't matter much, one way or the other. Those were good men. They didn't deserve to die like that."

"But, you always rode for the Running H."

"Not anymore I don't."

"Here's your money Bacon, let's get them loaded." Tossing the twenty on the bar, the old cowman looks at the gathered faces. "You boys have a drink on Sam and Nate."

Pole and Rusty, sitting wrapped in blankets on the front porch, spot the wagon first as it crosses the flat canyon floor. The tall man squints into the western sun, trying to make out the man driving the team. He knows it's not Wade or Newhouse.

"I better go fetch Wes. That's our team and wagon, but if I ain't mistaken, there's something wrong. Pole looks again at the nearing wagon. "That's Bacon Hollister driving. He's a Running H hand."

"I've known Bacon all my life," Rusty smiles. "He's always been a friend to me."

"He's still a Halleck man."

"What happened to Wade and Nate?" Rusty stares at the wagon as it nears.

"Don't know," Pole walks to the rear of the house and hollers for Wes. "Something's wrong, for sure."

The whole crew stares unbelieving into the wagon, as Wes pulls back the blankets, revealing the dead men's faces. "What happened, Bacon? Who killed Nate and Sam?"

Jenks sharp eyes center on the old man.

"Leland's what happened." Bacon swallows hard as Jenks turns on him. "Shot 'em both down, in cold blood."

"Did the Marshall arrest him?" Wes looks down at Sam Wade's blank eyes.

"He was outta town, besides there were no witnesses. The men that were there are scared. They said it was self-defense."

"You see it, Bacon?" Jenks looks down at the man.

"I seen it, as I said, it was pure murder." The man swallows hard. "Leland shot them boys in the back."

"Charlie, get him a cup of coffee." Wes looks at the little man's cold hands.

"Thought you rode for Halleck?" Jenks eyes the old man coldly.

"Not anymore; I liked them boys." Bacon takes the steaming coffee. "I don't like Leland or any back shooter."

"Why did you bring them home?" Harley steps threateningly toward Bacon.

"Nobody else would." The old man eyes Harley calmly. "Leland probably would have killed anyone else but me that tried."

"Leland in town?"

"Yes, Sir Mister Tobin, sitting bold as brass outside the hotel as I drove out of town." Bacon nods. "He's just waiting on you to come in."

"Why didn't he try to stop you?"

"Can't say, reckon he knows I've been with the Running H many a year. He just followed me with those dead eyes of his as I left Tucson." Bacon thanks Charlie for the second cup of coffee. "I figure he wants you to get the message."

"Well, I got it, real plain." Wes starts for the corrals.

Monte takes him by the arm. "It'll wait till morning Wes, then we'll all ride into town."

The cold eyes seem to look right through Monte, making him release his grip on Wes' arm. "When a rabid dog needs killing Cousin, you do it right then."

"We'll saddle up then."

"Not this time, Monte. I'm riding in alone." Wes turns for the corrals. "Alone."

Pole pulls from Rusty, following Wes to the barn. Reaching for a lariat, he unhooks the gate and plays out his loop as he enters the catch pen.

"You hear me, Pole?" Wes looks over at the gangly rider, "I said I was riding alone."

"I heard you, pardner, but them words don't mean squat to me." Pole whirls his loop, settling it around the neck of his good bay horse. "Saddle up if you're going and let's ride."

"You must like these cold, dark nights."

Rusty waves as the two men leave the ranch buildings at a high lope. This time, she says nothing to Pole. She knows, by the look on his face, it would do no good. She is a Flannery, and many times in the past, her family fought. She knows men have to fight, it's in their nature, and a woman's place is to stand loyal and proud by her man. She had seen the look on her own father's face many times in the past as he rode out to fight.

Her shoulders straighten as Pole rides ramrod, straight beside Wes, as they race away from the ranch. Slowly, her hand lowers, returning to her side. Today he might die on the streets of Tucson, but he would die a man, and she is proud of her man.

Monte and Ellen step up beside Rusty as they ride off. "I should saddle up and go help them."

"No Monte, you're not a gunman, you're a rancher." Rusty speaks without looking at him. "Your job is here on the ranch."

"They might need me, or think me a coward."

"Wes would never think that of you, and today they have each other, and that's all they need." Rusty looks up at Monte.

"I'm his Cousin first Rusty; I've forgotten that, for the last time." Monte looks down at Ellen.

Smiling, Ellen nods at Monte. "Go with them, Monte. The Sandigras problems are your problems. I'll be here waiting when you return."


Except for the oil lamps, lighting the streets, Tucson is dark as the horses trot up to the livery stable. Banging on the closed doors with his boot, Pole waits until he hears movement inside before dismounting. The iron hinges squeak noisily as the old stableman opens them, just enough to peek out.

"What you fellers a wanting?"

"It's Pole Nichols from the Sandigras. We want to put our horses up for the night."

"Who's with you?"

"It's Wes Tobin. You remember Wes, don't you Silas?" Pole steps closer to the door. Both doors swing open, enough to let the two saddled horses walk through, then close noisily behind them. Coal oil lanterns put out an eerie light in the dimness of the stable. The unmistakable smell of horses and horse liniment, fill the large, warm stable. Saddles line one whole side of the livery, while horse stalls and hay cover the rest of the building.

"Rub 'em down and give them hay and grain." Wes starts loosening his cinches.

"It's past five in the morning, boys. You rub your own animals down. The feed's right in that bin there." The bony old finger points at a wooden feed bin. "Right there."

Wes has to admit, the old coot is a feisty one. "Yes, sir, we'll do that."

"Leave a dollar on the table for your board, before you go up the street."

"How come you think we're heading up the street?" Pole asks. Maybe we're going down the street."

The old hostler spits a stream of tobacco as he tosses each man a currycomb. "Halleck and some of his bunch just rode into town. Those would be their horses stalled over there."

"So?"

"Don't play me for a dang fool, Pole Nichols." Silas shakes his head. "Leland killed your men this morning; shot one in the back. That's why you two rode all night to get here."

"That so?"

"Yes, it is, and that's why Halleck brought his men into town; to back Leland." The old hostler looks over at Wes and Pole. "You're both walking into a hornet's nest over there."

"Is the Marshall back yet?"

"Was."

"What do you mean was?" Wes pours oats into the manger. "Where is he?"

"Halleck rode in a couple hours ago, walked to the Marshall's Office, next thing I knew, Linder was leaving town like a scalded dog."

"Stacked deck huh, old man?"

"Yep, and without a cut," Silas laughs. "That ain't all either. That Rowdy Flannery is with Leland. If I were you fellers, I'd follow the Marshall out of town, and at the same speed."

"Well old man, you ain't us." Pole spits. "Tell us, what's Rowdy Flannery doing with Leland?"

"How should I know?" Silas shakes his head. "That redhead is a mean one. Those two have been closer together today, than a two-headed snake."

"Well, thanks for the advice, old man."

"Do as you will Tobin; I warned you." Silas turns for his bunk. "You leave the dollar, just the same; don't want you to leave out, owing me."

"Leave out where, old man?"

Silas stops in his tracks, turning to where Pole stands, feeding his horse. "To hell you dang fool. That's where Halleck and Leland intend to send you fellers."

Wes checks his pistol and turns for the door, after tossing a dollar on the table. "You hear him Pole? Rowdy Flannery, your new brother-in-law is with them. Are you sure you want in?"

"What do you think?" The tall man walks around Wes and heads for the door. "He sided with the wrong bunch."

"Thankee kindly young feller." The hostler pockets the money as Pole and Wes exit the stable. "Good luck to you two."

Wes hesitates at the door and turns around. "You seen Leland?"

"Yep, right at dark, he was sitting bundled up, outside the hotel with the redhead. Can't say where they might be now." Silas grins. "Don't 'spect him or Halleck will be hard to find though."

"Much obliged, Silas." Pole nods as he follows Wes through the stable doors. "If I happen to make it down there, I'll put in a good word for you."

"Very funny Pole Nichols, but I'm figuring on heading the other way." The old hostler shakes his head and turns to his bed. "Dang fools."

# CHAPTER 16

Even at five in the morning, piano music and raucous laughing emits from the well-lit saloon, as Pole and Wes walk slowly up the street toward the noise. Several drunken cowboys stagger through the door, making their way down a side alley, paying no heed to Wes and Pole, walking up the wooden sidewalk.

"Those ain't the ones we want. I'll bet the Running H riders are still inside getting themselves a belly full of courage." Wes steps up to the doors of the saloon. "You take the right and I'll watch the left."

"What's the play?" Pole checks the loads in his pistol.

"I'm after Halleck and Leland." Wes looks across at Pole. "If they're in there, you stay back and let me take them."

"I can't do that Wes. You know I've got a stake in this too."

"Alright, but don't you get yourself killed, not even scratched." Wes nods. "Rusty would have my skin, and watch out for Rowdy Flannery."

"What will she think if I have to kill her brother?" Pole looks at the double door. "How would I ever face her?"

Wes looks over at the tall man. "Let's hope it don't come to that."

"She's a good woman, Wes." Pole steps up on the sidewalk. "You should get you one; sure makes a difference in a man."

"I had one." Wes turns toward the saloon. "Didn't do right by her."

"Shucks pard, you had no way of knowing the Comanche would raid while we were gone."

"I shouldn't have left her."

Pole nods. "I know you blame yourself, but she's back in Texas, probably married by now."

"We don't know for sure if she ever escaped the Comanche." Wes walks away. "We never heard anything of her in all these years."

"I pray she did, old hoss." Pole shrugs and looks toward the saloon. "It's hard to do, but you need to let it go."

"I need to know." Wes tosses his burned smoke away. "Someday I aim to find out, one way or another."


Halleck and five of his riders are sitting around a poker table as Wes and Pole enter the saloon. Hearing the door open, they all turn to see if it is Tobin, the man they have been waiting for. One of the younger riders lunges to his feet, grabbing for his pistol.

Halleck puts his hand out to stop him, but as the rider pulls his weapon, Pole's bullet catches the man dead in the chest, knocking him backward into another table. The rest of the men quickly place their hands back on the table, palms down. Their whiskey courage drains away as they look into the smoking barrel and cold eyes of the tall man.

"Your turn, Halleck." Wes looks down at the rancher. "Stand up and meet your maker."

"How about me, Mister Tobin?" The voice comes from the back of the room. Wes didn't notice Brock Leland sitting back in the darkness. "I believe it's me you want."

Wes sidesteps until Leland comes into his sight. Studying the layout of the backroom, he watches as Leland stands easily to his feet. From the corner of his eye, Wes watches as Rowdy Flannery steps off to Leland's side, making it hard for Wes to watch them both.

Leland and Rowdy Flannery stand slightly crouched, ready to draw their weapons. The room is silent. Not a sound comes from the bystanders. All eyes focus on the drama as it plays out before them. Everything in the room seems suspended in time as the three men face off at one another.

Suddenly, before the men can put their weapons into action, the side door of the saloon swings open, banging against the wall as Boston Flannery's huge body steps into the room. Rowdy Flannery pales as he sees the giant figure of his father, standing in the doorway.

"Step away boy, you ain't running with this bunch." Flannery holds a Spencer Carbine loosely in his huge hands. Rowdy can't believe his eyes, Boston Flannery standing in front of him, big as a mountain. What is he doing here? How did he find out?

"Stay out of this Pa. I'm fixing to kill me a man." Rowdy never takes his eyes from Pole. You can read the hate in his face. "Pole Nichols is a dead man."

Boston Flannery looks over toward Pole. "He's your brother-in-law boy, you're sister's husband. He's family, you don't fight with family."

"He shamed us, old man; you let it happen." Everyone can see Rowdy is ready to draw. "Now I'm fixing to rid the Flannerys of that shame."

"There is no shame boy, they're married." Boston pleads with his oldest. "Married son, leave it be."

"I told you old man, stay out of this."

The rifle raises slightly. "I'm running the Flannery Clan, Rowdy, and you're a Flannery. Now I'm asking you, back out of this."

"No longer you ain't, Pa. I'm taking over the Flannerys soon as I finish off my new brother-in-law." Rowdy glares across at Pole. "Now get back to your rocking chair old man."

"You were in with Leland when he killed those two Sandigras riders, weren't you?"

"It was a fair fight, everybody seen it."

Boston Flannery shakes his head sadly. "You're a liar boy, you told Leland they were coming into town. You're no good, boy."

"What if I did? I told you, it was a fair fight."

Pole jerks slightly as the roar of the heavy carbine sounds in the closed room. Rowdy Flannery is slung backward, into the wall as fire and lead spits forth from the Spencer. A bewildered look comes briefly into the redhead's eyes, before he slumps slowly in a crumpled heap on the floor.

Looking to where his son's body lies, Boston Flannery steps back and motions at Wes. "You gentlemen continue, forgive me for interfering."

Pole can't believe what he has just seen, Boston Flannery shot his own son down, without blinking an eye. Shaking his head, he quickly looks over at Wes and nods.

"I've got these polecat's Wes, you take care of that sidewinder." Pole nods at Leland, then rests against the bar with his thumb in his gun belt. "You gents just sit easy and live, move and I'll blow all of you into kingdom come. I would enjoy that very much."

Leland smiles. "Your friend has a lot of confidence in you, Mister Tobin."

"You're a dead man, gunfighter."

"You sure?"

Wes steps sideways. "You talk too much to be a bad man, Leland."

"Most men in boot hill would say different."

"I'm waiting, and my back ain't turned to you." Wes speaks softly.

Both guns roar at the same time. There isn't a breath between them. Witnesses swear they couldn't tell which man fired first. The guns came out so quick, no one in the room could actually say who drew first.

As the shootout is talked about, the story grows legendary. The swiftness and the speed of both men, grow with each telling.

Wes looks over at Leland, who staggers sideways, from the impact of the forty-four slug, standing slumped against the bar.

"You're faster than I figured, Mister Tobin." Leland tries to raise his pistol as Wes walks toward him. "Much faster."

"You killed two of my riders."

"I did that alright, and it almost worked, brought you running anyway." Leland's final breath comes ragged and with a final gasp of air, he stiffens and rolls sideways to the floor.

"Almost only counts in horseshoes or haven't you heard." Wes holsters his pistol, turning to where Halleck stands staring down at his dead gunfighter.

"I wouldn't have believed it." A voice comes from the crowd. "Leland dead, Tobin outdrew him."

"He got lead in Tobin." Another looks at the hole in Wes coat. "He's bleeding."

All eyes turn to watch expectantly as Wes walks to where Halleck waits, a sickly paleness covering the face of the big man. Not a Running H hand moves to help their boss. They have seen the speed of the tall man's gun and now the look of death in Pole's face. To move the slightest muscle would get them all killed.

"Your turn, Mister Halleck. Both of your gun hands are dead, now you can do your own fighting." Wes studies the big man. "And dying."

"I don't stand a chance against you, Tobin."

"More than Wade and Newhouse had against your killer." Wes looks into Halleck's face. "I'm gonna kill you whether you draw or not, just like they died, but you'll be looking at me."

"I ain't drawing against you." Halleck unbuckles his gun belt and lets it fall. "I don't think you'll shoot me in cold blood, Tobin."

Wes looks down at the gun belt, then up at Halleck. "You're yellow Halleck, hiring other men to do your killing. But you're wrong, I will shoot you down right where you stand."

Halleck kicks the fallen gun belt away from him. "I don't think so, not in front of all these witnesses."

Wes unbuckles his own belt and lets it fall. Pole looks down at the gun belt, then turns his full attention on the Running H riders. "I've got these gents covered, pard. First one of you fellers move, you'll all be dead men."

Halleck smiles as the gun hits the floor. He is thirty or more pounds heavier than Wes, and two inches taller. Raising his huge fists, the rancher advances on the smaller man. The big rancher knows he is no match for Tobin with a gun, but he has never been beat in a rough-and-tumble fistfight. He's been afraid to face Tobin with a gun, but with his fists, he fears no man. No one has ever been his equal. His courage and confidence comes back with a rush as he starts forward.

All eyes turn from the scene before them, as Monte's huge frame comes through the swinging doors and enters the saloon. Walking to where Halleck stands, with his fists balled up, ready to square off against Wes, Monte smiles coldly.

"If this is Mister Halleck, he's mine, Cousin." Monte removes his heavy coat. "All mine."


The rage still sweeps through Wes as he thinks about the senseless killing of the two riders because they rode for him. Now before him, stands the man responsible, the man that brought in the hired gun. He is the one man causing all the trouble in the canyons.

Slowly, the rage evaporates from him. Nodding, Wes picks up his gun belt and buckles it slowly back on. "Halleck's all yours, Cousin."

Rushing forward, into the bigger man, Monte unloads two hard rights to the man's midsection that only slows the rancher for a second. Both men are mountains of muscle and sinew, confident in their own strength. Now only one would be left standing, the one with the stronger will and determination.

A roundhouse right sends Monte crashing backward, across a poker table and onto the floor. Halleck rushes forward, cat quick, extremely fast on his feet for a big man. Monte hardly has time to roll to his feet, away from the boot heel that lands where his head was. Halleck follows him across the floor, landing lefts and rights as Monte dances backward, trying to roll with each blow. The Running H riders forget the drawn guns covering them and start yelling encouragement to their boss.

Halleck manages to grab Monte in a headlock and starts forward, trying to run his head into the iron stove. Breaking away at the last minute, Monte trips the big man, who goes down hard, his own head smashing face first, into the hot stove. The hard toe of Monte's boot catches the rancher brutally in the rib cage twice, before he manages to roll quickly away.

"You fight dirty, little man." Halleck's face blisters from the red-hot stove. "I ain't done yet."

A hard right smashes into Halleck's face, causing blood to spurt from a flattened lip. "I aim to beat you to death big man, you hear me, to death." Monte growls.

Halleck blinks and looks at the man before him, a man who he has misjudged as a fighter. Monte is bigger than Wes, but still seems small, compared to the huge Running H owner.

Swinging from his hip, he catches Monte with a hard uppercut, sending him reeling across the floor again. Both men come back to their feet, smashing at each other like two enraged bulls. Pushing and shoving, they fight back and forth across the saloon. This is a fight without rules and no one dares to interfere. Each man tries to give out all the punishment he can to the other.

Blows rain down on the combatants, causing blood to flow freely, down each of their faces. The two men use everything; fists, elbows, knees, and boots. Halleck is all muscle and the heavy blows glide off him. Monte finds himself tiring as he backs slowly across the room, trying to conserve some of his strength.

Halleck grins viciously, charging forward as the blows from Monte lessen and became softer. Swinging with all his might, Halleck misses his target and stumbles forward, right into a hard right hand from Monte. Blood and teeth fall from the rancher's smashed face. Going down to one knee, he shakes his huge head, making blood fly across the room. Staggering to his feet, he moves shakily toward Monte.

Both men are battered, bloody, and exhausted, but the fight continues with neither giving an inch. Again, Monte surges forward as he pounds the tiring rancher unmercifully. He shakes his head as a hard right hand catches him flush on the jaw. Halleck might be a coward with a gun, but with his fists, he is a mighty tough man.

Halleck is tiring as the raining blows from Monte are taking their toll. The rancher's huge arms are heavy and hard, as all their strength goes into every blow. Free-for-all fighting like this, takes every ounce of a man's strength and vitality.

Monte is a fighter. He knows most men don't like the sight of their own blood and become fearful as they run out of stamina. Halleck is fixing to get whipped but the sight of his own blood doesn't bother him. However, this is the first time he has ever been stretched out in a fight. He knows his endurance and strength is quickly fading from too much soft living, letting others do his work is starting to show. It puts fear in his gut, knowing he is too tired to defend himself, and his opponent is still coming on.

Drunkenly, the big rancher pushes forward, swinging with both hands. Monte feels Halleck is whipped so he starts picking his shots, landing them at will against the heavy body and the bloody face. The watching men wince as the blows rain on the unprotected man as Monte puts every ounce of strength in each blow, trying to destroy Halleck.

Finally, Halleck staggers, going to his knees as Monte lands one final punch to his ear, sending the big rancher sprawling.

"He's whipped, Cousin." Wes steps between the two fighters. "You've won, he's almost dead, let it go."

Monte gulps in deep breaths as he stands bowed over the bloody rancher, trying to right himself. A fog lifts from his brain as the words penetrate his tired body. Nodding, he slowly turns and leans dizzily against the bar.

Staring down at the broken and bloody face of Halleck, Monte shakes his head and looks over at Wes. "And I once called you cold blooded, Cousin."

"You men pick that pile of horse manure up and get him out of here." Pole waves his pistol at the Running H riders, watching as they carry the limp form of Halleck through the front doors. "And don't let me see any of you anywhere near the Sandigras."

Wes looks about the room and walks to where Boston Flannery kneels beside his son and removes his hat. "I'm sorry, Boston."

Shaking his huge head, Flannery lifts Rowdy from the floor, looking down at his son's face. "This was a long time coming, Mister Tobin. It's much better this way. A man has to be loyal to his clan or suffer the consequences."

"How did you know to come in?" Wes is curious.

Flannery looks up at Wes. "His brother's told me he was up to something with Leland. When he rode out this morning, I followed him here to Tucson."

"How did he know Sam and Nate were coming into Tucson?" Wes looks around the room.

"I reckon he had one of our hands, watching the road in here from the Sandigras.

"You've been outside all this time?"

"I've been asking around." Boston holds the lifeless body in his huge arms. "The people here in Tucson know me. They won't lie to me. Rowdy was in on the shooting of your men. Oh, he didn't actually shoot them, but he was in with Leland and planned it all."

"I heard he was."

"Why? I raised the boy the best I knew how." Flannery shakes his head slowly. "Why?"

"You want Pole to tell Rusty?" Wes hesitates, "Exactly what happened?"

Boston nods slowly, turning for the door. "She's a Flannery, she'll understand. Tell her we'll bury him come first light tomorrow. I'd like, for her mother's sake, for her to be there. We'll wait on her."

"We'll tell her." Wes nods. "Thanks, Mister Flannery. We're all sorry for your loss."

"Maybe we can have peace now, Mister Tobin."

Looking over, where Bacon Hollister stands, leaning against the bar, Wes nods. "You've got a job with the Sandigras if you want one, Mister Hollister."

"Thank you, but I reckon I'll ride out with Halleck. He'll be needing me now." The old puncher shakes his head sadly. "He's no longer the king of the mountain around here."

They are ready to leave town right at daybreak, after getting statements in writing from the men present at the bar. Picking up their horses at the livery, they start to ride out of Tucson as the sun comes up amid the curious stares from most of the town. It appears everyone turns out for their departure. The gunfire from the saloon and the two big men tearing at each other in the early morning, wakes up almost everyone in town.

Marshal Linder returned to town and stands in front of his office as they pass. Wes reins up and looks down at the town law. "You got a problem, Marshal?"

"I've been told it was a fair fight." Linder looks up at Wes. "No, I don't have a problem."

"Halleck's done. He won't be needing your services anymore in Tucson."

"I'm duly elected marshal here," Linder glares up at Wes.

"You just got dis-elected." Wes lights a smoke, deliberately baiting the ex-Marshal. "When I come back, I'll kill you if I find you're still here in Tucson."

Pole watches, as Monte kneels beside the clear running stream outside Tucson, washing the dried blood from his puffy face. Monte rinses out his handkerchief and dabs at his swollen face. Pole rolls himself a smoke and looks over at the big man. "I don't think he ever tried to fight you that hard, pard."

"No, I don't think he did." Wes nods. "Lucky for me."

"We should have visited the doctor before we left town." Pole hands Wes a lit cigarette and looks over at Monte. "You okay, Monte?"

"I'm alright, I've had worse." Monte tries to remove the dry blood from his face.

"I doubt that, Cousin," Wes smiles. "Halleck was a tough nut to crack, but you got it done."

"I ain't proud of it Wes, but it needed doing."

Wes looks back, toward Tucson and then at Pole. "Well old friend, what do you think, you ready to head home?"

"I think I'm hungry and we're three hours from the ranch and food. And, I need to see Rusty."

"That's gonna be rough to tell her what happened." Wes looks out across the desert.

Pole nods. "I know, but we'll get through it."

Wes rolls a smoke, striking a sulphur on his legging's. Looking off to the east, toward Texas, he pulls hard on the cigarette. "Rusty put sourdough biscuits and meat in your saddlebags before we left the ranch."

"She did?" Pole flips his smoke and rushes over to his horse. "You want some Monte?"

"No, reckon not."

"Too sore, huh?"

Wes watches as the tall man bites into a biscuit. "Boys, we've made a small treaty with the Apache and we've made friends and married into the Flannery Clan. Halleck's beaten and his gunfighters dead, he's whipped."

"What are you saying, Wes?" Pole bites into a biscuit, looking across at his friend.

"The Sandigras Ranch has earned the right to live here in peace." Wes exhales smoke and looks off across the desert. "We have won."

"And?"

"I won't be riding back with you and Monte old friend."

"What? Where are you going?"

"Back to Texas."

"After the girl?" Monte looks flabbergasted at Wes. "Cousin, she's long ago married or dead."

"Maybe, maybe not." Wes nods. "I've got to go find her."

Wes walks to where his horse stands ground tied and picked up the reins. "You boys take care. Send up a smoke fire if you need me."

Pole shakes his head and looks over at his friend. "You ain't in any shape to ride out alone with that bullet in you. You have no supplies, nothing."

"I'm fine Pole, it only nicked the skin. I've got some salve in my bedroll." Wes pats the blanket roll behind his saddle. "Good-bye, boys."

"You weren't planning on riding back when you left the ranch, were you?" Pole shakes his head, looking at the blanket role. "You've got your possibles with you."

"I wasn't sure, now I am."

Pole looks at the extended hand. Shaking his head, he finally takes hold of it, pumping the arm hard. Monte steps forward, taking Wes in a bear hug. "We'll be seeing you, Cousin."

"Someday Monte, look for me to come riding in." Wes mounts his good sorrel and looks down at the two men. "You take care of my dog, you hear?"

"We'll do that Cousin," Monte promises.

"You will be back?" Pole hollers, as Wes spurs his horse and rides away. "You will."

"He's gone to look for Molly Hawkins, Pole."

"Yeah, he just stays long enough to see the Sandigras and all of us safe and settled." Pole stares across the barren desert land. "That's what he did."

"Yes sir, he did, he's quite a man."

Pole smiles, "Yes he is, Mister Jonas Webb was right."

Only the lonely sound of the moaning wind, crossing the high flatlands, calls back to the two men as they watch Wes disappear into the chaparral and scrub brush of Arizona.


## The End